Cast of C

Lady Lupin Lorrimer Hastings. The lovely 21-year-old daughter of an earl, Loops is as kindhearted as she is scatterbrained and had barely set foot in a church when she married the handsome 43-year-old vicar of St. Mark's.

The Rev.

Duds ?   l,
who

Diana L Acc   n
cynical 38- *Retu'n*   r   the   derer.   *of Return*

June Stuar   s attra ive but hot-tempered young

Miss Phylis Gardner. A very proper sort, she had never given her parents any reason to worry and seems to live for the Girl Guides.

Charles Young. The 27-year-old curate who is mad for foreign missions.

Mr. and Mrs. Grey. Pillars of the parish, he is the meek treasurer of the Temperance Society, she the forceful president of the Mothers' Union.

Dr. and Mrs. Brown. He was a kind man, much liked by his patients, but his timid, anxious wife was only concerned with the servant problem.

Miss Thompson. A hearty Guider whom Lupin is convinced is actually a man.

Miss Violet Oliver. The Guides district secretary, she "has a face like when one looks in a spoon" and is continually writhing, wriggling and hissing.

Miss Watson. The dedicated headmistress of the day school.

Miss Gibson. The equally dedicated Sunday School superintendent.

Gladys Simpkins. She had a red face that was all nose and legs like bolsters.

Miss Young. The curate's older sister, who would like to see Diana hang.

Jack Scott. Andrew's nephew, in the Secret Service and attracted to June.

Father Gibson. Miss Gibson's High Church nephew, whom she'd like to see installed as curate of St. Mark's.

Inspector Poolton. An otherwise levelheaded policeman who doesn't mind letting Scott and Lupin look for clues.

Stephen. Lupin's boyfriend, who exits our story when Andrew enters it.

Various servants, townspeople, and civic officials.

Books by Joan Coggin

The Lady Lupin Quartet

Who Killed the Curate? (1944)
The Mystery of Orchard House (1946)
Why Did She Die? (1947)
Dancing with Death (1947)

Girls' Books

Betty of Turner House (1935)
Catherine Goes to School (1945)
Jane Runs Away from School (1946)
Catherine, Head of House (1947)
Audrey, a New Girl (1948)
Three New Girls (1949)

Who Killed
the Curate
?

A Lady Lupin Mystery by
Joan Coggin

The Rue Morgue Press
Boulder, Colorado

The editors thank William F. Deeck
and Katherine Hall Page
for bringing the Lady Lupin
mysteries to their attention.

PRINTED IN THE UNITED STATES OF AMERICA

About Joan Coggin

*There's nothing wrong with this parish that a few well-timed
funerals couldn't cure.*

So goes an old joke often attributed to Episcopalian clergy, although we
suspect ministers in various other denominations have thought pretty much
the same thing. Certainly, the victim in *Who Killed the Curate?* didn't lack for
enemies, though he wasn't all bad, and his death no doubt was beneficial to
any number of the parishioners. But it's a new arrival, not a sudden departure,
that truly improves life in St. Mark's parish at Glanville on the eastern coast
of Sussex.

That arrival is the lovely twenty-one-year-old Lady Lupin Lorrimer, the
wondrously ditzy daughter of an earl, who marries the forty-three-year-old
vicar of St. Mark's, the Rev. Andrew Hastings. As scatterbrained as she is
kindhearted, Loops, as her friends call her, is totally unprepared for the chal-
lenges presented by the various activities usually assigned to the wife of a
vicar, including the Church of England Temperance Society, the Girl Guides,
and the Mothers' Union. Yet she soldiers on, gladly abandoning for the most
part her previous life of parties and indolence to be with her soulmate.

Even though her friends affectionately think her often a fool, they all
agree that she has a peculiar talent for getting at the truth, however circuitous
a route she might take. This comes in handy as Lupin finds herself playing
detective four times over the course of ten years. The passing years temper
some of Lupin's youthful enthusiasms but never her charms. *Who Killed the
Curate?*, though published in 1944, is set at Christmas 1937, and *The Mystery
of Orchard House*, published in 1946, is set a year after those events. The
final two books in the series, *Why Did She Die?* (1946) and *Dancing with
Death* (1947), are set just after World War II. The first and fourth are the
more clearly identifiable as traditional detective stories, although all four fit
comfortably in the genre. All were originally published by Hurst & Blackett,

a relatively obscure and long-since defunct London publishing house, in what must have been fiendishly small print runs, as they are extraordinarily difficult to find on the used-book market. None was ever published in the United States.

Murder mysteries often have sported clerical sleuths or church settings, but Lupin may well be the first clergyman's wife to take up crime-solving as a hobby. More recently Mollie Hardwick produced several books featuring English antiques dealer Dorian Fairweather, who married and then divorced an Anglican vicar over the course of seven novels. American Katherine Hall Page, an avid fan of Joan Coggin's books, discovered them years after she launched her own series featuring caterer Faith Sibley Fairchild, who is married to an Episcopalian minister in a small Massachusetts town.

Both Hardwick's and Page's books often revolve around church politics and social life, although perhaps not to the extent that Coggin explores those themes in her first mystery, and their protagonists are nowhere near as clueless as Lupin is during her first encounters with Andrew's parishioners. The amusing byplay between Lupin and her doting, mostly understanding and totally smitten spouse resembles in some small measure the interaction between the vicar and his flighty, flirtatious wife in Agatha Christie's 1930 novel, *Murder at the Vicarage*, the first Jane Marple mystery.

Christie's story is told from the vicar's point of view, but life in that vicarage is a bit different from Glanville. As Charles Osborne remarks in *The Life and Times of Agatha Christie*: "The domestics in St. Mary Mead are a dim lot, and rather unsympathetically described by Mrs. Christie. This may be because she wishes her readers not to consider them as 'real people' and therefore potential suspects." Servants are far more favorably treated in Coggin's books—Lady Lupin sometimes wonders why they even bother to consult her before making a domestic decision—and more than once come under suspicion. Despite her lineage, Lupin is a truly democratic soul who can be found gossiping with the servants and goes to great pains not to offend the working class, as in *The Mystery of Orchard House,* where she tries to conceal her blue blood from a garage mechanic who's a Communist.

Lady Lupin's generous nature is apparent in other ways. The murderers she encounters are often much more likable than their victims, and on several occasions Lady Lupin suggests that she's willing to give the alleged culprit a head start before reporting in to the police, so long as a signed confession is left behind that clears the other suspects.

In addition to her four mysteries, Coggin, using the pseudonym Joanna Lloyd, wrote six girls' books set at the imaginary Shaftesbury School and based on Coggin's own school years at Wycombe Abbey. These stories are as charmingly told as Coggin's mysteries, and indeed the young Catherine, who figures in several of these books, bears a remarkable resemblance to Lady Lupin. In *Catherine, Head of House* (1947), Catherine's friends recall when she put her books in the laundry basket and took her linen bag to school. Catherine hopes that no one will run away from school during her tenure as head, since it's unlikely that she'll notice their absence. You can almost hear Lady Lupin in Catherine's lament:

> "I hope someone will notice. I remember one day when I was at home I brought some fish home but I forgot to give it to Mother. I was reading *Endymion* for the first time, so I just put in the drawer. It was some days before I remembered it. I don't know if I would have remembered then, only there seemed to be something a little funny about the room, and Mummy said she thought the drains must have gone wrong, and Jack thought it was a dead rat. Anyhow, someone found the fish but it wasn't fit to eat. It was rather a waste. I often wish I had a better memory."

What makes this passage even more interesting is that misplaced—or spoiled—fish constitute a running joke in several of the Coggin mysteries. Although Catherine is absentminded and easily distracted, there's no doubt that she has a first-class mind and, indeed, is set to head off for university to study to become a history don. Coggin herself, on the other hand, was said "not to be academically brilliant" although she "enjoyed her school days." And Lupin's mind certainly does not work in conventional ways. Over the course of the four books she manages to overcome most of her ignorance about church and religious life—quite an achievement when you consider she once had Jews confused with Jesuits—but she still happily butchers literary quotations and tends to go off on tangents (you can probably guess who misplaces the fish). Coggin pokes more than a little fun at some of the parish activities Lupin is expected to embrace, such as leading the Girl Guides, an English version of the American Girl Scouts, which Coggin herself participated in as a "Guider," or adult leader, for many years.

Born in Lemsford, Hertfordshire, in 1898, Coggin was the granddaughter on her mother's side of Edward Lloyd, founder of *Lloyd's Weekly London Newspaper*, which no doubt is why she used Lloyd as a pseudonym for her schoolgirl books. Her mother died when Coggin was eight and the family moved to Eastbourne, one of the easternmost towns in Britain, where she was to make her home for the rest of her life.

Glanville is no doubt Eastbourne, somewhat reduced in size, and St. Mary's church there is probably the model for the Rev. Hastings' own St. Marks, also a Norman building. The original jacket art, reproduced on the cover of the present volume, shows Lady Lupin in a winding street near a church that greatly resembles the real St. Mary's. Whether St. Mary's "boasts" the same ugly stained glass windows of St. Marks is subject to examination. Glanville, like Eastbourne, was heavily bombed by the Germans during World

War II.

After she was graduated from Wycombe Abbey in 1916 in the middle of World War I, Coggin worked as a nurse at an Eastbourne hospital. Although she suffered from a mild form of epilepsy, Coggin did not let it inhibit her lifestyle. After the war, she returned to those activities expected of a young woman of her class and upbringing—the social round of bridge, tennis, golf and books. She also worked with the blind.

In the 1930s, she turned to writing, producing her first girls' book, *Betty of Turner House*, in 1935. With the exception of that book Coggin's writing career was limited to a five-year period between 1944 and 1949, during which she produced nine books. For the last 30 years of her life she apparently did no more writing and died in 1980 at the age of 82.

Her contribution to crime fiction was slight but memorable. *Who Killed the Curate?* is arguably one of the funniest mysteries you'll ever read, with a belly laugh on virtually every page. Lupin herself may remind readers of Gracie Allen of Burns and Allen (who, oddly enough, were perhaps among the first real-life celebrities to be featured in a detective novel—S.S. Van Dine's 1938 *The Gracie Allen Murder Case,* which may also be the first detective novel deliberately written with an eye toward a movie sale). She's certainly the spiritual godmother of the Pauline Collins character in the very funny BBC comedy series *No, Honestly* from a few years ago. The Collins character came many years later, of course, and although Coggin may well have been familiar with Gracie Allen's routines, there is little doubt that Lady Lupin sprang full-blown from Coggin's own imagination. She's that rarity in cozy crime fiction—in spite of her many eccentricities she seems more real than most of the people we encounter in real life. Or maybe that's just wishful thinking.

Tom & Enid Schantz
Boulder, Colorado
December 2001

CHAPTER 1

"How is my face?" asked Lady Lupin Lorrimer.

"Not too bad," replied her friend, Duds Lethbridge. "That spot hardly shows at all unless you get right under the light. You might put on a little rouge, though."

"I have just spent a guinea in having it massaged and made up," replied Lupin coldly.

"Oh, have you? Well, never mind, if you hadn't wasted it on that you would probably have wasted it on something else."

"Need we stay long at this ghastly party tonight?"

"No, I shouldn't think so, but I suppose we shall have to stay until after the speeches."

"Speeches! There aren't going to be any speeches, are there? Do you know, Duds, I don't feel frightfully well. I think perhaps I'll lie down and just have a little something on a tray. I may be feeling better by the time you and Tommy get back from the party, and we might all go on to a quiet nightclub or somewhere."

"Don't be a cad. It's not Pamela's fault that she is having a twenty-first birthday party. It is much worse for her than it is for us. Besides, we all backed you up last April, although it meant going down to the moldy old country and staying in your ancestral castle, which may be historic and romantic, but has the worst sanitation I have ever struck. If they are going to start pulling down the slums, they ought to begin with some of the stately homes of England."

"Well, anyway, I did have the decency to have it in the quiet home circle. I didn't drag in all my uncles, aunts, nannies and cousins seven times re-moved and plant them down in the middle of the Savoy. And they'll all be so horribly cheerful and hearty, I know. I shall probably burst into tears."

"Yes, the last generation are disgustingly cheerful. I wonder why it is."

"I suppose they never had any worries when they were young."

"Talking of worries, are you going to marry Stephen?"

"I suppose so. But need you talk about it now, when I have enough to depress me already? What with Pamela's twenty-first, and my face not being a success! Oh, dear, how awful to think that I shall soon be married, and making speeches at my children's twenty-first birthday parties."

"Don't! What a ghastly notion!"

"What is a ghastly notion?" asked Tommy Lethbridge, Duds' husband, walking into the room at that moment.

"Lupin and Stephen's children having a twenty-first birthday party."

"I didn't know that they had any children," said Tommy.

"They haven't yet," replied Duds.

"Oh well, that's all right then. We'd better be getting along. Oughtn't you to brush your hair or something, darling? I gather it's going to be quite a big party."

"This happens to be the very last word in hairdressing."

"It looks like a mistake to me. Never mind, perhaps no one will notice you in the crowd. What a frightful evening this is going to be!"

They arrived at the Savoy and were taken to a private room where a large number of guests had already arrived and were trying to buoy up their flagging spirits by drinking cocktails. Pamela, the heroine of the evening, was looking depressed, surrounded as she was by numbers of uncles, aunts, cousins and relations by marriage.

Lupin was thankful to see Stephen. He was rather a nondescript looking young man and brains were not his strong point, so she felt at home with him. At the moment she was feeling shattered and much in need of the support of a familiar friend.

"My dear," she said, sinking into a chair, "the most frightful thing has happened. I am sitting next to a clergyman."

"No," he replied reassuringly, "you are seeing things. On one side of you there is an empty chair, quite empty, and on the other side there is me. And I am not a clergyman, not at all; in fact quite the contrary. Have a drink of water or an aspirin or a cocktail or something?"

"Don't be a fool. I don't mean now, I mean at dinner. Pamela has just broken it to me, and I wish I hadn't sent her that perfectly fascinating beauty case; it really was a dream-blue leather with her initials on it, and masses of little pots and bottles all with blue stoppers—I longed to keep it for myself and this is what I get in return; it makes one think of that thing of Wordsworth about a crocodile's tooth—or was that Tennyson?"

"I don't actually remember at the moment, if you know what I mean; not offhand, that is. But I say, my dear old thing, I think you must be making a mistake. Clergymen don't come to the Savoy; they have meetings and—er—visit the poor and go to church and all that sort of thing; you must have got it wrong."

"Yes, they do, for twenty-first birthday parties; they unbend on these occasions and become positively frolicsome. We must leave early and go on to the Crimson Canary or somewhere. He would hardly follow us there, would he?"

"Hardly! No, definitely not. Good notion of yours. We'll push off early. As a matter of fact there is something rather important that I want to ask you, and I may as well ask you there as anywhere else."

"Oh, dear, I mean do you; I don't know if you'll feel up to being asked anything after this dinner party, though I suppose, as Duds says, it's worse for Pamela. I remember at mine last April, all the uncles and aunts kept remembering the most shaming things I had done or said as a child, and, just as I was shivering with shame, Nanny came up and said no wonder I was cold, and that if she had her way I should have been wearing woolen combinations. It was too humiliating. I wonder which is Pamela's nanny? She is sure to be among those present. As if it is not bad enough to be twenty-one and know that one's life is nearly over without having everyone gloating over it."

Duds and Tommy came up. "I say," said Tommy, "I hope we are not butting in at an awkward moment, but the funeral procession is just starting, so I suppose we had better mingle with the merry throng."

"Loops is sitting next to a padre at dinner," explained Stephen, "so she is feeling just a little shaky. Aren't you, darling?"

"Oh well, I am sitting next to Pamela's girlfriend from the country. I have promised to be kind to her, but it will be more to the point if she is kind to me. She is one of those fierce-looking girls with masses of teeth and a voice that carries. I think she is more used to talking to horses and dogs than to human beings."

"I have been let in for Uncle George, the one with the red nose. Pamela says it's indigestion, but people always say that. I know he will tell me funny stories all through dinner, and I shall want to cry. However, I shall try to keep a stiff upper lip, and think of the old school tie and Rudyard Kipling."

"Well, it won't be for long. Lupin and I are going on to the Crimson Canary afterwards. I'd ask you to come too, but as a matter of fact . . . well . . . er. . ."

"That's all right, we quite understand, Duds and I were in that predicament ourselves once. We won't butt in."

Lupin had not heard a word of this conversation. She had just caught sight of the most attractive man she had ever seen. She could only see his side face, but his profile gave her quite a funny sensation. She was not as a rule of a susceptible nature, but something had certainly happened to her this time. She wandered in to dinner as in a dream, only to find that he was seated beside her, and that he was wearing one of those black waistcoats without any buttons and a round collar, and that the card in front of him stated that he was the Rev. Andrew Hastings. The whole thing gave her such a shock that she found herself eating smoked salmon when she had really meant to have caviar.

"I expect you often come here," said a very charming voice, from close beside her.

She awoke from her reverie with a start. "Where?" she said, surprised. "Oh, here, yes of course, rather, I mean not very often. I mean I sometimes go somewhere else." What a fool she was making of herself. Not that she was ever what might be described as bright, but she was not often at a loss for something to say, and she was in the habit of being rather a success with young men. But then, Andrew was not young. He must be nearly forty, at least. He was going gray on the temples, which made him more attractive than ever. She racked her brain for an intelligent remark.

"Have you many poor in your parish?" she asked.

"No, not many. I used to have plenty when I was in London, but now I have quite a small parish in Glanville."

"Oh, I see." Whatever did one talk about to clergymen? She tried to remember what the vicar at home talked about when he came to dinner.

"Do you have trouble with the choir?" she asked, feeling inspired. She seemed to remember some conversation about the difficulty of getting choirboys, or getting rid of them or something, that had gone on for hours once, and she hoped that she might be starting her neighbor on a congenial conversation which would break the ice.

"No," said Andrew thoughtfully, "I do not have much difficulty with the choir."

'Bother,' thought Lupin, 'I'm being a perfect frost.' She made one last effort. "Have you a parish magazine?" she asked desperately.

"Yes, we have. Have you ever read a parish magazine?"

"Well—er—I don't know, I mean I don't know that I have actually read one, as a matter of fact. I have often seen them knocking about. I am sure they must be awfully interesting. I—er . . ."

Suddenly she realized that Andrew was laughing at her; his eyes crinkled up deliciously when he laughed. She began to laugh, too.

"I am afraid I don't know much what to talk about to clergymen," she admitted. "But I know the vicar at home had some trouble with the choir, though I don't know what it was. I am not in the country an awful lot except in the winter, of course, and I am not frantically good at good works and things. We always have a treat for children in the summer, but I haven't been there for it for the last few years. I mean I like to think of children being happy, but I would rather not be near them when they are being it. They do get so sticky."

Andrew agreed that he really preferred children being happy just at a little distance. He was quite easy to talk to after all, Lupin found. "What relation are you to Pamela?" she asked suddenly.

"I am her godfather," he replied.

"I shouldn't have thought you were old enough to be her godfather."

"I was forty-three, last birthday."

"Oh, dear! still even then . . ." Lupin screwed up her forehead, "if you married when you were twenty and had a child, she'd be twenty when you were forty and that only leaves three years for Pamela, and we know she's twenty-one." Andrew began to laugh. "I know I'm not very good at arithmetic," admitted Lupin. "I once got a sum out as three-fifths of a square woman. I suppose I've gone wrong this time somewhere, added instead of subtracted or something."

"I think you have mistaken godfather for grandfather," suggested Andrew.

"Oh, of course, so I have; that solves it all. I have a godfather, too, a dear old man with fluffy white hair. He gave me fifty pounds for my twenty-first birthday; wasn't it sweet of him?"

"Very. I am afraid I haven't done so well by Pamela."

"Well, I expect you have got a lot of children of your own by this time, as you married so young."

"But I didn't; you are still thinking I am a grandfather. I am not married at all as a matter of fact."

"Not at all?"

"No, not at all."

Lupin didn't know why, but somehow she felt rather pleased that he wasn't married.

"I thought clergymen always were," she said, "except of course when they're celebrates. Do I mean celebrates?"

"Celibates, I expect. I'm afraid I'm neither one nor the other; just an ordinary unmarried clergyman."

Lupin was enjoying herself, she did not know why, for she had not expected to enjoy this party; but it had turned out to be the best party she had ever been to. She looked round and thought how nice everyone looked.

"I thought you were going to go on talking to that padre all through dinner," grumbled Stephen.

"Padre? Oh, he's Pamela's grandfather, I mean godfather."

"He would be. How soon do you think we can get away?"

"Get away? Where to?"

"Yes, get away, do you want to stay here forever?"

Lupin smiled, rather inanely, Stephen thought. It was quite a fascinating idea; she did not think she had ever enjoyed a party so much before. It would be very nice just to go on sitting here, talking to Pamela's grandfather, no godfather, forever. She turned to him. "You know," she said, "I think Pamela's really got the best of it, in spite of the fifty pounds, re godfathers, I mean. Mine is a dear old man, but he got up at my twenty-first birthday party, and a lot of my friends were there, you know, not just relations, and said he always thought of me as, 'Rose, of the rosebud garden of girls.' You wouldn't do a thing like that to Pamela, would you?"

"No, in fact I think fifty pounds quite inadequate for such a remark. It was worth at least two hundred."

"A hundred? Two hundred! I haven't lived it down yet." By the time the speeches had started, she and Andrew felt that they had known each other all their lives. Uncles and aunts and cousins several times removed droned on about how it seemed only the other day that dear Pamela was a little girl playing with her dolls. But Lupin did not mind; she and Andrew exchanged glances and tried to keep serious faces. She did not try to catch the eye of any of her other friends. She had forgotten that she had any other friends. She and Andrew might have been alone on an island of aborigines. At last, however, even in her happiness, Lupin spared a pitying thought for poor Pamela, for she was a kindhearted girl; and the sight of Pamela's expression of shame and misery would have moved a harder heart than hers. Anyone would think that she had just been discovered cheating at cards or robbing a blind man rather than attaining her majority. She sank, lower and lower in her chair, and fingered her pearls nervously as if they had come into her possession in some nefarious manner, instead of having been a perfectly voluntary twenty-first birthday present.

At last the speeches were over, and the guests went down to the ball-room. Andrew and Lupin walked together forgetting that there were other people present.

"Will you dance with me?" asked Andrew. "I am afraid I am not very proficient. I don't get much practice except occasionally at a parish social."

"What is a parish social?" asked Lupin with interest.

"It is a gathering of the parish for social purposes," explained Andrew.

As a matter of fact, although Andrew did not know many of the modern steps, he really did dance quite well, and between dancing and sitting out, the evening was passing very happily, when Duds came up accompanied by Tommy and Stephen.

"I say, Loops, don't you think it is time we were wandering along to the Crimson Canary, if we are going there?"

"The Crimson Canary?" replied Lupin in a surprised voice, as if she had never heard of such a place.

"What is the Crimson Canary?" asked Andrew.

"It's a nightclub," explained Tommy, "quite a new one, rather a good place."

"It's rather like that thingummybob you were telling me about," said Lupin, "I mean one meets there for social purposes, but as a matter of fact I have never seen a padre there, you might feel a bit—well, I mean I know how I'd feel if I found myself at a parish gathering."

"Are you trying tactfully to convey to me that I should be out of place at the Crimson Canary?" asked Andrew gravely. "Not that I agree for a moment that you would be out of place at a parish social. I should love to see you at one. Perhaps one day I shall."

Duds and Tommy stared. Stephen was feeling rather depressed and gazed moodily in the opposite direction. "I don't think you'd really like it," said Tommy at length, "I mean you don't know Loops like I do . . . ."

"Shut up, Tommy," said his wife, "I am sure Lupin would be a great success at a parish social, but perhaps you had better not come to the Crimson Canary. It has never been raided yet, and I don't see why it ever should be, as it is as quiet a little spot as you could wish to find, but it still would be awkward for you if anything unfortunate occurred."

"Yes, wouldn't it?" agreed Lupin. "Let's stay here, what is the point of going away? After all it's poor old Pam's twenty-first birthday party. It seems rather a shame breaking it up and going rushing off, and in any case I am rather tired of the old Canary. I have been there at least twice . . . ."

"Righto," said Duds, "but I think Tommy and I had better do something about Stephen. He seems a bit down and out, you know."

Lupin looked at her vaguely, "Stephen?" she said. "Isn't he feeling well, poor old thing? I am sorry. Yes, you take him on. It will do him good. Mr. Hastings will see me home, not that I need seeing home or anything like that." She had quite forgotten that Stephen had been going to ask her an important question that evening. Pamela's birthday party entirely changed the lives of Andrew Hastings and Lupin Lorrimer. Coming together for one moment from entirely different worlds, it would have been natural for them to have met and passed on, but instead they remained together regardless of the surprise of their friends. By the end of the season their engagement was announced and in September they were married in the little Norman church at Lorrimer.

CHAPTER 2

LUPIN had sometimes left a note for her mother at the vicarage at Lorrimer, but that was the nearest she had ever got to the inside of a clergyman's dwelling. Now she was actually to live in one, and the idea seemed fantastic. In fact, during her engagement and honeymoon, she hardly realized that she was about to become a vicar's wife. Andrew was just Andrew, and she forgot all about his calling, so that it was with a certain sense of surprise that she arrived at her new home early in October. The house was neat and compact, surrounded by a tidy little garden in which geraniums and lobelias played a prominent part. The church and vicarage stood at the end of a broad and pleasant road, named Vicarage Road, in which were several moderate-sized houses with tiny gardens like her own and carriage sweeps before the door.

Glanville was a small seaside town, and it boasted three churches besides various chapels and other places of worship. To Lupin, who had hitherto spent her life in London or in the country it was like some foreign land. In fact it was just as exciting as going abroad. She longed to show it to Duds and Tommy, and to Stephen too, as soon as he had got over his disappointment; but if he were still in love with her, it would hardly be tactful to ask him there, and point out her and Andrew's geraniums, or their cozy little dining room, or their nice sunny bedroom. Lupin had been used to a social life, but when she married Andrew and knew she was to live at Glanville, she took for granted that most of her social activities would cease, but she soon found herself mistaken. On arriving at her new home, she found herself inundated with invitations: dinner parties, luncheon parties, tea parties and sherry parties seemed to form a large part of the life at Glanville. The evening on which she was to go to her first dinner party found her rather nervous. She had bought two black evening dresses while they had been in Paris on their honeymoon, laboring under the delusion that they were suitable for a vicar's wife. Andrew was not so sure of their suitability, but he liked to see her in them.

"How do I look, Andrew?" she asked, turning from her looking-glass as he came into her room. Her fair hair had been brushed until it looked like silver, she had really put on very little rouge or lipstick, and her dress was black; but somehow she did not look a bit like a clergyman's wife. Andrew burst out laughing, then he caught her in his arms and kissed her until she had to recomb her hair and repowder her face.

Andrew sighed as he watched her. "To think," he said, "that after sixteen years of blameless priesthood, that this should happen to me! You don't look like a wife at all, least of all a vicar's wife. Come along, we mustn't be late. When they say seven forty-five in Glanville, they mean seven forty-five."

They were dining tonight with one of the churchwardens and his wife, or rather the wife and one of the churchwardens, for no one noticed poor little Mr. Grey when his wife was anywhere near. She was a large imposing-looking woman of about fifty, with a deep voice and a gift for organization. She, bringing her husband with her, had arrived in Glanville several years before. They had taken a house in St. Mark's Parish and now might almost be said to be the parish. Pushed by his wife, Mr. Grey had become churchwarden, secretary of the men's club and treasurer of the local branch of the Church of England Temperance Society, while she was president of the Mother's Union, on the parochial Church Council and on the board of school managers.

If Mrs. Grey had had a family of children, she might have spent her energies and gifts in advancing them in the world, but as she was childless, her powers were all at the service of the parish. It was not a big parish, there were few very poor in it, and no really spectacular sinners; but Mrs. Grey did not let these facts daunt her, but worked untiringly within the scope allowed her. No one could have a cold in the head without her arriving with bottles of vapex and endrine; no one could disagree with a neighbor without her offering to act as an intermediary, and if anyone missed the morning service on Sunday for any reason whatever, she was on their doorstep first thing on Monday morning with jellies in case of sickness and arguments in case of religious doubts. She seemed very much attached to her quiet little husband, was very hospitable, and was on the whole popular with her neighbors, although some of them may have wished that she was not quite so zealous on their behalf.

The Browns, who were also at the party tonight, were perhaps the Greys' chief friends in Glanville. Dr. Brown was the other churchwarden at St. Mark's. He had a ruddy complexion and a hearty manner; he was also invariably in good health himself, which gave confidence to his patients. He was a kind man and always ready to put himself to any amount of trouble in the service of a friend or a patient. People had often remarked that he and Mrs. Grey would have made a well-matched pair, while his mousy little wife would have been an appropriate mate for poor Mr. Grey.

Mr. Young, the curate, was usually to be met with at Glanville dinner parties; men were few and far between there, and so, being quite unattached and fond of dining out he was usually asked to make the numbers even. He was rather a good-looking young man of about twenty-seven; his eyes were a little too close together and he had a nervous habit of blinking when he was speaking, but several of the church workers were reported to be in love with him.

The remaining member of the party was a Miss Phylis Gardner, a nice-looking woman who might have been any age between thirty-five and forty-five. She lived with a couple of aged parents in one of the biggest houses in Glanville. She was always nicely dressed, had charming manners and had never given her parents a moment's trouble. Her chief interest was Girl Guiding, in fact it was more than an interest, it was almost a religion and she held jealously to all its rules and regulations, disliking every change to the movement that the years brought along. She was the district captain for Glanville and longed for the time when every girl in the town should be in uniform (with skirts, black stockings and hard hats—she had no use for the easier uniform which was now being introduced), saluting Union Jacks, singing "Land of Hope and Glory" and signaling Morse and tying knots in their spare time.

Lupin got on fairly well during dinner. She sat between Mr. Grey and the doctor. One was a great gardener and had won prizes for begonias, vegetable marrows and melons at the local flower show. And the other was a golfer and had won quantities of spoons and medals. Occasionally Lupin got mixed up, as when she asked the golfer what the soil was like, but that went quite well as he was able to explain how soggy the fairways became in the winter; and then she asked the gardener whether the turf was good, but that also went all right, as he thought she was alluding to the square yard of grass in his garden, which he dignified by the name of lawn, so was flattered by the question.

Afterwards in the drawing room it was much worse. Mrs. Grey was evidently determined to take her under her wing. With a bachelor vicar she had had a pretty free hand during the last ten years. Luckily this new wife did not look as if she were likely to give much trouble and Mrs. Grey was quite ready to run her as well as the parish. The thing to do was to treat her quite kindly but firmly from the start.

Miss Gardner, too, was very kind. She implied in a perfectly tactful manner that Lupin was not a very suitable clergyman's wife but that she for one was prepared to overlook it. Mrs. Brown did not take much notice of Lupin, but then she was not really interested in anything except the servant problem.

"Well," said Mrs. Grey, after she had ensconced Lupin in the most comfortable chair in the room, with a cushion at her head, a footstool at her feet and a firescreen between her and the fire—for which she was sorry, as she was rather cold. "It is very nice to have a vicar's wife at last."

Lupin felt that she had been rather remiss in not becoming one sooner.

"Do you think, Mrs. Grey, that I might ask Lady Lupin that great favor we were talking about this morning?"

"I am sure you might," replied Mrs. Grey heartily. "I know Lady Lupin is out to help us all she can. Miss Gardner is very interested in the Guides," she went on to explain.

Unfortunately Lupin thought that she said guys, and that she was referring to the fifth of November which was a few weeks ahead. "Yes, I like fireworks," she replied.

There was an awkward pause, broken at length by Mrs. Brown. "I had a maid who was a Guide, a lazy little girl she was, too, and always telling lies."

"I am very sorry to hear that," replied Miss Gardner, looking very hurt and depressed, "but you mustn't judge all the Guides by one. Our great trouble is the difficulty of getting the right kind of Guider; one does want sahibs for that sort of work, I am, sure you agree with me, Lady Lupin."

As Lupin had not the very vaguest idea of what she was talking about, she could not really say if she agreed or not. "Oh er—rather, I mean I am sure there is a lot in what you say," she murmured noncommittally.

"Have you got any yet?" asked Mrs. Brown suddenly.

"Any what?" asked Lupin, surprised.

"Girls."

"Oh no, none at all, nor any boys either as a matter of fact. I mean I haven't any children."

"I mean maids," replied Mrs. Brown coldly.

"Oh, I see, yes, I think so, I mean yes, I have."

"I hope you are going to join the Mothers' Union," said Mrs. Grey.

Lupin began to feel uncomfortable. She and her friends had always been pretty unreserved among themselves, but these women were enough to make anyone blush. It wasn't as if she knew them very well either. "Well, I don't know," she said, "I mean perhaps later on, you see I have only been married six weeks."

"Now, Mrs. Grey," said Miss Gardner playfully, "you must let me get in my piece first. We are very much hoping, Lady Lupin, that you will consent to become our district commissioner."

"Yes, I hope you will," said Mrs. Grey, hoping through Lupin to get her finger into the Guide movement from which she had been excluded so far. "A splendid movement, the Girl Guides. By the way did you know that the Sunday School superintendent was talking of leaving?"

Lupin knew the answer to this one. "No," she replied, "I didn't."

"Well, of course, there may be nothing in it. She has often threatened to resign before, but do you know what I should do if I were you?"

"No," said Lupin eagerly, for it was difficult for her to imagine such an unlikely situation.

"Take her at her word, and take it on yourself, I could soon put you in the way of it."

"I think if Lady Lupin consents to becoming our commissioner, she will find it takes up all her time," put in Miss Gardner.

"Will it?" asked Lupin dubiously. The idea of having all her time taken up did not attract her.

"It is the busy people who have time for everything," remarked Mrs. Grey.

"They would," thought Lupin, without any wish to emulate them.

"Miss Gibson, our Sunday School superintendent, is an excellent woman. No one admires her more than I do, but she is not a woman of the world."

Lupin had not realized that that was one of the qualifications necessary for a Sunday school superintendent, but she made polite if noncommittal murmurs.

"At any rate she is a gentlewoman," said Miss Gardner, "you are lucky to have one. In our parish . . ."

"I can't think how she gets that maid of hers to stay with her," said Mrs. Brown, "I know for a fact that she gives her margarine. I always have butter in my kitchen, don't you?" she asked Lupin.

"Well," said Lupin, "I don't as a rule, not often, I mean, you see Andrew likes me to have it with him, and I don't somehow feel Sara would like it very much if I went butting into the kitchen at teatime—our parlor maid, I mean, she has been with Andrew so long and is rather strict, but of course—er . . ."

"Of course, personally, I think the Mothers' Union is the most important work of all," went on Mrs. Grey, "if only you can get hold of the mothers, you will get the children. What are your views, Lady Lupin?"

'Oh, dear,' sighed Lupin to herself, 'here they go again. Why do they want to get hold of the mothers, and as for getting the children, haven't they ever heard or seen children? . . . Don't they know that the only place for children is somewhere a nice long way away.' Aloud, she tried to prove herself a good vicar's wife. "Yes, of course," she said, "it must be a splendid thing as you say. I suppose they decide how many babies they should have, and how much money they should be given for housekeeping and . . ."

Luckily the men came in at this moment. Lupin's dinner companions hurried to her side. Mr. Young also approached her. Although she was not very clever, men usually seemed to enjoy her company. The curate stood looking down at her with a questioning look, as though trying to make up his mind whether she would make a good clergyman's wife or not. Lupin could have told him that at once, but she was determined to do her best, so she looked up at him with what she hoped was a bright expression, and remarked: "I hear you have a Sunday school in the parish."

Mr. Young's face clouded. "There is, of a sort," he admitted darkly.

Lupin turned to Dr. Brown. "I am longing to try the golf course here," she said, then remembering that it was the other one that played golf, she added, "if I can spare time from my garden, that is."

"I hope you are going to take an active part in the work of the parish," said Mr. Young, "we have been looking forward very much to your arrival."

"How kind of you, so have I! Yes. I am taking a very active part. I am going to be a district thingummybob on Guy Fawkes' day, and then there is the Sunday School and the Mothers' Union."

"Are you interested in foreign missions, Lady Lupin?"

Lupin had, of course, heard of foreign missions, but it is no use pretending that, up to date, she had given much thought to them: still, now she came to think of it, there had been a missionary box in her nursery at home, in fact Nanny had made her put a penny in it each time she refused to finish her porridge. "Yes," she said, rather pleased with herself for being so *au fait* with the movement. "So is Nanny."

"Nanny?" asked Mrs. Grey with interest.

"My nurse, I mean."

"Is she still with you?"

"Yes, I mean no, she lives at home, not here, you know."

"Nurses need a lot of waiting on," said Mrs. Brown. "Last time we had one in the house, both my maids gave notice."

"Then you were brought up to take an interest in missions, as a child," exclaimed Mr. Young, eagerly.

"Yes, I suppose so," said Lupin, doubtfully, remembering one time when she and her brother had tried to shake some pennies out of the box, and another time when they had filled it up with buttons. "And I've never learned to like porridge," she added reminiscently.

"I can never get a cook who can make it properly," grumbled Mrs. Brown. "If it hasn't lumps in, it comes out thin like paste. And they won't be told."

"That's what we want in the Sunday School," exclaimed Mr. Young.

"Do you give them porridge at Sunday School?" asked Lupin rather bewildered.

"Porridge!" laughed Mr. Young, "that's a good simile of yours, Lady Lupin, that's just what they do get, stodgy, unimaginative lumps of information, just like porridge! We want to inspire them, to give them some idea of the adventure of Christianity, to tell them stories of men who go out into the wilds and spend years without ever seeing another white man. I should like to see a missionary box in every home; I should like the children to spend their leisure hours in reading lives of missionaries; I should like every boy and girl in the parish to grow up with the wish to be a missionary themselves."

'That's what Miss Gardner meant about sahibs,' thought Lupin. 'They come from India I'm sure, and so do missionaries, though how they manage to go for so many years without seeing a white man, I can't imagine, considering half the people one meets are either just going to India, or have just come back from India. I always thought it was full of white people, playing polo, dancing, or getting engaged to someone, or going up the hills for the hot weather, just a round of gaiety from what one reads in books; however, I suppose I've got it wrong.' "Of course the sahibs must be most useful," she said aloud to Phylis, "not that I've ever been to India, myself."

Phylis looked slightly surprised by this remark but she was never at a loss. "I believe you went to Brittany for your honeymoon, didn't you?" she asked.

"Yes, we had a perfectly radiant time, motoring about and bathing and—er—well, just playing the fool generally, and then we spent a few days in Paris on the way back. I'd like to have a honeymoon every year. And there was the most wonderful food, you know, in the tiniest places, and wine that cost nothing and made you feel like a bird with two tails, and then there was the scenery of course and all that."

"We spent our honeymoon in Devonshire," said Mrs. Brown, "but it rained all the time and the doctor got an awful cold, and the cream made us both sick."

"Devonshire," said Mr. Young, "that is a very delightful county. I spent a great deal of time there as a boy, and often think I should like to go back again. Do you know Devonshire at all, Mrs. Grey?"

A dull flush mounted slowly over Mrs. Grey's already florid countenance. "Yes," she replied in rather a strained voice, "I know it quite well."

Miss Gardner began to talk brightly about Scotland, while Lupin wondered why Mrs. Grey had seemed so embarrassed at the thought of Devonshire. Probably it was just the heat of the room that had made her so red. It was stiflingly hot. But Mr. Young had a rather curious smile on his face, perhaps he and Mrs. Grey had some secret joke about Devonshire. Lupin turned to Mr. Grey. "The flowers are wonderful in Devonshire, aren't they?"

she said. Then realizing by his lack of enthusiasm that she had made a mistake again, she went on hurriedly: "I happened to notice them when I was playing golf at Broadstone, because I drove into a clump of—er—foxgloves. Isn't Broadstone in Devonshire, Andrew? Oh, Dorset, I knew it began with a D, but I was bit off my golf that day so got muddled up. I mean I must have pulled or sliced or something, because the foxgloves would hardly have been in the middle of the fairway, would they? As a matter of fact I rather think it was heather not foxgloves, but it would have been a good drive if it had been straight, and of course I lost my ball—a perfectly good Silver King."

"I always use a Dunlop," said Mr. Grey. "It's a funny thing, but if I play with any other ball it seems to affect my drive. There is a very good one-and-sixpenny ball on the market, and several of my friends advised me to use it, so I bought half a dozen, but I don't think I drove one of them past the two hundred yard mark, and then when it comes to putting. . ."

"And you will think of becoming our commissioner?" begged Miss Gardner.

"A wonderful work the Girl Guides!" exclaimed Mr. Young fervently, "We have an excellent company in our own parish. The captain is Miss Lloyd, a splendid worker. Have you met her yet?"

"No, not yet, I am going to tea there on Tuesday."

"Poor dear Diana," sighed Miss Gardner, "she is a very great friend of mine."

"She ought to get married," announced Mrs. Grey, "so ought June Stuart. I have no patience with two girls living together like that. It's not natural."

"My opponent was two up at the turn. The second hole is a short one over a stream. . ."

"I think you will find with a little trouble you will be able to grow delphiniums . . . ."

"I hope you will visit the Sunday School and form your own opinions; I am sure we should find your advice most helpful."

"I suppose you don't know of any London girls who want a place at the seaside; it is a good home for any girl—good food, good wages . . . ."

"You will find the Guiders an enthusiastic, willing set of girls, though as I was saying, not quite the kind we really want—except for Diana Lloyd and June Stuart, there are none whom you would exactly describe as pukka . . . ."

"You are going to be my right hand in the Mothers' Union, I know that."

Lupin looked imploringly at Andrew. He nodded his head. "Oh, dear!" she said, "is it really as late as that?" Though inwardly she felt sure that the clock had stopped. "How the time does fly when one is enjoying oneself! But I am afraid we must go; you see tomorrow is Sunday and Andrew always gets up early on Sunday to go to church, you know. Thank you so very much, we have had a lovely evening and I am longing to see your garden, Mr. Grey—your greens, I mean. Good night, everyone."

"Good night, Lady Lupin. I am very glad that you are taking such an active interest in all our work. You will find plenty to do, what with the Guides and the Mothers' Union and the Sunday School. We are going to make use of you, you know; you won't find time hanging heavy here. We are busy people in Glanville and there is plenty of recreation, too, so you mustn't think it's all work and no play. We have our dramatic society and our bridge club, and if you arc interested in Shakespeare you will enjoy our Shakespeare Circle. Good night, Vicar. We won't let Lady Lupin feel dull, don't you worry."

That night Lupin dreamed that she was sitting peacefully in Duds' flat when it suddenly dawned on her that she ought to be taking a Sunday School class in Glanville. She leaped to her feet but could not find her handbag anywhere. Nervous and flustered, she began to search for it. She could not possibly go without it; what was she to do? She was late already and had quite forgotten the lesson that she was to teach the children. To be or not to be, that is the question . . . but how did it go on? Ah, there was her bag at last. She opened it eagerly, only to find it was a manicure case. What, was this? a canteen of knives and forks. Someone had given it to her for a wedding present. If only she could get her ball on to the green all would be well but it was an enormous bunker and the bunker was full of delphiniums. She would be dreadfully late, she knew. "To be or not to be . . ." she couldn't remember how it went on. She had tried to get out of the bunker but her feet would not come out of the sand; the flowers were twining round her ankles. "The Mothers' Union are waiting for you," said Mr. Young. He was looking at her in a funny sort of way and she felt frightened. If only Andrew were here! She was in London now and there was Andrew on the other side of the road; but every time she tried to cross to him the traffic policeman held her up. She looked at him imploringly, only to find that he was Mrs. Grey. "The Girl Guides are coming," she cried, and everyone began to cheer. Miss Gardner was in white satin and she carried a Union Jack. Stephen was in plus fours. 'Why on earth hadn't he put on his wedding garments?' thought Lupin. "Stephen," she cried...

"I wish you wouldn't call out other men's names in your sleep, darling," complained Andrew the next morning at breakfast. "The best vicars' wives don't do that sort of thing."

Lupin looked thoughtful for a moment. "How do you know?" she inquired.

CHAPTER 3

IT WAS a delightful autumn afternoon when Lupin started off to have tea with Diana Lloyd and June Stuart. At the end of Vicarage Road a ridge of hills stood out in dark relief against the clear, pale blue sky, and just above hung the sun—a huge red ball. Lupin turned to the left, and walked down a road leading to the sea. The tide was out, and black rocks stretched far away toward the silver sea in the distance. Everything was very quiet, very still; a faint, intangible scent hung over the afternoon, composed of frost and seaweed and bonfires. Lupin did not consciously appreciate the beauty of her surroundings, but all the same it filled her with a sense of pleasure and well-being. She was looking forward, too, to her tea party; she was particularly anxious to meet Diana and June, as she knew they were very great friends of Andrew.

She really knew very little about Andrew's background. There had been that first wonderful evening at the Savoy, when they had so surprisingly fallen in love with each other. There had been other hurried meetings, when he had managed to snatch a few hours in which to come up to London to see her, and there had been that one short and wholly delightful visit to Lorrimer Castle. But what his life had really been like before he met her she had no idea. The Browns and the Greys were, of course, ordinary parishioners for whom he could not be accounted responsible, but he had spoken of these two girls with real affection, and had appeared eager that Lupin should make friends with them.

Lupin rather wondered why Andrew had not married one of them as he was so fond of them and must have been thrown much with them, but she had not a scrap of jealousy in her composition, and the thought of Andrew's affection for them only made her determined to like them herself. After all, one could not marry all the people one was fond of. She was very fond of Stephen; she would have married him if she had not met Andrew. Perhaps Andrew would have married Diana or June if he had not met her. She hoped she had not spoiled anyone's pleasure, for she was a kindhearted girl and liked everyone round her to be happy and comfortable, and it must be very sad for anyone not to be married to Andrew. She was just wondering whether Stephen could be persuaded to take to one of them when she arrived at their house.

It was a small white house overlooking the sea and was surrounded by a small garden, not quite so tidy as most of the Glanville gardens, but much more attractive. As Lupin walked up the garden path, with Michaelmas daisies rioting on each side, and noted the many shades of the veronica bushes beneath the windows, the dark red fuschias in the distance, and the old man's beard climbing over the wall, she felt a moment of dissatisfaction with her own neat geraniums. She was shown into a large and pleasant room, running the length of the house. The windows faced south and west, so that you could either look out to sea or on to the Downs, whichever you preferred. Bookshelves ran halfway up the walls on the remaining two sides and there were other books lying about on chairs and tables and window seats. A big bowl of bronze chrysanthemums scented the room with their clean, bracing autumn scent. There was a bright fire before which June Stuart was toasting crumpets.

Lupin had seen both June and Diana in church and had liked the look of

June very much. She was only twenty and that in itself was an asset in Glanville, where most people were middle-aged, and she was very pretty, and altogether Lupin had hopes of her proving a kindred spirit, She was even prettier without her hat, as her head was covered with reddish-brown curls; she had bright hazel eyes, and her face was flushed from the heat of the fire.

"I can't shake hands," she said, "mine are all over butter!"

"Good!" exclaimed Lupin. "I do love lots of butter, and are those really crumpets?"

"Yes, they are. Do sit down, and I'll call Di. She is working at the moment. I am afraid there are books on most of the chairs, but you can put them on the floor."

Lupin would have preferred June not to call her friend quite so soon. It would have been nice if they could have chatted alone for a bit while Diana finished her work. For one thing Diana was quite old—thirty, if not forty—then she wrote books and worked in the parish so altogether she was rather alarming. She wondered why June had chosen a friend so much older than herself; surely she must find it dull. Of course, Andrew was rather old, too, but then husbands were different, and Andrew was especially different; no one could find him dull. Her thoughts were interrupted by the entrance of Diana.

Diana was actually thirty-eight, five years younger than Andrew. She supplemented a small income by writing children's stories. She would like to have written other things and had had one novel published but it had not been a success financially and as she needed the money she felt obliged to stick to the children's stories, for which she had a gift. However, she had lately determined to have one more attempt at something different and had actually started a detective story.

In spite of her advanced age, Lupin had to admit that Diana was rather good-looking in a dark, haggard kind of way. She might have been almost lovely when she was a girl. She had a thin, clever face with green eyes that seemed too big for it. All her features were good but there was something a little bitter about her mouth. It may have been that she had been unable to realize the literary ambitions with which she had started out. Lupin was afraid that it was because she had been unable to marry Andrew and she felt rather guilty about it.

However, Diana's manner when she came into the room was friendly enough. "How do you do? I am so glad you were able to come. I expect you are having a weary time, having tea with all your parishioners in turn, but it is a great occasion for us to have a vicar's wife among us at last."

"I'm afraid I'll be an awful disappointment to everyone. I'm not really a proper vicar's wife at all. I seem to have come here under false pretenses. I'll do my best, but it's no good pretending that I know much about vicars' wives, except that they usually seem to be having dozens of children all the time."

"That is not a characteristic that I should advise you to emulate," said Diana. "I should think a few would go a long way."

"That's just how I feel," said Lupin in a heartfelt voice. "Mrs. Grey, or was it Brown—anyway, it was some color or other, was mad for me to join the mothers' trade union or something. It won't be her fault if I don't restore the falling birthrate. She seemed quite hurt that I hadn't done something about it already. But you can't very well come back from your honeymoon with a family, can you?"

"Not very well, I suppose. Do you find the other functions of a clergyman's wife enjoyable?"

"Functions?"

"She means jobs," explained June. "She can't help talking like that."

"Oh, jobs, you mean the things I have to do? They're all perfectly ghastly. Of course, I expect they are all very interesting when you know how, but when you are an absolute beginner, you feel the most frightful fool, like when you first played golf and had to drive off in front of several retired colonels and women champions."

"I don't see why you ever should," objected June. "Surely you would let them all go through."

"Yes, but you can't do that when it is the Sunday School and the super, what do you call it, is watching you."

"I should like to see you and Miss Gibson playing golf together in the Sunday School," murmured Diana.

"Well, there we were, " went on Lupin, "and there were masses of children goggling at me as if I were King Herod, and some alarming young women, who had obviously never given their mothers a moment's anxiety since they were born; I think they were the teachers. Miss Gibson said, 'Here's Lady Lupin,' as if she were breaking bad news, and all the children began to giggle, except one who burst into tears, and I don't blame it. The teachers said, 'Hush, hush, what will Lady Lupin think of you?' and then Miss Gibson said would I like to ask them a question; I felt absolutely paralyzed, and all I could think of to say was, 'What is your favorite pudding?' As a matter of fact it went most awfully well and the children looked more intelligent than you would have thought possible and they all began to answer quite brightly; but I don't think it was an enormous success with Miss Gibson and the teachers. Then just as I was leaving, Miss Gibson asked me if I was interested in temperance, and I said I thought it was horrid to drink too much; I started to tell her about one night at the Crimson Canary, when some people got tight, but even that didn't seem to bring us really together."

"Do you want to be brought together?" asked Diana. "Personally, as regards Miss Gibson, the less we are together the merrier we shall be."

"But you're not the vicar's wife," said Lupin; then went scarlet and wished that the floor would open and swallow her up, as she remembered her suspicions of Diana's feelings toward Andrew. She took a gulp of hot tea and gave a hiccup. "Oh," she said, after a pause, "I ought to have said 'pardon,' I learned that at the Day School yesterday; one of the children started hiccupping, and the teacher said, 'Say pardon, Ivy.' It was a new one on me; tell me do you think one should say it after each hiccup, or at the end of the session?"

"About every three, I should think," replied June. "It's a pity you didn't say it because we could have shown our breeding by saying 'granted.' Mustn't it be lovely to be refined? Do tell us more about the Day School."

"There isn't much to tell, I was far too frightened. I felt I was back at school again myself, and whatever one may say about one's school days being the happiest in one's life, everyone must know they're absolute purgatory. Well, I just followed the headmistress round and stood about on one leg, and then in one room, when she told the children who I was, one of the boys said, 'Loopy Hastings,' and instead of being tactful and pretending not to hear, the wretched mistress hauled him out and made him apologize, and of course, we both felt too embarrassed for words. I know I kept looking loopier and loopier, at last I felt I couldn't bear it any longer and simply made a bolt for it. I felt Miss Watson would haul me back and make me write out something a hundred times, so I ran all the way to the vicarage. Then tomorrow there's Guides, do you know anything about Guides?"

"I hear you are to be our commissioner."

"Am I? What is that?"

"The head of all the Girl Guides of Glanville."

"Oh, dear, tell me. Will I have to do a good turn every day?" she asked, alarmed.

"I don't know," said Diana, "I never mean to, but they are thrust on one. June and I sometimes try to go through a day without doing a good turn, but we never succeed. As soon as we step out of the house someone falls off a bicycle at our feet and we have to bandage them up. I think it must be something to do with having joined the Guides; a curse is on us from the beginning. I should never have joined if I had known."

"Even if we go up to London for the day, dressed in our best and meaning to enjoy ourselves," added June, "the same thing happens. We haven't been there five minutes before someone has asked us to help them across the road, or to hold their hand on the moving staircase, or to take them to the lavatory. It is damping when you are hoping you look a bit gay. I always put it down to Diana being a clergyman's daughter. People can always tell. I wonder if it happens to clergymen's wives too."

"Oh, dear, I do hope not. Then you are in the Guides as well."

"Oh, rather, we *are* the Guides in fact, aren't we, Di? Didn't Andrew tell you? There is hardly a girl in the parish that hasn't passed through Diana's hands at one time or another. She is what is known as wonderful with girls.

While I have a way with the brownies!"

"Then what is Miss Gardner?"

"Oh, she is the district captain," explained. Diana. "You see there are several companies here, and she goes round to them all in turn and measures their shoelaces to see that they are all the same length, and to find out whether they know the alphabet in Morse, and that they get a lump in their throats when they sing 'God Save the King.' "

"Oh," said Lupin, "it does sound difficult, but what have I got to do?"

"You keep peace among the Guiders. It will take you all your time, for there are about thirty of us altogether, counting the Brown Owls. You look after us, and make us all into one big, happy family."

"Do I?" It didn't sound too good to Lupin and she wondered what Brown Owls were but she did not like to ask. She could not quite make Diana out; she was friendly enough and rather amusing, but it was difficult to tell when she was being serious and when she was not. However, she did not gaze at Lupin with raised eyebrows as if she were some peculiar specimen, as did most of the people in Glanville, and for this she was truly thankful.

Diana and June often went up to London for a night or two to do some shopping and see some plays, and they were able to talk about things Lupin understood; it was a relief not to have to appear intelligent about the Sunday School, the Mothers' Union and the church missionary society, and the time passed away very happily. Lupin was quite sorry when it was time to go. She walked home through the gathering dusk, feeling thankful that she had made two friends in this strange place. Diana, of course, was rather old, and there was no doubt she was a bit too clever for comfort, still she was quite like a human being, and June was a girl after her own heart. She had felt at home with her from the beginning, just as she did with Duds and Pamela. She must ask Stephen down. He would be sure to fall in love with her.

Thinking of Duds, and Pamela and Stephen, Lupin began to feel a little homesick. She wondered what they were all doing. If she were in London now, she would be at a cocktail party, then she would dress and dine, and go on somewhere else to dance. No one would expect her to make the Guides feel like one big happy family; nor to talk brightly to the Sunday School teachers; nor to run a working party in aid of foreign missions. How lovely it would be to be dressing for a party, putting on a really exciting frock and starting out into the friendly lights and noise of London. Then she suddenly remembered Andrew—if she were in London she would not have him. One had to take the rough with the smooth! And she would rather have Andrew than any amount of friends and parties.

The lights were shining from the vicarage windows. It looked welcoming in the dusk. The evening air was cold and Lupin gladly hurried into her nice warm house. Andrew was in his study, and the sight of him made up for everything.

"Well, I've been to tea with your girlfriends," she said. "I like June most awfully. Diana was nice, too, but a bit frightening. Didn't she go to Oxford or Cambridge or something, or has she taken a degree or written a book? There were masses of books everywhere, and some of them looked a bit stiff, but we had a lovely tea, crumpets, with plenty of butter. I must ask Sara to let us have more butter, or do you think I'll get fat? Duds says there is always a danger of getting fat in the country. Not that Glanville is exactly country, and Diana is thinner than anyone I've ever seen, in spite of the butter, but I'd rather be thin when I'm her age than have middle-aged spread."

"Diana has never taken a degree, I can promise you that," Andrew reassured her when he was able to get in a word. "I admit she has written some books, but they are chiefly children's books. I don't think that you will find her unpleasantly clever when you get to know her well. I should particularly like you to be friends."

CHAPTER 4

LUPIN found herself, to her great surprise, sitting in the chair at her first Guiders' meeting. On one side of her was Phylis Gardner, looking anxiously important in a high collar and a green tie. On the other side was Miss Oliver, the district secretary; she had a long, thin face, like the reflection one sees in a spoon, and she appeared to suffer from some strange affliction that prevented her from keeping still; she tipped her chair first one way and then another, she twined herself round the back of it, then leaned forward, hugging her knees. She turned her head from side to side on her long neck and altogether seemed so uncomfortable that Lupin longed to suggest her going home and having a hot bath and applying some soothing lotion. Facing her were about thirty Guiders, varying in age from nineteen to ninety-one, or thereabouts, as it seemed to Lupin. Among them were Diana, who looked exceedingly bored, and June, who caught Lupin's eye, and began to giggle.

They all sat for a few minutes in perfect silence, except for the creaking of Miss Oliver's chair and the breathing of one or two of the Guiders who suffered from adenoids. Lupin was just trying to think of some suitable remark to make, when Phylis leaned forward and hissed in her ear:

"You haven't called on the secretary."

Lupin blushed. What a terrible solecism with which to start her career as district Guider or whatever she was. Of course she ought to have called on the secretary. Why had she never thought of it? As a matter of fact such a thought had never entered her head. Of course the secretary was Miss Oliver, and the reason she was fidgeting in such a strange way was not insects, but hurt feelings. Lupin turned to her anxiously.

"I say," she said, "I am afraid I have never called on you. I am so sorry, but I am afraid I am not much of a hand at calling. I never can find any cards, in fact last time I called on anyone, I left the Queen of Spades by mistake. I don't know how she got into my case, but anyway I do hope you will come to tea one day."

Miss Oliver went scarlet, and squirmed more than ever. Phylis gave a sarcastic little laugh. A Guider, who looked exactly like a man dressed up, said, "Ha, ha, ha, ha," in a deep, bass voice. A sweetfaced Guider sitting near the front gave a sad smile, as much as to say, "Laugh while you may, tomorrow is awaiting you," and June burst into an uncontrollable peal of laughter.

"Ask her to read the minutes," whispered Phylis.

Lupin gazed blankly round the room, then, luckily, she remembered that minutes were something that secretaries did read at meetings, why, she did not know, and she turned to the embarrassed Miss Oliver. "It would be most awfully kind of you to read the minutes," she said, desperately.

She did not hear much of the minutes, she was too busy trying to avoid June's eye and in repairing the ravages to her own complexion. Suddenly to her horror she realized that every eye in the room was fixed on her powder case and lipstick. Blushing more than ever, she muttered, "I am sorry," to no one in particular, and thrust them back into the capacious pockets of her new uniform.

Phylis Gardner handed her a piece of paper. On it was written: 'Is it your wish that I sign these minutes?' Lupin looked at it wonderingly, and could make nothing of it.

"I don't mind at all," she said out loud, just as Miss Oliver had informed them that it had been decided to hold a church parade service during the autumn months. There was a stunned silence, then Miss Oliver resumed her reading. Lupin felt that she was in the middle of a nightmare. She looked at the earnest faces and the many open mouths (most of the Guiders seemed able to attend better that way), and wondered how she had got there, and if there was any chance of escape. If anyone had told her a few weeks ago that she would ever find herself taking the chair at a meeting of Girl Guiders, she would have been ready to bet a hundred to one that the thing was impossible. But the thing was even worse in reality that it had been in imagination. Most things you dread are not so bad when they actually happen, but this was a hundred times worse. There seemed to be an almost sinister atmosphere in the room, at least that is how it struck her. Suddenly she realized that there was complete silence once more, and that all eyes were turned on her. Miss Oliver was holding the book toward her, Miss Gardner proffered a pencil. Lupin muttered something indistinct, and signed her name slowly and carefully. It was something to do, and she had no idea what was supposed to take place next. At length, however, there seemed nothing for it but to plunge. She looked at her agenda paper, held it this way and that, and then, in a nervous and husky voice she remarked, "Well, now, there seem to be some things here that we ought to discuss and what not—I mean—I suppose that is what we are all here for, and the sooner we get the things fixed up, the sooner we'll be able to get away, if you know what I mean. Not that it isn't very nice here, of course. Still, there it is. Here, for instance, it says something about a competition for a shield—some sort of competition I expect," and she looked anxiously at Phylis.

"Might I say a little about this, madam?" asked Phylis.

"Please do," replied Lupin earnestly, as she leaned back in her chair and felt for her cigarette case. She had just selected a cigarette and was about to apply her lighter, when she caught June's eye. June shook her head slowly, and Lupin realized that she had been on the verge of committing yet another solecism. She grinned back gratefully, replaced the cigarette, put the case back in her pocket, and tried to follow what Phylis was saying.

"As you all know, a shield is offered each year for the company which gains the highest number of marks in a competition. This year it was thought that the competition should be based entirely on the Second Class Test."

'Why Second Class?' wondered Lupin, her thoughts wandering a little. 'I suppose it is a second class shield. A pity they don't have second classes on the railway now. It would be so very uncomfortable to travel third, and yet it seems a little extravagant for a vicar's wife to travel first.' Then she remembered an elderly woman she had once met who had nursed in Italy in the War, and had been awarded the Order of Chastity, Second Class. She began to giggle, then pulled herself together and murmured, "Very nice idea, I am sure," but no one seemed to hear.

"Who thought it?" Diana was asking in her bored voice.

Phylis flushed. "It was the wish of our late commissioner, Mrs. Lowe."

"Oh!" The short word implied profound contempt for Mrs. Lowe, and for any thoughts which she might have had.

"It was suggested that it might be divided into four groups—Morse, Knots, First Aid and Nature Study."

"I wish it could all be on Nature Study," remarked the sweetfaced Guider, "the more we can get our little people in touch with the great world of nature, the nearer we are approaching to the ideal of our splendid movement."

"I think it should all be on First Aid," suggested somebody else, "especially gas masks, and what to do in air raids."

"I think it would be a pity to mix the Guides up with anything like that," said Miss Oliver, wriggling as she spoke. "After all, it is an international movement, and I think we should keep ourselves out of a war."

"I wonder if the hostile aircraft will know that we don't want to be mixed up with them?" said Diana, thoughtfully. "They may not be able to distinguish Guides and non-Guides from the air."

Lupin laughed, and most of the Guiders followed her example. Miss

Oliver looked very angry and as if she might start hissing by mistake. The sweetfaced Guider said, "Oh, war, to think of human beings wanting to kill each other when the world is so very beautiful!" which remark did not do much to further the discussion.

"I should suggest," said Phylis, "that we get a doctor to draw up a syllabus for the First Aid test." Everyone seemed to agree to this, and Lupin murmured, "Jolly sound scheme—I mean, a good idea—I should if I were you."

Phylis went on. She obviously realized that if the meeting were to be conducted satisfactorily, she had better conduct it herself. "Has anyone any ideas as to how the Morse should be tested?"

"Yes," said Diana, "I should give full marks to any company who refused to waste their time over it."

"You consider it a waste of time then for children to learn perseverance, concentration and accuracy?" asked Phylis.

"Yes," replied Diana.

"Oh, Morse is jolly good fun," said the man-Guider, whose name, Lupin afterwards learned, was Miss Thompson.

"So long as they do it under God's blue sky," murmured the sweetfaced Guider.

"I expect that they will do it under God's tin roof in the gymnasium at six o'clock on a winter's evening," pointed out Diana.

Phylis muttered something out of which Lupin thought she caught the word 'blasphemous.' She began to feel more uncomfortable than ever, as she remembered her job was to make them all feel like one big happy family. "Well, she said, "I like to see children happy."

"Then you should not have joined the Guides," said Diana.

"What exactly do you mean by that?" demanded Phylis.

Diana smiled. "Just what you think I mean," she replied sweetly.

"Couldn't they act a play?" suggested an intense-looking Guider with a loosely knotted tie and a great deal of hair.

"No," replied Diana.

"Why not?" hissed Miss Oliver.

"I don't know," said Diana. "For the same reason that I can't walk on my head, I suppose."

"All children can act," said the intense one. "It is only a question of drawing it out of them."

"Yes, let's have a drawing competition," said Lupin, waking up for a minute.

"For Guides or Guiders?" asked Diana.

"I think we want to encourage self-expression," said Miss Oliver, writhing.

"Why?" asked Diana

"Yes," said the sweetfaced Guider, "we want to bring out all that's best in their little minds."

"If you bring out the best, you will probably bring out the worst as well," pointed out Diana.

"You will bring out what you look for; I expect the highest, and I get it."

"In acting a child releases his ego; he fulfils a natural urge. Why does a child show off?"

"Because it wants a smack—" began Lupin. "I mean—why does it, do tell us?"

"Because he wants to impress himself on his environment. In acting he can do this in a legitimate way. Surely, as a writer, Miss Lloyd, you can understand this. Why do you write?"

"To earn money," replied Diana.

"We are rather wandering from the point," said Phylis, who did not care for abstract discussions.

"Well, I wish to propose that the Guides act a play for the competition," said the intense Guider.

"I'll second that," said Miss Oliver.

"What about handicrafts?" asked the sweetfaced Guider—"clay modeling or woolwork?"

"What about an original poem?" suggested someone else.

"What about ballet dancing, or a set of Greek verses?" asked Diana, brightly.

After a pause, when some giggled and some looked angry, and Phylis Gardner was obviously counting ten before she spoke, the sweetfaced Guider poured oil on the troubled waters by saying reprovingly, "All that matters is to love the little mites."

"And play the game," said Miss Thompson, who hadn't followed this conversation and barely knew what self-expression meant, but who had great faith in the team spirit.

Lupin caught hold of this last idea eagerly, "Yes, let's play a game," she said, "discussions so often lead to … well, what I mean is, one man's meat is another man's fish or something. Anyway, what about a nice game. Isn't there something where two people go out of the room and think of something, and then come back and guess what it was they thought of?"

There was a surprised silence, broken by a suppressed giggle from June.

"Jolly sporting idea," said Miss Thompson.

"We have rather a lot to discuss," pointed out Phylis.

"Oh, well, just as you like. I was only wondering whether it wasn't leading to—er—um—a bit of discussion, you know. Can't we toss up for it, or vote, or something. A secret ballot they call it, I believe."

The latter idea took on rather well. The voting took place, and the nature of the test was decided on more or less amicably. Lupin did not take quite in what they were going to do. Her interest was flagging by this time, but so far as she could make out, the children were going to plant acorns in flower pots, tie a lot of knots somewhere with something, do breathing exercises and have a motor accident. Her collar was tight and so was her hat, and she wished that she was sitting in Duds' flat drinking cocktails and talking harmless scandal. It would be nice to put on a new frock and go out somewhere to dine and dance. There was a new show that Duds had written about that sounded marvelous. Perhaps Andrew would take her to see it at Christmas, but it was dull going to see things when they had been on for months and everyone else had seen them and forgotten about them.

"What do you think . . . Lady Lupin?"

Lupin gave a jump. Bother! They had all stopped being a happy family again. Phylis was bristling, Miss Oliver was hissing, and Miss Thompson snorting. Even the sweetfaced Guider was smiling in a somewhat twisted way. Diana was regarding her fingernails in a detached manner. She had probably been baiting them all. Lupin was glad that Andrew was not married to her; she might have baited him, and Andrew, like herself, preferred a quiet life.

"I think it must be nearly bedtime," she replied.

Everyone laughed, and harmony was restored, "I think Miss May would like to say a word or two about the Brownies," murmured Phylis.

"How nice," said Lupin wearily.

A Guider with a whimsical expression and in a very large hat got up at the back of the room. "I don't know if any of you have fairies in your gardens," she began. Lupin supposed she must have gone to sleep and be dreaming. She sat up straight and pinched herself. "But I assure you," went on Miss May, "that Glanville is swarming with fairies."

'Good heavens, she is drunk,' thought Lupin, and she looked anxiously at Phylis. But. Phylis was thinking about the Shield Competition; she was not very interested in Brownies.

"Fairies and gnomes and elves and pixies—all little people living in a magic world touched by the pipes of Pan."

Lupin wondered if there were anyone in Glanville who was not touched with something. Diana's face was perfectly serious, but she gave Lupin the suspicion of a wink. June rushed wildly from the room, her handkerchief held to her face.

"These little people, dressed in brown, live in Glanville and are always on the lookout for good turns to do."

Lupin remembered meeting a band of small girls in what she supposed was a Brownie uniform a few days ago; they had thrown stones at her car as she went by; she wondered if that had been one of their famous good turns.

Miss May droned on. Several of the Guiders excused themselves. She was certainly good at clearing a meeting. 'I suppose they always put her on,' thought Lupin, 'when they feel the meeting has gone on long enough.'

Diana sat on, seeming to take a cynical enjoyment in what Miss May was saying. The sweetfaced Guider had a slightly forced expression of interest, and Miss Thompson gaped woodenly before her. At last, after what seemed several hours, Miss May concluded with: "And so we all join hands in the Fairy Ring and sing our Brownie song."

"Well," said Lupin, stifling a yawn, "I am sure that was all very interesting. Thank you so much for telling us all about the—er—them."

"Dear little mites," began the sweetfaced Guider, "what a unique opportunity for those who have the molding of their beautiful little minds."

Lupin made an effort. She couldn't bear any more of it, and this woman was obviously a bit put out that someone else should have poached on her preserves and talked about sweet little children. If left to it she would try to get her own back, which would take another few hours.

"Yes, indeed," said Lupin, "very nice—children, I mean—in moderation, that is. I expect you will all be wanting to get home now; must be fresh for the good work tomorrow—all these children and fairy rings and pipes of Pan—splendid work and all that. Shall we be toddling now?" and she turned to Phylis.

"There was only one thing more that I wished to say," said Phylis. "I am sorry so many Guiders had to leave before the end, as I have one piece of very good news for everyone. Our late commissioner, before she left, made us a delightful present, a Union Jack, to be kept in Guide headquarters and to be used by any Guider whenever she likes." (Lupin wondered on what occasion a Guider would be likely to wander into headquarters and use a Union Jack.) "I have only one request to make, and that is that you will always leave the Union Jack as you would wish to find it."

Lupin was thankful that June had gone home, as she knew that if she had caught her eye she would not have been able to control herself. She stole a look at Diana, who was regarding Phylis with a perfectly serious expression, but with a slightly raised eyebrow. Phylis reddened angrily under her gaze.

"Color Party, fall in," cried Phylis. Three Guiders leaped to attention, knocking over two chairs in so doing; everyone else shuffled awkwardly to their feet; Lupin edged toward the door.

The color party were jerking at a string; a small, tight bundle was bobbing about at the top of a pole. Suddenly it jerked from its moorings and revealed itself as the new Union Jack. It took off the sweetfaced Guider's hat and she forgot to look sweet for a moment, then the post fell down, catching Phylis on the side of the head, and the flag fell to the floor with one of the color party on the top of it.

Phylis bravely ignored the blow, and sang through the first verse of the National Anthem in a reedy voice, seconded by Miss Thompson in a different key.

"This is where we leave," said Diana. "Good night, Phylis. Are you sure you are not hurt? Be careful to leave the Union Jack as you would wish to find it."

"Oughtn't we to do anything to help?" muttered Lupin halfheartedly.
"I don't think so. She is more angry than hurt."

"Never again . . . never again," said Lupin, as she drained her whiskey and soda. "If I have to take part in a bullfight I hope I shall behave like a well-bred English gentlewoman. If you put me down in the jungle, surrounded by wolves, I may prove worthy of my ancestors . . . but a meeting of Girl Guiders—no, it simply can't be done."

"Wait until you have met the Parochial Church Council," replied Andrew grimly.

CHAPTER 5

LUPIN poured herself out another cup of coffee and set herself to the difficult task of assimilating a letter from Duds. Her handwriting was not easy to decipher, and the paper on which she had chosen to write was extremely thin. She and Tommy were spending a belated holiday in the South of France, as Tommy, usually the essence of good health, had contracted a severe attack of influenza and had been ordered south to convalesce in the sun. They seemed to have lost most of their money at the casino, but Tommy had run away . . . Good heavens! . . . Tommy had run away with a 'sweet . . . sweet something' at the hotel . . .

"What is it, Sara?"

"Miss Gibson to see you, my lady."

"Damn—Dash, I should say. You may clear away, Sara."

Lupin lit a cigarette, glanced in the mirror and wondered whether a green velvet dressing gown was a really suitable garment for a vicar's wife to appear in at ten o'clock in the morning. However, there was nothing to be done about it now. What could Duds have meant about Tommy? Had his influenza gone to his head?

"Good morning, Miss Gibson," she said, brightly. Duds had told her that a vicar's wife must be bright at all costs. "I expect that you have come to see me about the Guides." Miss Gibson's face froze. Lupin had evidently made a bad shot. "I mean the Mothers' Union," she hazarded, but that was obviously not one of her better efforts either.

"I am sorry to have brought you downstairs, Lady Lupin. If I had known you were unwell, I should have deferred my visit."

"But I am not unwell, I've seldom felt better." Then she remembered the dressing gown. "Well, I was feeling a little bit done up as a matter of fact. We had a Guiders' meeting last night and—er. . ."

"I have nothing to say against the Guides," announced Miss Gibson, "I am sure that it is a splendid movement, although I don't quite know what good it is supposed to do. I always notice that the Guides behave worse than any other children in the Sunday School, in fact they are seldom there. If they were taught anything, I should say nothing, but they merely monopolize the Church Room, waste electric light and gas, and frequently leave the door unlocked so that all the boys can break in and destroy everything, not to mention smashing the windows. Luckily I keep the missionary box in my own house, but several of the hymn books have been defaced."

Lupin began to think of Duds' letter again and to wonder with whom Tommy could possibly have run away; she pulled herself together.

"Well, there is Morse," she said, "and drawing the Union Jack, and being able to recognize a tree when you see it, and tying wet ropes together and breathing through the mouth—or is it the nose? Anyhow, breathing, you know, so important." Then she had an inspiration. "What about the Sunday School? Is all well with it, if you know what I mean?"

"All is not well with the Sunday School, Lady Lupin."

"Dear me, now; isn't that too bad! Won't you have a cigarette?"

"Thank you, I don't smoke."

"Well—er—a cup of coffee—or an egg?"

"I breakfasted at 8:30, thank you. What I came round about was to say that I cannot continue as Sunday School superintendent if Mr. Young is allowed to interfere with my classes."

"No, absolutely. I see your point."

"He came in last Sunday morning and asked the girls in the third class to repeat their duty to their neighbor. The Duty to their Neighbor is not taken until the girls reach the fourth class, so of course none of them knew it."

"No, of course not."

"It was most annoying."

"Absolutely. . ." (Tommy ran away with the sweet . . . Could Duds have meant the pudding?)

"And that is not the worst."

"Oh, dear!"

"I don't know if I ought to mention it."

"Well, don't if you'd rather not."

"But I think you ought to know . . . Why do you think that Mr. Young visited the girls of the third class last Sunday morning?"

Lupin felt that she knew the answer to this one. "To tell the girls their duty to their neighbor."

"I am afraid not; it was to see Miss Simpkins."

This did not strike Lupin as likely. Sometimes one had to see Miss Simpkins; it could not be avoided. But one would hardly set out deliberately to look for her. She was not a 'thing of beauty' or 'a joy forever'—quite the contrary. "Perhaps he did not know that she took that class," she suggested.

Miss Gibson did not exactly snort, but she gave what would have been a snort in anyone who was not both a Sunday School superintendent and a gentlewoman. "There is something there I don't like," she said.

Lupin was with her there. "I know," she said, "her nose. I dare say it's indigestion."

"I was not alluding to Miss Simpkins's nose."

"Her ankles," suggested Lupin. "I quite agree."

"I was alluding to her relationship with Mr. Young."

"I did not know they were related," said Lupin.

Miss Gibson had never really liked Lady Lupin. She realized now that if she were not a Christian she would positively dislike her. "They are not related," she said, in an awful voice, as she rose to take her leave. "You will do as you think best about telling the vicar," she added.

After seeing Miss Gibson out of the front door, Lupin put her head in at the study. "Andrew," she said, "did you think that Mr. Young and Miss Simpkins were related to each other?"

Andrew looked up from his sermon. "No, darling," he replied.

"That's all right, they're not."

She walked back to the dining room and picked up Duds' letter once more. 'Tommy ran away with a sweet. . . shane, swain, shade. I know,' she thought, suddenly, ' "Sadie," that's an American name. It must be some American girl staying at the hotel. But this is too frightful, poor old Duds. What does one do? I suppose I ought to fly at once to my stricken friend, but I'd better get dressed first, anyway, then I'll have to find out how to get there. I don't like leaving Andrew all alone. I wonder what he'll think about it all. Perhaps I'd better ask him first, or shall I get dressed first? Bother,' as the front doorbell resounded through the house.

"There is a person from the school, wishing to see you, my lady," said. Sara, in a disapproving voice.

"From the school, what school?" Someone from her own old school. At any ordinary time she would be delighted for a chat about the dear old school days, but this morning she was too worried about Duds, besides, every minute counted if anything was to be done.

"I think she said her name was Watson," volunteered Sara, distastefully.

Miss Watson, the headmistress of the day school, how frightful! "Show her into the dressing room," she said. And she wasn't dressed, this was awful, but how could one get dressed, when people never stopped coming in?

"Oh, good morning, Miss Watson, I am so sorry I am not dressed, but every time I've tried, someone—I mean, something—has stopped me, and I am rather upset this morning."

"Don't mention it, Lady Lupin," replied Miss Watson, stiffly. "I wouldn't have disturbed you for the world, but I thought it best to ask for you rather than for the vicar in case of a misunderstanding."

"Yes, of course. Though as a matter of fact, I am much more likely to misunderstand than he is."

"I shouldn't like to give your servants any reason to talk."

"I don't think they need much reason. I often hear them chatting away together, and as for the cook . . ."

"What I wish to speak about, Lady Lupin, is Mr. Young's interference in the day school. Of course, I know it is a church school, and I am delighted to see the vicar at any time, but the vicar is one thing, and a curate is another."

"That makes two," replied Lupin, brightly.

Miss Watson quelled her with a glance. "When it comes to dropping in at all times and during all lessons to talk about missions, I feel I must put my foot down, though no one is more interested in missions than I am."

Lupin couldn't help thinking that this was a lie, as obviously Mr. Young was, for one, but she did not like to point this out, and her mind reverted to Duds. Tommy, of all people! It made one quite nervous. Would Andrew? No, he hardly could, being a clergyman; it was lucky she had married a clergyman as it had turned out, even though it did mean one couldn't have one's breakfast, nor put on one's clothes in peace. It was lucky she had got through her bath without anyone breaking in to talk about Mr. Young. He always seemed to be popping up somewhere where he wasn't wanted.

"I'm afraid I shall have to appeal to the N.U.T."

The last word caught Lupin's ear. "T.N.T. I believe I've got some upstairs. Mrs. Grey told me to get some and to gargle with it night and morning. I never have. Don't tell her, will you? I'll get it for you."

"I wasn't talking of T.N.T., Lady Lupin."

"No, I don't believe it was T.N.T., now you mention it, but it's something like that; good for colds, anyway."

"I was alluding to the National Union of Teachers."

"Have they all got colds?"

"I wasn't aware that I had mentioned colds."

"No, nor you did, but I thought you sounded a little hoarse, but—er—I was so interested in what you were saying. I suppose you wouldn't like to say it to the vicar; he is more used to these sort of things than I am."

"I should be very glad to explain my difficulty to the vicar, but I thought I'd better tell you first what I wished to speak to him about, in case you wondered."

Lupin led her to the vicar's study. "Here's Miss Watson," she said. "She wants to talk to you about foreign missions." As she walked back she found Sara showing Diana up to her sitting room.

"I'm afraid I've arrived rather early in the day," apologized Diana, "but June and I are going to play golf. As you have already had Miss Gibson and Miss Watson this morning, I dare say you are feeling a little under the weather."

"Well, I am rather. I couldn't understand what they were talking about."

"I can tell you about Miss Gibson. She came to drop hints about Mr. Young and Gladys Simpkins. Why she has hit on poor Gladys, I can't imagine. She must be nearly old enough to be his mother, apart from anything else. She was in my Rangers until I had to superannuate her, so I can really vouch for her morals. Not that being in my Rangers gave them to her. I should not be surprised at anything any of the others did, but poor Gladys. Well, you've seen her, I expect."

"Yes, the one with the nose and thick ankles." Lupin wondered if she had better fly to the South of France; she would get there sooner that way, on the other hand, did she want to get there sooner? It would be very unpleasant when she did get there.

"Of course, Miss Gibson has always had her knife into Mr. Young, she wanted her own nephew here as curate, but as the vicar said, one in the parish is quite enough."

"Yes, two curates would be rather expensive." (Perhaps she had better not fly. She must try to be economical, now that she was a vicar's wife. Besides, her maid would probably be sick.)

"He meant 'Gibsons,' not curates."

"Oh!" Lupin felt rather dazed. She had visions of two Miss Gibsons wandering in and out of the vicarage and marshalling the children to Sunday School. "Won't you have a cigarette?" she said feebly.

"Thank you very much." Lupin noticed that Diana averted her eyes in a pained manner from a photograph of her and Andrew taken after their wedding. She felt rather apologetic; it was bad luck on the woman not being married to Andrew.

"I'm sure you are a great help to—er—everyone," she murmured.

"Especially to Phylis Gardner," replied Diana.

Lupin remembered the Guiders' meeting and began to laugh. "You did rattle her rather," she said.

"I can never resist it," said Diana, "it's very feeble of me, I know, but those Guiders' meetings always annoy me. They are all so horribly smug, and I don't believe that any of them care two pins about the children."

'I believe she really likes children,' thought Lupin, surprised. 'What a pity she never had any.' Then her mind reverted to Tommy and Duds. They had always been such a devoted couple. When Lupin returned to Diana once more, she found she had left the Guides and was talking about Miss Gibson.

"Of course, she is a sincerely religious woman, but she wants everyone else to be religious in her own particular way, and if she could have got her nephew here by hook or by crook, she would have felt she was furthering the cause. The vicar is too broad-minded for her."

"Yes, he is broad-minded, isn't he?" But Lupin did not think that he would approve of Tommy running away with a 'sweet Sadie' from the hotel.

"She is the sort of woman whom I can imagine committing murder for the sake of her religion."

"Sweepstakes!" exclaimed Lupin.

"What?" Miss Lloyd gazed at her in astonishment.

"I'm so sorry. I don't know what I was thinking about. I am so much interested in what you are saying. Please go on. I had not realized that Miss Gardner was so High Church. Was that why she was annoyed at the meeting?" (What a fool she had been. . . Tommy had won the sweepstakes at the hotel. As if he would have left Duds for anyone called Sadie.) She began to laugh, but managed to turn it into a cough. Tears of suppressed laughter came into her eyes.

Diana looked at her quizzically. "We must all seem very funny to you, " she said.

"No, no," said Lupin, becoming serious in a moment. "Please do not think that. I was really most awfully interested. It's only that I had a letter from my great friend this morning saying that her husband had run away with someone or something, and I've just realized that it was only a sweepstakes after all, and I've been working myself up for nothing."

Diana had been rather distressed when Andrew had brought home this pretty little fool as his wife, but now she realized that, although she was no doubt foolish, she was like a foolish but attractive child. Her distress at appearing rude was genuine, and her frank explanation was very childlike. Although Diana might seem cynical to those who did not know her well, she had a tender side for children and animals.

"How very trying for you, having to listen to me talking about Miss Gardner and Miss Gibson and High Church and Low Church when you had got that on your mind—and before me you had Miss Gibson telling you about Mr. Young and Gladys Simpkins."

"Yes, she arrived just as I was reading the letter, and I hadn't time to finish it."

"Well, finish it now, I'll leave you in peace. I was only going to ask you to enroll some Guides. I know you'll hate it."

"No, wait. I'll read it to you—here it is. 'Tommy has run off with a sweepstakes at our hotel, so we are feeling quite rich.' There, that is absolutely all right, but I hadn't got as far as that when Miss Gibson came in, and it did look like 'Tommy has run off with a sweet Sadie in our hotel.' "

They both began to laugh, and as they lay back in their chairs with tears in their eyes, Mr. Young was announced. The curate looked at Diana and smiled. She gave him a cool nod. Lupin pulled herself together.

"How do you do?" she said. "It's a pleasant morning, isn't it?"

By this time Mr. Young had seen Lupin's dressing gown, and was looking embarrassed.." I only came to ask you if you would very kindly give away the prizes at my Bible class on Wednesday, December second?" he explained nervously.

"Of course, I shall be delighted," replied Lupin shakily. She was so relieved about Tommy, and the whole thing was so ridiculous, and the sight of the curate shying at her dressing gown was so funny that she felt she might burst out laughing again any minute.

"Lady Lupin is not feeling very well this morning," explained Diana.

"Oh, dear, how unfortunate. I am very sorry to hear that. We can't have this, can we? I am afraid you have been overdoing things, Lady Lupin. We all take advantage of your good nature."

"Mrs. Grey," announced Sara.

"Hallo, everyone, jolly morning, isn't it? Well, Lady Lupin," and she beamed all over her good-natured face. She caught sight of the curate, and her face changed. "Good morning, Mr. Young," she said, coldly.

"Good morning, Mrs. Grey. I regret to say that Lady Lupin is not feeling very well this morning."

Mrs. Grey looked at Lupin with interest. "Come, come," she said, cheerfully. "Let me take you upstairs, Lady Lupin," and Lupin meekly allowed herself to be led from the room. "Feeling a little sick, I expect?" continued Mrs. Grey, knowingly. "Just pop into bed with a hot water bottle, and you will soon feel as right as rain. Shall I ring for your maid? I wanted to have a chat about the Mothers' Union, but another time will do for that," and she stamped off.

'Oh, dear, I know what she thinks,' sighed Lupin to herself, 'how disappointed she will be!'

Mr. Young and Diana faced each other in the drawing room. "So you and Lady Lupin are becoming great friends?" he remarked.

"We have hardly had time for that yet," replied Diana.

"No, I suppose you have hardly had time to tell her all your secrets."

"No, but I may later on."

"I wonder. It would be interesting to know how she would receive your confidences, and then, another thing, she is not exactly what I should call reticent. I mean she would not intend to betray any secrets, but they might pop out."

"This is rather an unprofitable conversation, isn't it? I am going home now."

"I must be going, too. I have a lot of parish business to attend to. I'll just see if the vicar has any orders for me. It would be a pity if he had to leave the parish, wouldn't it? He is doing so much useful work here."

"I can see no reason why he should leave the parish."

"No? Perhaps not, but misunderstandings do arise sometimes, don't they, and a vicar has to be so very careful."

Diana did not answer, but walked toward the door. Young took a step toward her. "Why not end all this?" he asked. "If I were married to June, our interests would never clash again, and you would have peace of mind at last."

"What makes you think that June would ever marry you? She has never shown any sign of caring for you."

"I think if you were to put the facts before her, she would marry me, and I would make her a good husband."

"I would rather see her in her grave," replied Diana, and she walked out of the room and out of the house. As she paced slowly along the road, she pondered on ways and means. How was she to raise another hundred pounds by today week? Slowly her little capital was being reduced. Soon there would be nothing left; she did not make enough by her books to live on, besides, that too would probably be taken from her. Why had she talked to Andrew so freely that evening in the garden? Surely she might have known that a garden has ears. If only she could tell Andrew. . . .

"Di, Di, what ages you have been. I waited for hours, but Bill got so impatient I simply had to start."

Diana's face cleared as she looked at the slim, tweed-clad figure with her bare, curly head of reddish gold. Bill, the cocker spaniel, rushed to greet her, and Diana banished her worries for the time being. It was a lovely autumn morning. She would enjoy it and forget everything else; whatever happened, she would have this to remember—the blue sky, the frosty tang in the air, the scarlet hips and haws, the gold of the beech woods, and June's arm through hers.

"Did you see Lady Lupin?" asked June.

"Yes," and Diana told June all about Tommy and 'Sweet Sadie' and they both laughed as if they had not a care in the world. "I was lecturing away about the Guides and Miss Gibson's religious views, and the poor child never heard a word I said. I had just got to a really impassioned indictment of Miss Gibson, when she burst out 'sweepstakes.' "

"I wish I had been there, you are so funny when you go all parochial. I expect you terrified the poor girl."

"I don't think I am really parochial," said Diana, thoughtfully, "but I am interested in the different people in the parish, and the way things affect them."

"Oh, that's because you write books, but about Lady Lupin, I like her, don't you? Of course, she is quite bats, but she is very ornamental, and kind, too, I should think."

"Yes, I should think that she is kind. She was terribly upset when she thought that she had been rude to me. She insisted on reading her letter to me, to show me why she had been so absentminded. Rather a nice child; Andrew might have done much worse."

Left to herself at last, Lupin sat down and wrote to her friend:

Dearest Duds,

I have had an absolutely ghastly morning. First of all, I got your letter saying that Tommy had run away with someone, and just as I was wondering what we'd better do, the head Sunday School teacher came round to tell me that the curate wasn't related to one of the others, teachers I mean, not curates, and no sooner had she gone than in came the Guide captain, and said that the curate was her nephew and that he might murder her for the sake of her religion, and in the middle I suddenly realized you had said 'sweepstakes.' You can't think how thankful I was. I mean it's different for cinema stars and people like that, but if quiet husbands like Tommy are going to start behaving like Mormon elders, where will one be? I was so relieved, I believe I must have got light-headed. Anyway, I think the curate came in next, but he was so embarrassed when he saw my dressing gown that he could not bring himself to say much, but Miss Lloyd told him I was ill, which I must say was pretty decent of her because I hadn't been listening to a word she said. Then the head of the Mothers' Union came in and thought I was going to have a baby and enrolled me as a member on the spot. I do wish you would write more clearly.

Best love,
Loops.

CHAPTER 6

ANDREW had just come in from a round of visits and was lying back in his armchair, smoking a pipe. Lupin was perched on the arm, with a cocktail in one hand and a cigarette in the other. She had slipped into a white satin shirt and a pair of black velvet trousers on returning from her afternoon of good works. She had visited the Infant School that morning, and attended a Mothers' Union meeting in the afternoon, uncomfortably conscious that she was there on false pretenses, and had been to two tea parties. She looked thoughtfully at Andrew.

"I suppose it's worth it," she said.

"My profile?" he asked, complacently, "of course it is."

Lupin knitted her brows. "Andrew, how is it that plain parsons ever get married?"

"I suppose they have hearts of gold," hazarded Andrew, bending down and patting John, Lupin's West Highland terrier, who was stretched out at his feet.

"I suppose so, but I don't think I'd marry anyone for a heart of gold. I mean, after a dreary day of good works it wouldn't cheer me up to look at someone with a heart of gold."

"Well, you don't have to."

"No, thank goodness, but you know, Andrew, Mrs. Grey is sure to find out sooner or later that I'm not going to have a baby, and then where shall we be?"

"I don't quite understand why our offspring should be any business of Mrs. Grey."

"But they seem to be. They gave me a footstool at the Mothers' Meeting."

"Miss Gardner, my lady. I've put her in the drawing room."

"Oh, dear. Take some sherry in, Sara. I say, Andrew, do I look a pukka sahib?"

Andrew looked at her thoughtfully. "Not much—rather more like the principal boy in a pantomime."

Miss Gardner was in Girl Guide uniform, a fact which seemed to make Lupin's trousers even more conspicuous. John, who had followed her into the drawing room, greeted the visitor vociferously. Miss Gardner was not used to dogs, but her manners were always perfect, and she said "Good doggie then," without showing any sign of distaste for the sharp claws and white hairs on her neat uniform. Lupin did her best to be bright.

"Well, this is a pleasant surprise," she said. "Come here, John."

"I hope that I have not called at an inconvenient time."

"Not at all," said Lupin, wondering if any time would have been convenient.

"As a matter of fact I was taking a walk this afternoon and thought I'd like to have a look round your church."

"Very nice," said Lupin. "Come here, John."

"I was looking at a window in one of the side chapels, when I happened to see the colors. Good doggie then."

"Yes, there's a lot of color in them, isn't there?"

"And I could not help noticing that the Company color was on the right of the King's color."

This was very difficult. "Will you have some sherry?" suggested Lupin.

"Not in uniform, thank you. You may think it strange of me coming to you, but I had a reason. Down then, good dog. Diana Lloyd is one of my best friends, in fact, I am devoted to her, but it's no good pretending that she is not just a tiny bit touchy, if you know what I mean. Lie down then, there's a good doggie. But you are so tactful; I know that you will arrange the whole thing. There is no need to mention my name, you'll see for yourself when you are next in church and then perhaps you could draw her attention to them."

Lupin poured out a glass of sherry, then came to the conclusion that she had better keep her head as clear as possible. "Yes, rather, of course," she said vaguely. "Lie down, John, will you? You're a bad dog. I'm sure to see her in church, but we don't sit very near each other. Still I might catch her eye and point to the window. It's a pity that I haven't learned that Morse business yet, those dots and dashes, you know. I mean, I could tap it out on the pew." She realized that a cold blue eye was resting on her. It reminded her of a codfish that she had bought the other day which had not turned out an unmitigated success. "But perhaps that wouldn't quite do," she added, "I mean, I always think that when one is in the fishmonger's, in church I should say; well, what I mean is that when one is in church, one is in church, so to speak, isn't one?"

"Poor Diana," said Miss Gardner, sadly, "she is a strange soul, a dear, but . . ."

"Yes, rather, very dear, but perhaps I ought to say something to Andrew first. I mean we could hardly do anything to the window without telling him, could we?"

"The window?"

"Miss Stuart," said Sara.

Lupin turned with a sigh of relief; she would have welcomed almost any-one at this particular moment, but June Stuart was the one person in Glanville with whom she felt at home, Bill followed June into the room and John flew at him before anyone had time to say "How do you do." Several minutes were spent in trying to separate the dogs, and during this time a table was knocked over, a flower vase broken, and a good many books and other oddments hurled on to the floor. At length peace was restored, June was seated one side of the room, holding Bill by the collar, and Lupin on the other, holding John,

"I was coming back from my Brownies and ran full tilt into Miss Gibson. I knew she was going to ask me to take one of her beastly Sunday School classes, so I said I'd got to come and see you. Is that what they call a cocktail suit? I never knew anyone really wore them. Yes, I'd love some sherry and a cigarette, please."

"Childie dear, in uniform?"

"I'll take it off if you like, if you don't think the vicar will be embarrassed at the sight of my undies, they're quite pretty."

"He isn't often embarrassed," said Lupin, "but I don't see how I'm to give you the sherry without letting John loose again. Would you mind hold-ing him for a minute, Miss Gardner?"

Miss Gardner did mind, but could not very well say so, and put a hand gingerly into his collar. John wriggled violently and nearly pulled her off her chair.

"I shouldn't be surprised if Miss Gibson follows you in here; this house is rather like the Grosvenor Hotel—very nice of course, I like seeing people." (What a pity a vicar's wife always has to be so untruthful, she thought to herself.) "Oh, and June will tell Diana about the window, I mean it will come better from her."

Miss Gardner looked a little annoyed. "Oh, it was nothing, dear, only I happened to be looking at the windows of your church."

"Why?" asked June, surprised. "They're pretty frightful, aren't they?"

"And I couldn't help noticing that the colors were the wrong way round."

'How wise of Miss Gardner to refuse the sherry,' thought Lupin, 'she evidently has a weak head.' "Would you like some orange juice?" she asked.

"Oh, I see," said June, "I expect the verger has been playing about with them. He hid the Union Jack once, and put the candle extinguisher in its place. I carried it out by mistake, and everyone saluted it, before they realized what it was. How we laughed."

"Or some tomato juice?"

"But, childie, surely the verger shouldn't be allowed to touch the colors?"

"Well, he must dust the church sometimes, mustn't he, Lupin?"

"Yes, of course—er—er—most unfortunate. Will you try some bicarbonate of soda?" and she looked anxiously at Miss Gardner who was gazing at her with what almost seemed like disapproval. To rest her eyes, Lupin looked at June who was sitting on the end of the sofa sideways to her. For a moment she was struck with something about her face that reminded her of someone or something, she couldn't think of whom, or of what. She felt that the likeness was only just eluding her; she would capture it in a moment.

Andrew came into the room and Lupin forgot what she was thinking about. John escaped from Miss Gardner and flew at Bill again; Andrew removed him and picked up some of the debris which bestrewed his path.

"Oh, Andrew," said Lupin, when she was at last able to make herself heard, "here are Miss Gardner and June. They want to tell the verger to dust the candles because the colors seem to be wrong in one of the windows."

"They're wrong in most of the windows," replied Andrew cheerfully. "How do you do, Miss Gardner? Well, June?" and he smiled at her affectionately. "I gather you have been having a dogfight."

"Yes, I'm sorry, it was my fault. I oughtn't to have brought Bill in."

"They'll have to get used to each other," said Andrew. "What exactly do you want me to do about the windows, Miss Gardner?"

"I didn't mean to bother you about it," replied Miss Gardner, rising to take her leave. "It's nothing really, but I happened to notice that your Guide Colors were in the wrong position, and I thought Diana Lloyd would like to know."

"I don't think she would really," said June, "not frightfully, I mean."

"Well, let's put them right without telling her," suggested Andrew. "I'd like a little stroll."

Lupin was left alone, so she went back to the study to see if any of her cocktail was left. Andrew seemed very devoted to June, and small wonder, she was most attractive. Lupin rather wondered why he had not married her. Still, she was very glad that he hadn't, and it was a good thing he liked her, as she and June were becoming great friends. But what they all meant about the colors she could not imagine. She picked up a detective story which was lying on the table beside Andrew's sermon and was soon absorbed in it.

Andrew came in. "Do you regret having married me, darling?" he asked. "I'm afraid I've let you in for an awful life."

Lupin got up and sat on his knee. "No, I don't regret it a bit, darling, it's all rather interesting in a way, though I never understand one word anyone's talking about, but then I'm not much good at French either, except for knowing a list of the irregular verbs by heart, and they don't help one much in conversation, but I enjoy being in France."

"People are interesting, aren't they?" agreed Andrew. "I missed my big parish when I first came here, but I have got to know all the people here as individuals, in a way one can't when there are ten thousand of them."

"Oh, I am glad there aren't ten thousand here; where would we put them all? The other day, Miss Gibson was in the dining room, Miss Watson in the drawing room, and Diana in my sitting room. I was afraid the one who came next would have to wait in the downstairs cloakroom. So awkward if it had been Phylis Gardner!"

"Wouldn't it? Especially if you forgot to warn me! But you know I like Phylis, though there are some places I shouldn't wish to find her in."

"I think I should like her, if I weren't so frightened of her. In fact, I quite like them all in a way. It's great fun, and well, I like you rather," and she kissed the top of his head. "You know," she went on, rather soberly for her, "I'd have got bored if I had gone on forever in London, doing the same old things day after day, and night after night. One was always looking out for something new, well this is absolutely new."

"You feel at home with June, don't you?" asked Andrew rather wistfully.

"Oh, absolutely. I don't know what I'd do without her; she is quite human. I suppose we ought to go and dress. Sara won't like it if we're late." Just as she got into her bedroom she remembered there was something she had wanted to ask Andrew about June; whatever was it?

CHAPTER 7

LUPIN was closeted with her Guide secretary, Miss Oliver, who had rung her up to ask if she might come, and who had brought several fierce-looking documents for Lupin to glance through. It was a cold day, and they were sitting one on each side of the fire in Lupin's sitting room.

Miss Oliver always made Lupin feel uneasy. As a matter of fact, all the social workers with whom she came in contact made her feel uneasy, but Miss Oliver made her feel more uneasy than any of the others. It was not only the shape of her face, it was the way she sat, or rather fidgeted, in her chair, twisting herself about like a snake.

Lupin armed herself with the brightness of a vicar's wife. "How nice, I quite agree. You must be very clever at figures, I'm not very good. I was doing the weekly books this morning, and I had to go down to my husband in the middle and ask him how many shillings there were in seventy-three pence. So tiresome for him, because he was writing his sermon, and was thinking about Genesis, but he told me at once. Men are so clever, aren't they?"

"I like figures, they fascinate me."

"Do you really? How interesting. I once knew a girl who kept white mice. What is this? A notice of a meeting at the vicarage? Dear me, I think I shall be in London that day, but that won't make any difference, will it? You can all come here, and Miss Gardner will run it just as well as I should, better in fact, because she knows all about everything and it's still Greek to me."

"If you will forgive me for saying so, Lady Lupin, I don't think that many of the Guiders will turn up if they know that Miss Gardner is going to be in the chair. She may be very capable, and I don't wish to say anything against her, but her superior attitude toward all the other Guiders makes her very unpopular with them, and well . . . personally I should not come if she were in the chair."

Lupin was not remarkably intelligent, but she had a sudden flash of insight at this moment. 'Miss Oliver does not like Miss Gardner,' she thought to herself.

"Oh, what a pity. What about Miss Lloyd?"

Miss Oliver's face grew more enigmatic than ever. "I think it would cause a lot of unpleasantness," she replied.

"What about Ju . . . Miss Stuart? Surely no one dislikes her?"

"No, I don't think anyone actually dislikes Miss Stuart," said Miss Oliver reflectively. She seemed rather surprised to think that there was one Guider who was not actively disliked by all the rest, "But then she is not a free agent, she is absolutely under Miss Lloyd's thumb. I sometimes think she has some hold over her," she added mysteriously. "After all, it's rather funny. . ."

"Did you say Tuesday? Because it is Wednesday I am going up to London."

"Oh, that is a great relief, Lady Lupin, a very great relief," and Miss Oliver wriggled about in a kind of ecstasy. Anyone would have thought that a European war had just been averted.

Lupin's maid came in and spoke to her in a low voice. "I'm so sorry, do you mind if I go to the telephone for a moment?" It was a trunk call from Duds and it was a full twenty minutes before Lupin returned to her sitting room.

Duds and Tommy were coming for Christmas; what fun it would be! Of course, it would have been rather nice to go to Lorrimer, but one could hardly expect Andrew to leave his parish for Christmas, and it would be rather a thrill having her own friends staying in her own house, where she could do everything just as she liked. At Lorrimer she was always treated as a child by her father, her mother, and her brother, not to mention Nanny. Here she was a real grown-up person, a vicar's wife, looked up to by all.

At least, perhaps she was not looked up to quite by all. She had her doubts about Miss Gibson. No, she didn't think Miss Gibson exactly looked up to her, and then there was Miss Watson; well, you could hardly expect a head-mistress to look up to anyone, could you? How about Mrs. Grey? It's true she treated her much the same as Nanny did, suggesting she should take a dose and so forth, and it was no good pretending that Nanny looked up to her and Mrs. Grey wouldn't either when she found out that she wasn't going to have a baby after all! She was afraid Mrs. Brown rather despised her because she didn't have 'trouble with the maids.' 'Trouble with the maids,' always sounded such a grown-up sort of thing to have, but how one set about it she couldn't think. She had had a bit of an argument with Staines the other night about an evening dress; she had wanted to wear her pink and Staines had wanted her to wear her green, but you could have hardly called that trouble; in fact when she had put on the green, Staines had beamed proudly on her, and said how well it suited her.

Did Phylis Gardner look up to her? Did that slightly raised eyebrow beto-ken admiration? Did that twisted smile indicate approval, or was it keeping a stiff upper lip in the face of calamity? The latter, she feared. Yes, not to put too fine a point on it, Phylis thought that Andrew had committed a solecism in bringing her to Glanville, but did her best to gloss it over. Diana? Well, natu-rally if she had wanted to marry Andrew herself, she would hardly look up to her supplanter, if that was the right word. No, she didn't seem to be univer-sally looked up to in Glanville, but perhaps Duds wouldn't find that out dur-ing a short visit.

Crash! Something hit her and she barked her shin against the banisters.

"Oh, Lady Lupin, I am so sorry," said Mr. Young, rebounding off her on the stairs, and looking down on her, rather guiltily.

"So am I," said Lupin, rubbing her shin.

"I can't have been looking where I was going. Please forgive me. I came to see you about the Sunday School treat and was shown upstairs to your sitting room. Unfortunately I must go now, as I have an appointment at six o'clock. I do hope I haven't really hurt you."

"No, not a bit. I wasn't looking where I was going either! Lucky we didn't both fall over; if Miss Gibson had come in and found us both rolling about together on the stairs, she would have thought we had had one over the eight."

"Very awkward," laughed Mr. Young uneasily. "Then perhaps I could see you for a few minutes in the morning?"

"Perhaps," agreed Lupin vaguely. Now what had she been thinking about when she had collided with Mr. Young? Oh yes, of course, Duds. Was it wise of her to grow her hair long? Those curls at the back had suited her. She pulled herself together. "Of course, I shall be delighted," she said, then an-other thought struck her. "Was there anyone else in my room?" she asked.

"Do you mean in your sitting room?" replied Mr. Young, looking rather embarrassed. "Er . . . yes, Miss Oliver."

"Oh, dear, what a pity. I mean, I quite forgot. Need you go?" The thought of resuming the *tête-a-tête* with Miss Oliver was very distasteful to her. "Do come back and we'll have some sherry."

Andrew was coming in. He was a little surprised to hear Lupin's earnest entreaty. She had never seemed to care much for Mr. Young.

"Oh, well," said Lupin, "come to supper after the carols tomorrow evening. You can tell me about the treat then. June Stuart is coming, too."

Andrew walked a little way back with his curate as he had something to discuss with him, and Lupin reluctantly retraced her steps to her sitting room.

"I'm frightfully sorry," she said, "I don't know what you must think of me. It was a trunk call and I forgot . . . I mean, so awkward."

Miss Oliver had squirmed out of her chair. She was looking rather embarrassed. Lupin wondered if she had been flirting with the curate. The man must be a regular Don Juan! To Lupin's great relief she seemed anxious to go; she had been dreading a resumption of confidences about all the other Guiders and their misdoings.

"Oh, must you go? Well, we've settled everything, haven't we?"

"Yes, I'll send the postcards."

"Postcards?" queried Lupin nervously. Why on earth did the woman want to send postcards around? She only hoped that they would not be of a dubious nature. There was something strange about Miss Oliver, something to do with her face and her snaky movements and her intense voice. She was just the sort of person one read about in the newspaper, who sent improper postcards to clergymen. It would be most awkward.

"Announcing the meeting."

"Oh yes, of course, the meeting, rather, that will be great fun. I am looking forward to it enormously." She hurried her down the stairs and out of the front door. She took a deep breath of the frosty night air before closing it, somehow she felt a little stuffy.

A shadow appeared on the drive and before Lupin had time or presence of mind to shut the door, Miss Simpkins appeared on the threshold.

"Oh, Lady Lupin, could you spare me a few minutes?"

"Yes, of course, rather, come in."

Why on earth had she married a vicar? If only she had married Stephen she would probably have never even met a curate, or a Sunday School teacher or a Girl Guide. She took Miss Simpkins up to her sitting room where, to Lupin's intense horror, she burst into tears.

"Oh, Lady Lupin, what am I to do? I came to you because you are always so kind, but I don't know how to tell you."

"Dear, dear, dear," said Lupin, "how very unfortunate. Wouldn't you like something to drink?"

"No, thank you. I have never had anything to drink in my life."

"How thirsty you must get," replied Lupin absentmindedly.

Miss Simpkins did not appear to hear her. She rocked herself to and fro moaning. "I have always been a good girl," she sobbed.

"I am sure you have," replied Lupin with great conviction. Miss Simpkins' fortieth birthday was a thing of the past. She had dark hair streaked with gray, scraped well back off her face, which was of the kind that looks as if it had been regularly scrubbed with a hard scrubbing brush. Perched on a large nose were a pair of steel-rimmed spectacles; her legs in their cotton stockings were of exactly the same girth from as high as you could see them to the ends where they turned into feet. She held a responsible position in a large draper's shop in the town, and it certainly seemed, on the face of it, that she was correct in her assertion that she had always been a good girl.

"I couldn't tell anyone else," she gulped.

Lupin wondered why it was that people so often told her things that they could tell no one else. 'I must have a sympathetic nature,' she thought, with mixed feelings.

"A man took advantage of me," said Miss Simpkins in a funereal voice.

"What a brave man," exclaimed Lupin, supposing that he had palmed off a florin on her, instead of half a crown and got away with it. No mean feat with those spectacles trained upon him.

"He seduced me."

"What?" cried Lupin. "I mean, are you sure? Haven't you made a mistake?"

"It is hardly the sort of thing one is likely to make a mistake about, Lady Lupin."

"N—n—no, I suppose not; but whoever did it?"

"Wild horses will not drag the name from me," was Miss Simpkins' gallant answer.

"No, no, of course not," agreed Lupin hastily: "It's very difficult to tell, isn't it? I mean, I suppose it all happened in the dark?" What a shock the poor man would have got if he'd seen her! she thought to herself.

"I felt I must come to you, as you would know about these things."

"No, really, absolutely," stammered the bewildered Lupin, "I have never been seduced in my life so far."

"I mean that you will advise me what to do."

"I don't quite see what you can do; I mean, why do anything? I should try and forget the whole thing if I were you."

"It's worse than you think. I'm going to have a baby."

"No! Whatever makes you think that? I mean—don't tell me if you'd rather not. In fact, I don't think you'd better tell me at all. I really don't understand anything about these sort of things; I have never had any. You had better go round to Mrs. Grey; she seems to know all about it, though she hasn't had any either; at least, if she has she keeps them dark. Perhaps she will let you join the Mothers' Union. I'm afraid I simply must go and dress now, but I'll tell them to bring you some tea and when you've drunk that, you'd better trot round to Mrs. Grey."

"I shall kill myself."

"Oh, I shouldn't, if I were you. It's so cold; besides, it would all come out at the inquest, why you did it, and there'd be photographs of you everywhere—most unpleasant. I should have a nice hot cup of tea (how clever of me to think of that. I believe I am really cut out to be a vicar's wife after all; I know just what to do on every occasion!). Don't hurry away, but I'd certainly go on to Mrs. Grey as soon as you feel rested. Oh Sara, will you bring Miss Simpkins some tea. And will you ask Staines to take a cocktail up to my bedroom? And, by the way, whatever did you show Mr. Young up here for?"

"I didn't, my lady. I showed him into the drawing room."

('Am I going mad?' thought Lupin, 'or is everyone else? I feel just like Alice in Wonderland.')

She managed at last to get away from Miss Simpkins, who was still in floods of tears. She felt rather a brute but hoped that a 'nice cup of tea' would put her right. She found her cocktail in her bedroom and was sitting in a chair by the fire sipping it and reading a detective story when Andrew looked in.

"Oh! What do you think, Andrew?" she cried excitedly. "Duds is growing her hair!"

CHAPTER 8

"Isn't it a nuisance, Andrew? The housekeeping money has all gone."

"How much exactly, dear?" asked Andrew.

"Ten pounds, I think it was. I'd got it ready to pay the books and was going round to do them this morning."

"Where has it gone?"

"That's just what I don't know ... I mean, if I knew where it was I could find it, couldn't I? Yes, I know what you are going to say: Where did I see it last. Well, I know the answer to that one, it was on my writing table at teatime, because you were out."

"Why should it not have been there, had I been in?"

"Because I had tea in my sitting room, of course, and I went to the writing table to get a piece of paper to write to Duds and then she rang up, so I didn't have to write to her after all. They are arriving at four-nine, or was it five-nine? Anyway, it is something-nine. I'll have to ring up and find out."

"And the money was on the table then?"

"When?"

"When you were looking for your notepaper?"

"Yes, because there wasn't any notepaper, only pound notes, and I couldn't very well write on them, could I?"

"Not very well, When did you miss them?"

"The notes or the paper?"

"The notes."

"Just now. I went up to get them because I thought I'd go out and pay the books and get some flowers for Duds' room. I wanted to get some freesias because they are her favorite flower. It's funny, isn't it, about flowers. I like sweet peas best, I think, though of course one could hardly have them at Christmas, could one? But we must have some next summer. How do you think we had better set about it?"

"I will order some seeds. About the money; who has been in your sitting room since teatime yesterday?"

"Oh, millions of people. Well, wait a minute. Miss Oliver came in directly I had finished tea. Now you mention it, she did look rather embarrassed when I went back after talking to Duds on the telephone. And she was in a great hurry to get away, too. But then she always looks as if she had just murdered her grandmother and buried the remains among the cabbages, doesn't she?"

"Yes, I think she does rather give that impression."

"Then there was Mr. Young, but he wasn't alone there, because Miss Oliver was there, too. Of course, they may both have taken it and split it fifty-fifty."

"There is that aspect of the matter, although I should be loath to regard Young as a thief. I have known him for over a year and have every reason to regard him as honest."

"Then, of course, there was Miss Simpkins. I left her alone there drinking tea. Wasn't it clever of me to think of tea? I'm sure it's just the sort of thing a vicar's wife would always have on tap. Now I come to think of it, she would be glad of the money if she is really going to have a baby. Oh! I don't know if I ought to have told you that; it may be a secret."

"Very likely, but you surprise me."

"I was surprised myself. She said that she had been seduced—but why should anyone want to seduce her? I mean, if someone was bent on seducing a Sunday School teacher, there are one or two who really aren't bad looking in a quiet way. Of course, it may have been in the dark, but even then he must have bumped up against her spectacles. I suppose Miss Gibson would say it was Mr. Young but I don't see why he should want to do a thing like that, do you?"

"No. I have no more reason for supposing him immoral than I have for supposing him dishonest. He always seems to me to be a very earnest young man."

"Well, no one but an earnest young man would think of seducing Miss Simpkins, would they? I mean, she would hardly inspire affection in anyone lighthearted. But I don't really think she took the money. I am sure she is honest. Think of her ankles."

"Need I?"

"Then there are the servants. But why should they take this particular ten pounds? I am always leaving money about."

"That is very true."

"And they have never taken it before. Anyway, it couldn't be Staines; she has been with me all my life and Sara's been with you nearly as long, hasn't she? And Maggie is her niece. Besides, if any of them wanted ten pounds they would have the sense to ask for it, wouldn't they? It's not as if we weren't always quite pleasant to them."

"Well, there is nothing to be done for the moment. You had better draw another check for the books and go and get your freesias for Duds. I expect they will have some at Shaves."

"Yes, that will be best, won't it. I am simply longing to see Duds' hair, aren't you?"

"I can hardly wait! There is the telephone bell. I hope it is not Miss Gibson ringing up to say that she has been seduced. You have quite shaken my faith in the staff of the Sunday School. Is that for me, Sara?"

Andrew returned after a few minutes. "I say, darling, my nephew Jack Scott has just rung up to say that he has been given leave rather unexpectedly for Christmas, and as his parents are in the South of France . . ."

" 'Can we have him for Christmas'. . Was he that very good-looking one who came to the wedding? Do let's have him."

"I should not have thought that a young bride would have noticed that anyone at her wedding was good-looking, except her own husband."

"Why not? You noticed that my Aunt Maria was plain. Oh, I know, he is the one in the Secret Service. How frightfully thrilling! He'll be able to tell us all sorts of things. Oh, and I will tell you what, perhaps he'll find out who took the ten pounds. He will have to sleep in the room that we'd planned for the nursery if Mrs. Grey's hopes were fulfilled. Well, we won't want it over Christmas, anyway, will we?"

"I should hardly think so."

"Unless, of course, we lent it to Miss Simpkins. Oh, and Jack will be able to find out about that, too. He will be an awfully useful person to have in the house. I must ring up Diana. Miss Simpkins was a Rover or a Ranger or something under her, and she was sure she would never do anything wrong."

"I expect she is right. You probably misunderstood her. I expect she was talking about a child in her Sunday School class who hadn't been given her attendance stamp."

"Very likely, darling. I was rather busy, thinking about Duds' hair. Do ring up Jack and tell him to come and that he will have to sleep in the nursery, but that as far as we know he will have it to himself. He might not come if he thought he'd got to sing the little ones to sleep and get them drinks of water in the night. I know I wouldn't; they always wake up so early too, just when respectable people are trying to get their eight hours. What fun it all is; I do love a lot of people for Christmas. I wonder what Jack would like for a present? I am longing for Duds to see everything and everyone. I have asked Phylis Gardner to dinner on Christmas Day. I hope she will run true to form and talk about the Empire. I asked Di and June, but they are going to the Greys'. I wish I'd asked them sooner. But June is coming back tonight after the carol practice. Di couldn't; she has got an enrollment or something. Oh, and I asked Mr. Young, so I shall be able to ask him about the ten pounds. Oh no, I don't think I can very well, or about Miss Simpkins. No, I am not at home, Sara, I am out. Aren't you going to kiss me, Andrew? You won't see me till lunchtime."

It was a clear, frosty afternoon and Lupin walked up and down the platform accompanied by John. At last the train appeared and Tommy and Duds were soon discovered. They had two trunks, a suitcase, a hatbox, a dressing case, two bags of golf clubs, a brace of pheasants, a brown paper parcel, a few loose novels, several magazines and a large red setter, whom John regarded with resentment.

"My dear, where is your hair?" cried Lupin as soon as she caught sight of her friend. "It is quite all right, John. This is a very nice dog; he has come to stay; no, he isn't a horse, nor a lion; just an ordinary quiet little dog. You must be great friends."

"I had it cut off this morning. I hated it."

The dogs were skirmishing round each other and there were signs that a dogfight might take place at any moment.

"Well, I think it's the limit. Come to mother, John. One doesn't bite visitors, especially when they are bigger than you are. I've been looking forward to seeing you with it ever since you rang up last night, so has Andrew."

"Come here, Rufus, you will never be asked out again. Can't you behave pretty to the little dog. If I'd known I'd have kept some for you, but it was all swept up."

"Still, you might have waited. I am sorry, Miss Gibson." John had entangled himself with the skirts of the Sunday School superintendent, who was accompanied by a tall young parson.

"Have you a car or anything?" asked Tommy. "I think the porter would like to put some of the luggage somewhere."

"I suppose that is the High Church nephew," was Lupin's rejoinder. "Yes, of course, that blue one."

"How ecclesiastical you have become!" exclaimed Duds with admiration.

"How on earth did you know he was High Church? Oh, bother, Rufus has escaped. Look out, Tommy."

"Don't let him eat Mrs. Grey's Peke," begged Lupin. "I've got bad news for her as it is."

Whether the dogs found out that their views coincided about Mrs. Grey's Peke, or whether they merely decided to make the best of a bad job, is unknown, but it was certain that by the time they reached the vicarage, they had become quite friendly, and apart from occasional differences of opinion, they stayed fast friends throughout the length of the visit.

The vicarage looked very inviting with its blazing fires everywhere and with tea spread in the hall, with toasted muffins in the foreground.

"Oh, Andrew, what do you think?" cried Lupin as she ushered in her friends.

"I hope nothing has occurred to distress you, darling," said her husband.

"Yes, after all our excitement, too! Duds has cut her hair off again."

"Dear me!"

"Well, she looked a frightful sight with it on," said Tommy, frankly, "worse than she does with it off, I mean. I say, these muffins are good, Loops."

"Hurry up and eat them, then, because we have got to be at the carol practice by six o'clock."

"Did you say anything? I can't have been attending properly, you'll never guess what I thought you said," and Tommy laughed loudly. "I thought you said that we were going to a carol practice."

"Don't be tiresome. You know you have a very nice voice."

"He used to sing in the choir at school," put in Duds.

"How much sharper than a serpent's tooth is a wife in the bosom. Never mind, Andrew, I'll stay at home with you, and we'll have a nice heart to heart about women while the girls are singing carols."

"Andrew is writing a sermon for Christmas Day. Besides, one of the first things I was taught as a child was that when paying a visit, you have to fall in with the wishes of your hostess. I remember being made to fall in with a game of charades when I was staying with my cousins. I couldn't have been more than six, I think the word was marmalade. Anyhow, I had to pretend I was the Queen, and I cried, and was told it was very naughty to make a fuss when I was staying out."

There was to be a carol service in St. Mark's Church on Christmas Eve, and the choir was to be augmented by a large number of the congregation, together with several of the Girl Guides and the Sunday School. Lupin was rather glad to have an opportunity of showing off so many of the inhabitants of Glanville at one sitting, so to speak. Miss Gibson was there with her flock, and Diana with hers. Mrs. Grey and Mrs. Brown brought slightly reluctant husbands. Miss Gibson's nephew wore a somewhat supercilious air; perhaps there may have been some excuse for him, if he were used to good singing, as

the rendering of the carols was certainly more hearty than musical. Gladys
Simpkins came in late and appeared rather moved during the singing of "The
First Noel."

Mr. Young was conducting the practice with the help of the organist.
Lupin noticed at once that his usual enthusiasm and vitality were lacking. It
was the sort of occasion in which he would naturally have reveled. His eager
young face would have been alight as he rallied his followers; he could have
pictured the rather humdrum congregation, in the middle of a respectable
seaside town, as a band of intrepid missionaries spreading light in a land of
heathen darkness. But today, far from 'reveling,' he looked limp and tired and
could hardly bring himself to say, "Let us try once again," in a defeated voice,
when "Good King Wenceslas" had been rendered by two distinct schools of
thought as regarded both pitch and tempo. Perhaps he felt that the whole thing
was doomed to failure from the word go, but that was not like him. He would
enjoy leading a forlorn cause and at his best he would have soon had everybody singing in harmony. The choirboys were whispering to each other, a
thing they would never have dared to do under ordinary circumstances. If it
had not been for the organist, there would have been little or no practice; as it
was the whole thing seemed futile and halfhearted.

Lupin wondered what was the matter with Mr. Young. Had she kicked
him when he bumped into her on the stairs yesterday? Perhaps she had trodden on a corn, that would quite account for his defeatist attitude; and she had
never even asked him if he were hurt, what a pig she was! Of course, it might
be the presence of Miss Gibson's nephew that was putting him off his stride.
After all, she herself had got on quite well at the Mothers' Union until Mrs.
Grey came in, then she had dried up completely. Miss Gibson was fixing poor
Mr. Young with a particularly baleful eye that would be enough to upset anyone apart from the nephew. Of course, he ought to be used to her by now, but
she did look extraordinarily like a witch; was she putting a spell on him?

Lupin had looked forward to this evening. It was going to be such fun
pointing out everyone to Duds and Tommy, and she loved carols, but it didn't
seem to be working out according to plan. She felt unaccountably depressed
and everyone had somehow become rather sinister. Last Christmas she had
been at Lorrimer and everything had been cozy and normal and she rather
wished she were back there now. What was she doing here in this alien atmosphere, cheek by jowl with that witch-like Miss Gibson with her evil eye and
that lumpy, red-eyed Miss Simpkins? There was an inscrutable look on Diana's
face, which looked even more haggard than usual. Why was Andrew so anxious for them to be 'bosoms'? How could one be 'bosoms' with someone
who didn't even notice you were there half the time? Mrs. Grey was normal
enough, but Lupin wished that if she must sing so loud she would sing in the
same key as the rest of the congregation. She looked with a feeling of thank-
fulness at Tommy and Duds. If only they could escape together and go to a

nightclub or something homely!

She had been genuine enough when she told Andrew that the people of Glanville interested her; they did up to a point, and she had really tried very hard to be a good vicar's wife, but tonight she felt she couldn't go on trying any longer, she wanted to get away. Then she remembered if she stopped being a vicar's wife, she would have to stop being Andrew's wife and she wouldn't like that at all. When she was with him she felt happy and safe, and everyone else seemed nice and ordinary; it was only when she was away from him that they seemed alien and sinister. She hurried Duds and Tommy home and ran in to kiss Andrew before Mr. Young and June, who were coming back to dinner, arrived. "Oh, Andrew, I am so glad to see you, I felt so homesick in church. That must be Mr. Young and June arriving, I do hope he will cheer up a bit; if he is like he was in church he won't add to the gaiety of the dinner table."

June went up to Lupin's room to powder her nose. They had become very friendly during the last few weeks. "My dear," said June, "Charles has a boil on his neck."

"Do you mean Mr. Young? I didn't know anyone called him Charles. That accounts for all, poor thing, but I am glad it wasn't my fault. I was afraid I'd trodden on his best corn. But does that mean you are going to marry him? Because, if so, do think a bit. I mean, look at me, and after all I have got Andrew. Not that I want to be unkind about Mr. Young, if you are really in love with him, but it's pretty ghastly being a clergyman's wife . . . ."

"I am trying to tell you, if only you would listen for a moment, I have no intention of marrying him. I never had really, but this boil settles it. If one was really in love with someone I suppose a boil wouldn't put one off, so as soon as I found myself shuddering, I knew I wasn't in love."

"Well, I am thankful. I should have hated you to marry Mr. Young. I can't think what made you contemplate it."

"I didn't really, but you know what this place is. One hardly ever sees a man from one year to the next, and it is nice to be admired by someone, even if it's only the curate! But I'll tell you one thing, I don't think Di likes him. She is very nice to him, and asks him to tea, and that sort of thing, but I can always tell whether she really likes someone or not."

"Oh, can you? I can't. I have no idea whether she likes me or not. I think she is awfully difficult to talk with. Sometimes I have a feeling that she thinks I am a perfect fool."

"Yes, she does, but she likes you all the same, so you needn't worry. But about Charles Young, of course I wouldn't ever marry anyone if Diana didn't like them."

"Wouldn't you? I am devoted to Duds, but I should have married Andrew just the same, even if she hadn't liked him, and she would have done the same about Tommy Not that anyone could help liking either of them, but you know what I mean. After all, everybody can't like the same people. It would be awkward if they did, and you and Di won't get married at all if you both have to fall in love with the same man before you marry him."

"You have been talking to Mrs. Grey," laughed June. "Very unnatural for two girls to live together; what you want is a couple of husbands each and a family of children!"

Lupin laughed. "I can hear her; all the same there is something to be said for husbands, especially when it is Andrew."

"Now, Loops," said Tommy when they were all seated at the dinner table, "do tell us exactly who everybody was. I know Mrs. Grey, because she was at the station with a Peke, and my eardrums are still aching from the effects of her fruity bass. By the way, what is the disappointment you said you had got in store for her? My voice?"

"I'll tell you some time when we are alone."

"No, no, I would rather not hear it, if it is anything of that sort."

"Who was the one like a sergeant-major, who kept prodding the children?" asked Duds.

"Don't be tactless, darling," begged her husband, "she is probably the mother of one of those present."

"Not mine," said June. She caught Andrew's eye and smiled.

Mr. Young was sitting hunched in his chair, toying with a piece of fish. His boil was evidently making him feel unwell, but he looked up at Tommy's question. "Not mine," he said hurriedly, "not at all; quite the contrary."

"Do you mean that she is your father?" asked Tommy, who was rather literal.

"That woman was never anyone's mother," announced Duds firmly.

"What Mr. Young means," explained Lupin, "is that Miss Gibson can't bear the sight of him. You see, she has got a nephew of her own."

"I know," replied Tommy, "that tall one with a hungry face. He winced every time I opened my mouth."

"Well, you should use Colgate's," remarked Duds.

"Need you be coarse, dear?" inquired her husband. "It's not as if he were often asked out as it is. Then that was your sister sitting next to you, wasn't it, Miss Stuart?"

"No, she is not my sister; we are just friends and live together."

" Whatever made you think they were sisters?" asked Lupin. "They aren't a bit alike."

Tommy hesitated. "I don't know," he said. "No, they are not alike really, I suppose; I mean, one is dark and one fair, but somehow I jumped to the conclusion that they were sisters. Intuition, I suppose."

"But they are not sisters," pointed out Duds.

They played rummy after dinner, but the game broke up early. Mr. Young was obviously feeling unwell, but he had arranged to walk home with June, and nothing was going to prevent him doing so. In the end, out of compassion, June said she would leave, as she wanted to get home early.

"You are a brick," said Lupin as she saw her off. "He would never have gone without you, and I was expecting him to be sick at any moment—not that I would have minded, but John was sick in the drawing room this morning, and I feel it would have been too much to ask Sara to clean up twice, and it would be so awkward if she were to give notice. She has been with Andrew for years and knows all his ways much better than I do."

"I do hope I shan't come over all womanly and accept him out of pity," said June.

"No, don't do that. You don't want to spend the rest of your life in fomenting boils and holding basins. Give my love to Diana. Wasn't it funny of Tommy to think you were sisters?"

CHAPTER 9

CAPTAIN SCOTT arrived in time for tea the next afternoon. He was the son of Andrew's stepsister and was nearly ten years older than his new aunt. He was in the army and had done very well in his profession; for the last two years he had been working with the Secret Service and had done useful if unspectacular work. He was looking forward to a quiet Christmas at Glanville, and he had been working very hard lately. He was fond of his uncle and was anxious to get to know his wife, as he had thought her very pretty in the brief glimpse he had of her at the wedding. He found a thoroughly typical Christmassy atmosphere when he arrived at the vicarage, decorated as it was with ivy, holly, and mistletoe. The fire was blazing in the hall, and there was a pleasant smell of hot buttered toast.

Lupin and the Lethbridges had spent an active day over the decorations. Their energies had not been confined to the vicarage; in fact, they had spent most of the morning in the church, but it must be admitted that their efforts there had not been an unmitigated success. Duds, eager to make herself useful, had hurled herself on to the pulpit and had just succeeded in concealing it behind branches of holly and tendrils of ivy when an old woman arrived, who promptly burst into floods of tears. It appeared that she had decorated the pulpit every Christmas for the last fifty years, and to arrive and find it already done was more than she could bear.

"How lovely and Christmassy it all is!" exclaimed Jack Scott as he stretched his long legs out to the blaze and settled down comfortably to the business of making a large tea.

"Can you sing?" asked Duds.

"A little. Do you play?"

"What my wife means," explained Tommy laboriously, "is that you are about to take part in a carol service."

"Oh, I see. No, I am afraid I don't sing at all. I suffer from enlarged tonsils. In fact, my parents were afraid that they would lose me as a child."

"It's no good," said Tommy. "You will have to do it."

"But I only know 'Good King Wenceslas.' "

"That's all right. It doesn't matter what you sing. No one will hear you. No one hears anything but Mother Grey's voice; there is no competing with it. We'll stand together and you can sing 'Good King W.' while I weigh in with 'The First Noel.' They will go well together and will give a modern touch which will appeal to the young people. So important in these days of nightclubs and hot rhythm."

"Well, if you are all ready," said Lupin, "we had better be starting. The show is billed for six o'clock, but we all have to be ready in our seats before the public is admitted."

It was a beautiful night for Christmas Eve, clear and frosty with a few bright stars already to be seen. Even Tommy and Jack were rather moved by the atmosphere as they walked across the garden to the churchyard and entered the holly-decked aisle. At night, when the stained glass could not be seen, the church was really rather lovely, and the chancel, which was quite old, was beautiful. The augmented choir took their places in the seats allotted to them and awaited the entrance of the real choir and the clergy.

Lupin felt much happier this evening; she wondered what on earth had made her so depressed yesterday. All those ridiculous forebodings and imaginings seemed now like a bad dream; she must have eaten something that had disagreed with her. She and Duds had had great fun this morning talking about all their mutual acquaintances; Duds thought that Pamela and Stephen were beginning to take an interest in each other. That was satisfactory in a way, although she had rather earmarked Stephen for June; it seemed a pity, when she was such a dear, that she should have no one to admire her but a curate with boils on the neck and corns on the feet.

Mrs. Grey and her husband were already there when the vicarage party arrived; she greeted them with broad grins. 'If she knew about my fit of the blues,' thought Lupin, 'she'd think it was the baby.' Mrs. Brown appeared without her husband, but then he could always concoct a good excuse for staying away from anything. She looked neither more nor less depressed than usual …Then came the Sunday School children, marshaled by their teachers; foremost of these was Gladys Simpkins, looking moderately composed. Lupin tried to point her out to Duds with a whispered explanation until she saw that Mrs. Grey's eye was fixed on her with a somewhat shocked expression. Diana and June were on the other side of the aisle with some of their Guides; she did hope that June had not succumbed to Mr. Young's lovemaking last night. He certainly hadn't looked as if he were likely to become very ardent;

after all it wouldn't be easy to be ardent when handicapped by boils and blains, not to mention corns, and June looked quite normal, not as if she were committed to a step which would ruin her whole life.

Miss Gibson and her nephew were the last to arrive, rather to Lupin's surprise, as usually Miss Gibson was there first, marshaling not only the Sunday School but anyone else who was willing, or rather, not actively unwilling, to be marshaled. Looking at her in her present happy frame of mind, Lupin saw an ordinary elderly spinster who had probably been disappointed in love or else who suffered from chronic indigestion. There was nothing about her to frighten anyone; how silly she had been to think she was a witch! Soon Andrew would be coming in. What could be nicer than to spend Christmas in her own home with her own husband, to have her own friends staying with her and to sing carols in their own church? Certainly everything was for the best in the best of all possible worlds.

Now the public were starting to come in, this was chiefly gathered from the other parishes, as practically everyone in St. Mark's who was not dumb had been put into the choir. Phylis Gardner arrived with her church face carefully nailed on. She glanced at the flags as she took her seat, and Lupin earnestly hoped that they were in their proper positions. Miss Oliver sidled in. 'She might be going into a public house after closing time,' thought Lupin, 'or into a house of ill repute, whatever that might be, instead of into a place of worship. I wonder if she has got that ten pounds!'

Miss Thompson strode in swinging her arms, and the sweetfaced Guider drooped into a pew and held her handkerchief to her face. There was a pause after everyone had taken their places, one or two people shuffled to their seats, but the people of Glanville were usually punctual. The organist played a medley of Christmas airs. The children sucked sweets and kicked the pews. Tommy and Jack wore a boiled look, while Lupin tried to look like a vicar's wife. There was a feeling of tension in the air. People began to get restless.

"They'll start throwing things soon," whispered Tommy to Jack; then, catching his wife's eye, he hurriedly resumed his boiled expression.

Eventually the verger came in and whispered to Mr. Grey, who with a harassed expression turned to his wife for advice. He then approached Miss Gibson's nephew and spoke to him in a low voice, with the result that Mr. Gibson rose with a slightly consequential air and followed the verger to the vestry.

"Something has happened to Andrew," said Lupin audibly.

"Don't talk in church," replied Duds, "besides if it had, why should they break the news to a stranger? If they didn't like to tell you they could have told Captain Scott."

Jack, on hearing his name, went very red, and looked in the opposite direction so as to dissociate himself from those who did not know how to behave themselves when in church. Miss Gibson, feeling now more than ever that she was a priestess in St. Mark's, moved in her seat and fixed Lupin with a baleful eye.

Father Gibson, as he liked to be called, followed the choir into the church, then coming to the chancel steps, spoke in a well-bred, High Church voice: "I regret to say that your curate, Father Young," (an astonished murmur, and some giggles from those who knew no better, greeted this appellation of their curate) "has been taken ill. Your vicar has hurried to his bedside and has asked me, unworthy though I am, to conduct this service."

The carols did not go as well as might have been expected after such constant practice, but Mrs. Grey boomed on bravely, regardless of the rest. The choirboys were too absorbed in the news to give their full attention to the singing. Charles Young was quite popular with them and they were genuinely sorry to hear that he was ill, but they were unable to suppress a hope that there might have been some foul play somewhere. Most of the augmented choir sang remarks to each other, undercover of Mrs. Grey's unending booming.

"He must be pretty bad for Andrew to have gone—I mean, if he'd just been bilious he would not have needed Andrew."

"Well, he seemed pretty bilious last night. He must have been sickening for it then."

"Poor June, she'll be sorry. I rather wonder she wasn't sent for, too. Dr. Brown isn't here, I suppose he is with him. I hope he isn't really bad."

"I hope not. I don't expect he is really."

"I shouldn't be surprised if Miss Gibson had poisoned him, so that her nephew could conduct the service."

"Hush."

In the middle of one of the carols, Father Gibson knelt down. The vicarage party, anxious to conform, did the same, but had only just fallen on their knees when Father Gibson, his aunt and those of the congregation who 'were in the know' were all standing again. Jack, not realizing this, went on kneeling, his head buried in his hands. He was rather sleepy; he had been up most of the previous night, finishing off his work before coming on leave, and the church was very warm. Even Mrs. Grey's singing did not disturb him. She had remained on her feet throughout the carol, obviously scorning all popish ways.

"I suppose you didn't put anything in his soup?" sang Duds.

"No," replied Lupin, "I rather liked him."

Jack knelt on. He was not quite asleep, just pleasantly somnolent, with pleasant thoughts trickling through his brain. He liked the church and the carols, and he was looking forward to Christmas. On the other side of the aisle was the loveliest girl he had ever seen. The girl beside her was attractive, too, but she was a good deal older. There was a sort of likeness between them. He tried to make out what it was. Nothing to do with features or with coloring. It was more a matter of carriage and gesture. Probably you wouldn't notice it if they were sitting quietly. He had seen them exchanging smiles with Lupin. All being well, he would be introduced to them, but why were they standing? Good heavens! Everyone was standing. He was the only person in the church on his knees. He stood up, embarrassed. Tommy whispered:

"Finished your nap? Or do you want your early-morning cup of tea?"

It took Jack some time to recover his composure, but at last, in the middle of "In the Bleak Midwinter . . ." he stole another glance at June Stuart. Yes, she was just as lovely as he had thought. The church was rather dark, but a light fell across the girl's face illuminating her profile. He gazed at it in admiration, but it reminded him of someone else's profile: someone he knew well. He tried to concentrate on the carol; the girl would notice him staring, but who was she like? Suddenly it struck him. Her profile was very like that of his Uncle Andrew. What a ridiculous idea! But he could not get away from it. Andrew's face was manly enough, but this girl's face, side-face, anyhow, was extraordinarily like it, softened down, of course. It was a curious coincidence. He sat down for the sermon and tried to keep his eyes and thoughts away from the pew opposite.

Father Gibson only attempted a few words; they were quite well expressed and suitable for the occasion. Then, after one more carol, he pronounced the blessing, and the little service was over.

There was no doubt about the relief of the congregation as they hurried out to discuss the news. Was Mr. Young seriously ill? It looked rather like it, as the vicar had been sent for. He had certainly been looking ill the last few days, but no one had thought much of it. The fact of Father Gibson having taken the service came in for a good deal of comment. Some looked on it as the thin end of the wedge. He would be taking Mr. Young's place altogether and there would be vestments and incense before they knew where they were. As for Miss Gibson, there would be no holding her!

The vicarage party did not wait to gossip, and Jack was disappointed in his hope of being introduced to June Stuart. Andrew was in his study when they got in. He seemed rather distressed but spoke calmly as usual.

"Will you all come in here?" he said. "I have some bad news. Charles Young is dead."

Tommy and Jack shuffled with their feet, as men do when they hear of someone being dead.

"I am sorry," said Duds, "he seemed rather nice."

"He was always kind to John," added Lupin.

"He didn't seem frightfully fit, last night," muttered Tommy.

"Oh, it couldn't have been anything to do with the dinner, could it, Andrew?"

"I don't think so, darling, because we all ate it, too. But the doctor does think it is poisoning of some kind, and I am afraid there will have to be an inquest. The police may come round to question you all, as Young was here last night. I must go back now. I have wired to his sister."

"Andrew, he did not commit suicide, did he?"

"I don't know, dear."

Andrew left them and they all stood looking at each other rather blankly. At last Duds broke the silence.

"I don't want to seem heartless," she said, "but don't you think we'd all feel a bit better if we had something to eat and drink. There is nothing we can do for the moment, is there?"

Lupin was standing absentmindedly twisting her wedding ring round and round on her finger, while she tried to think of something. Yes, of course, there was the ten pounds that she had lost; she had forgotten it for the moment, but now it all came back to her. Had Charles Young taken it and then committed suicide out of remorse? But how awful! If only he had come and told her about it she would have said that it didn't matter a bit. Of course, ten pounds was ten pounds, and she and Andrew were not very rich. But they would both rather lose ten pounds than that someone should commit suicide over it. She should have said something about it to him yesterday—given him to understand that it didn't matter? It would have been so awkward to have referred to it. After all, she had no proof that he had taken it; in fact, she would never have thought of suspecting him if he hadn't committed suicide about it.

"Oh, dear, oh, dear!" said Lupin forlornly.

Duds put an arm round her. "Cheer up, darling," she said, "You really will feel better when you have had some supper."

"Supper? Oh yes, of course, it's cold. Cook wanted to go to the carol service. I shall never want to go to another carol service as long as I live. No, we won't dress; just wash … But then he was never alone in the room . . . ."

CHAPTER 10

BY MUTUAL consent they kept off the subject of Mr. Young's death during supper. But afterwards when they were all gathered round the fire in Lupin's sitting room, Jack touched on the theme which was in all their minds.

"Don't talk about it, Lupin, if you would rather not," he said, "but I believe you have something on your mind. Would you like to tell us about it? Just before supper you said something about his never being alone in the room. Were you alluding to Mr. Young?"

"Well, you see, on Tuesday, or was it Monday? It was the day before Tommy and Duds came, because Duds rang up about what time they were coming, didn't you, Duds? And about growing your hair, too, and today is Thursday."

"Yes, it was Tuesday that I rang you up."

"So it was. Well, Miss Oliver, I don't know if you saw her in church, she has a face like when one looks in a spoon, and she is always twisting about the place, and she is district secretary, Guides, you know. Anyway, she came at about five or thereabouts, I know I'd only just finished my tea, to talk about the Guides and arrange some frightful meeting or other. She is a tiresome woman, I hate people who wriggle, and she was rather nasty about June and Diana."

"Why?" asked Jack sharply.

"I don't know, I'm sure. I suppose she was born like it. Where was I?

"You didn't say, but I gather it was somewhere with Miss Oliver."

"Oh yes, so I was, unfortunately. We were in my sitting room. I know we were there because of the housekeeping money."

"What housekeeping money?"

"The money that was stolen, of course."

"You never told us about any money being stolen."

"Well, I suppose I had forgotten. One can't think of everything. There was Duds cutting her hair off after telling me she had grown it, and then the carol service, and now poor Mr. Young being dead. It would seem heartless to begrudge ten pounds."

"Quite! But do you mind telling us something about this ten pounds?"

"Yes; I mean no, of course I'll tell you. There is no secret about it. I cashed a check that morning to pay the weekly books; I hadn't time to pay them then, because I met Mrs. Brown in the library, and oh, good gracious!"

"What?"

"I promised her I'd ask if any of our maids knew of any who would like to go to her, and I never did, but they wouldn't, would, they? I mean, none ever do."

"Don't they? But about the check?"

"I meant to cash another check yesterday and pay them when I went out to get the flowers for your rooms, but I was determined to get freesias for Duds, and I went to two shops and they hadn't any, and then I saw some in another, but a man was just buying them, so I said, 'Oh, please let me have half, my friend is so fond of them,' and he let me have them all. He said, 'Your need is greater than mine,' or words to that effect, and bought some carnations instead, which was awfully nice of him, because they were much more expensive. I wonder if I'll ever meet him again. I am afraid he must have been a visitor. There are so few men in Glanville, and now poor Mr. Young. . ."

"I am very grateful for the freesias," said Duds. "I love the smell."

"Did you cash another check?" asked Jack.

"No, that is what I am telling you, I never did, and now I shan't be able to pay the books till after Boxing Day."

"Never mind, they are not likely to sue you over the holidays."

"No, but Andrew likes things paid regularly. I mean, it looks so bad if the clergy get into debt, and the newspapers do love stories about parsons. You know, 'Aged vicar marries twenty-year-old typist behind locked doors,' and 'Vicar's wife absconds with housekeeping money,' will thrill them like anything."

"But you haven't absconded," pointed out Duds, "and you wouldn't know how to, if you wanted to. Do tell us about the ten pounds that's missing."

"The first or the second?"

"Are two lots of ten pounds missing?" asked Tommy.

"No, the second lot hasn't been cashed. I told you so."

"We only want to know about the first lot," said Jack patiently.

"But I was telling you, only you would keep interrupting."

"Yes, of course, so you were. Now when did you last see the money?"

"At teatime. Andrew was at some dreary meeting, so I had tea alone in my sitting room, and I thought I'd write to you, Duds."

"Well, you never did."

"No, because you rang up before I had time."

"You had your tea," said Jack, "and then you thought you would write a letter, so you went to your writing table, over there."

"Yes, that is exactly what I did do, how clever of you to guess, but I suppose that it is because you are in the Secret Service; but anyhow, when I got there, there wasn't any notepaper, only just ten pound notes."

"I'd rather have them than notepaper, myself," remarked Tommy.

"Let's keep to the point. You saw the money, ten one-pound notes, I gather."

"I rather think one of them was two tens, no, it wasn't, because I wanted a ten-shilling note to pay the man who came to mend the carpet in the drawing room. It wasn't really John's fault; if it had been properly fastened down he'd have known it was a carpet, and he did it too beautifully—the man. I mean, not John."

"Had you a ten-shilling note?"

"No, I had to borrow it from Andrew. I hope I'll remember to pay it back."

"So there were ten one-pound notes on your writing table?"

"Yes, I told you so."

"And you saw them at teatime. What time was that, about four-thirty?"

"I suppose so. I had tea early, because I wanted it cleared away before Miss Oliver came."

"And you found no notepaper. Did you go out of the room to look for any?"

"No, I am afraid I didn't. I happened to see 'Death at the Grange,' and I remembered that I had just got to where the young man had been tied up in the cellar as well as being drugged and gagged and—"

"Yes, yes, very interesting," interrupted Tommy, "but let's think about the ten pounds."

"Yes, do let's if you don't mind," agreed Jack. "Now you had cashed a check for ten pounds the day before yesterday, and the notes were on your writing table at four-thirty on the same day. You are sure of that?"

"Yes, I know I saw them there, because I thought it was such a pity that they weren't notepaper."

"I'll give you some notepaper for them," offered Tommy.

"Shut up, Tommy," said Duds.

"I don't want any notepaper now," said Lupin, "besides . . ."

"You saw them at teatime on Tuesday," went on Jack, "and when did you miss them?"

"Yesterday morning, when I went to get them to pay the books."

"Who was in your sitting room during that interval? Say four-thirty on Tuesday, and ten or eleven yesterday morning?"

"If you had ever lived in a vicarage you wouldn't ask questions like that; people just walk in and out all day long. When Andrew asked me to marry him, he said he was afraid I should find it very quiet here, and what he meant I can't imagine! If I wanted quiet I'd rather retire to the Tower of Babel with a saxophone. I wouldn't not be married to Andrew for anything, but my advice to young girls who want to marry clergymen is 'don't,' unless you like spending your life in a railway station with total strangers coming up and telling you their life histories every moment. If Tommy dies, Duds. . ."

"Why should I die?" demanded Tommy.

"Well, if it was the fish, we'll probably all go."

"Yes," agreed Jack, "but if we don't you will be glad of the ten pounds, so cast your mind back to Tuesday evening, and try to think who were about the place then."

"It would be easier to think who wasn't, but here goes: Miss Oliver, the Guide secretary, poor Mr. Young, and Miss Simpkins, and I suppose one or two of the servants went in sometime, cleaning and dusting and whatnot."

"Tell us about Miss Oliver."

"I know the one you mean," broke in Tommy, "wriggles and has a face like a spoon. She was sitting on the other side of the church; she had rather a furtive look; she had probably got the ten pounds concealed about her person."

"I shouldn't be surprised; then, she always does look as if she'd got a guilty secret, so you can't tell and it's usually the innocent-looking people who commit crimes. Look at Crippen and that other man who was a church-warden. But I can't say that I like Miss Oliver; she kept throwing out dark hints about Diana and June."

"So you said before. Who are Diana and June?" asked Jack, though he really knew quite well.

"Great friends of ours; you must have seen them in church. June is lovely, and Diana is very good-looking in a middle-aged way. They were sitting on the opposite side in church. They live together, but Miss Oliver seemed to think there was something queer about it. I don't know what she meant."

"What awful rot," said Tommy.

"Yes, I know, but she is like that. Then she went on to Miss Gardner and said she'd rather not say anything about her. I should have thought Phylis's life was an open book."

"It looks bad."

"Yes, she seems to have got a grudge against most people, but I don't know why that should make her steal ten pounds."

"Nor do I."

"What about Young?"

"Poor man, I don't think he really stole it, and even if he did, one would not like to say so now he's dead."

"Unless it helped to clear up the mystery."

"But I don't see why it should."

"In a case of murder, not that we have any reason for thinking that this is murder, I expect the poor fellow took some poison by mistake. Everything is important; you can never tell what tiny detail may fit in. Now so far we have Miss Oliver and Mr. Young in your sitting room. Were they there together or separately?"

"Oh, wait a minute. I am so terrified of saying the wrong thing and hanging some innocent person, not that I should like to hang anyone even if they were guilty, but I was talking to Miss Oliver about some awful meeting and she said that she would not go if Miss Gardner or Diana were in the chair, and then Duds rang up and we started talking about her hair."

"Yes, I quite understand, and you left Miss Oliver alone in here?"

"Yes, and then when I'd finished on the telephone, I met Mr. Young on the stairs. He'd come to see me about something, I forget what, and he had been waiting in my sitting room, but couldn't wait any longer, and he told me Miss Oliver was still there."

"So he wasn't alone?"

"No, unless she left the room for any purpose while he was there."

"Who else did you say came in?"

"Miss Simpkins. I don't know if you saw her in church. She was with the Sunday School and has one of those red faces which are nearly all nose and legs like bolsters."

"I believe I saw her," said Duds.

"Was she ever alone in the room?"

"Yes, I gave her some tea and left her to it. Wasn't it clever of me to think of offering tea? It's just the sort of thing a proper vicar's wife would do. I was awfully pleased with my *savoir faire*, but I could not stay with her any longer. She was so weepy, and she doesn't weep becomingly."

"I have never known anyone who did," put in Duds.

"What was she weeping about?" asked Jack.

"She said that she had been seduced, and she would have it that I would understand—just as if I'd been seduced, too, which is one thing I never have been."

"Quite!"

"She said she was going to have a baby. It sounded unlikely to me, but, of course, there was that woman in the Bible, or is it Shakespeare?"

"If she were really going to have a baby, she might have been glad of the money."

"She didn't mention money; if she had I would have given her some. I always think it is much better to ask, don't you? I mean, then you all know where you are. If someone asks you, you can always say 'No,' if you want to; whereas if they take it without asking you can't."

"You don't think that it was Mr. Young who seduced her, and that she murdered him, do you?" suggested Duds:

"Or perhaps she hoped he would, and she murdered him because he didn't," contributed Tommy.

"Now don't start getting frivolous again," begged Jack. "This is a very serious matter. I don't know if Lupin's ten pounds have any bearing on the death, but we may as well try to clear them up. It looks as if it must have been either Miss Oliver or Miss Simpkins. Mr. Young was never alone there, so unless he and Miss Oliver decided to steal them together. . ."

"That's just what I said," said Lupin. "I ought to have been a detective myself, I have got such a logical mind."

"And then Miss Oliver killed him," put in Tommy, "so as to get his share."

"You'd hardly kill someone for ten pounds," objected Duds. "I think he came in and found Miss Oliver stealing the money, and threatened to denounce her."

"In any case we are not investigating the death," said Jack. "We are trying to find Lupin's ten pounds. I suppose all your servants are honest?"

"I suppose so. I think servants always are. It always says so on the references, anyway. Hard-working, too. I often wish they weren't. It gives me such a restive feeling, when people are forever turning out the rooms just as you want to sit in them, and . . ."

"We seem more or less limited to Miss Oliver and Miss Simpkins."

"I know," exclaimed Lupin suddenly, "Miss Gibson."

"What, the Sunday School superintendent?"

"Was she in your sitting room?"

"Why should she steal ten pounds? Is she hard up?"

"No, not ten pounds, the murder. Diana Lloyd once said that Miss Gibson

was the sort of woman who might commit murder for the sake of her religion.
I remember quite well. It was the day Duds wrote and told me that Tommy
had run off with the Sweet Sadie at the hotel."

"I never," said Tommy.

"But why should it help her religion to murder a clergyman?"

"No, I know; it was all cleared up in the end, but I was very worried at the
time."

"What are you talking about?" asked Jack.

"Well, Duds does write so badly, she was trying to tell me that Tommy
had won the sweepstakes at their hotel, but, of course I thought he had eloped
with someone and was in a frightful state, because I mean, it isn't the sort of
thing that does a girl any good, her husband going off like that with someone
else, and I had really made up my mind to go to her at once ..."

"But whatever had Miss Gibson to do with it, did you think Tommy had
run away with her?"

"No, no, she isn't that sort of person at all. Didn't you see her in church?
I shouldn't think that anyone had ever run away with her, not that you can tell,
After hearing Gladys Simpkins' story I would believe anything."

"I wish I had some idea of what we were all talking about," sighed Jack.

"Yes, I won a thousand francs," said Tommy reminiscently, "but Duds
lost most of it at the casino the next day."

"I want to know about Miss Gibson," said Jack.

"Why?" asked Lupin surprised. "Are you thinking of taking up Sunday
School teaching?"

"You said just now that she was the sort of person who might have committed murder for the sake of her religion."

"Oh no, I never said a thing like that. I mean, it's not a very nice thing to
say is it? Though, of course, it shows how religious she is."

"Who did say it then?"

"Who? What? Oh, you mean who said that about Miss Gibson? I was
telling you, Diana Lloyd. She had come to see me about the Guides; she is a
thingummybob, you know. She has a company of Guides in the parish, and of
course most of them are in Miss Gibson's Sunday School. Which reminds
me, Miss Gibson did say something about Miss Simpkins and Mr. Young. I
remember now, though I forget what it was. I wonder if he did seduce her, I
should hardly think so, being a clergyman . . . ."

"But what did Diana Lloyd say about Miss Gibson?"

"I told you, that she might commit murder for the sake of her religion.
You see, she wanted her nephew, you know, the one who did the doings this
evening, to be curate here. I think he is either High Church or Low Church,
whichever one Young isn't—wasn't, I mean. Oh, dear, it is awful, isn't it? I
mean, to think that he was dining here only last night!"

"I should hardly think you would go about killing people just because they were High Church, would you?" asked Jack.

"Well, there was the Inquisition or something, wasn't there?" said Lupin vaguely. "And Bloody Mary; but of course they were all Roman Catholics or Protestants. I should hardly think people would do that sort of thing nowadays. It was only Diana saying that made me think of it. It was sort of prophetic, wasn't it?"

"What about Diana?" asked Duds. "Perhaps she was meaning to do it all the time, and said that to put you off the scent."

"Oh no. She would never do a thing like that," said Lupin hurriedly. "She is awfully nice. Andrew has known her for years and is devoted to her. I rather wonder why he never married her, but I am glad he didn't, and anyway, why should she kill him? I mean, one doesn't go about killing people even if one doesn't like them."

"Didn't she like him?" demanded Tommy.

"No, I don't think she did, not much. At least, she didn't want him to marry June."

"There you are," said Duds. "She was afraid that June would marry him, so she murdered him."

Lupin knitted her brows for a minute or two while she digested this new theory: "But I didn't murder Tommy," she objected. "I mean, I shouldn't have done even if I hadn't liked him; after all it was you that had got to live with him, not me. Besides, June wouldn't have married him in any case; she told me so last night, because of the boil on his neck."

"We seem to be getting further and further from the ten pounds," said Jack wearily.

"Oh, I've just remembered someone else who didn't like Mr. Young," said Lupin. "Miss Watson, the headmistress of the day school. She is the most frightful woman; you remember Miss Jackson at school, Duds . . . ."

"Well, if we are going to have an account of the dear old schooldays, I'm off," declared Tommy.

"No. I was only explaining what Miss Watson was like. One wouldn't have put anything past Miss Jackson, and Miss Watson is just such another. Do you remember that half-holiday, Duds, when she kept us in? Oh, sorry, but anyhow, Miss Watson couldn't have done it because she wasn't here."

"Murdered Mr. Young or stolen ten pounds?" asked Tommy.

"Neither, but she was very mysterious one day about Mr. Young and some missionaries and a misunderstanding with Andrew and the servants talking about something. I didn't take much notice at the time, but it seems all to work in now, or at least it would if she hadn't gone home last week for Christmas."

"She might have come back in disguise," suggested Duds, "and murdered Mr. Young and gone away again."

"I suppose she might, but it would be rather a waste of time. I mean, if she were going to do it, why not do it while she was here instead of wasting her holidays? I often wanted to murder people when I was at school, but I always forgot about it once I got home. I should never have taken the trouble to buy a disguise and go back in the holidays, besides they wouldn't have been there, either, if I had."

"But Mr. Young was here."

"Yes, he was usually here when he wasn't popping up in the Sunday School or the day school or something. Of course, I can quite understand it getting on their nerves. He gave me a fright when he cannonaded into me on the stairs the other evening. I've still got the bruise. Still, he won't pop up anywhere any more, poor dear. I do think there is something dreadfully sad about people being dead. I mean, especially when they have been alive so lately. Oh, dear, I do hope I didn't hurt him; I was so busy thinking about myself; but perhaps I knocked him in a vital spot and that's what it is."

"Is what?"

"What finished him off, of course. I mean, led to his death. I wouldn't have had it happen for the world."

"I don't know if it's polite to tell one's aunt not to talk rot, but you are getting absolutely morbid. Do let's leave Mr. Young's death out of it and stick to the ten pounds."

"Inspector Poolton," announced Sara.

"How nice of you to come," said Lupin. "Will you have some whiskey? I'm afraid we're all a little upset this evening. A friend of ours has been murdered. Won't you really? Well, cigarette, then?"

"Yes, I quite understand, Lady Lupin. I'm sorry to disturb you at such a time, but as .a matter of fact, it was about Mr. Young's death that I wanted to see you. Might I have a word or two with you alone? I understand that the deceased dined with you last night."

"Oh, dear, oh, dear, I was afraid that everyone would think that. Must the others go? They really did eat the same dinner, at least two of them did—Mr. and Mrs. Lethbridge. In fact, they ate rather a lot, much more than poor Mr. Young. Oh, and this is Captain Scott, he is in the Secret Service, so I dare say he will be a great help to you, but he didn't have any of the dinner because he wasn't there. He only came this afternoon, but he has nearly found the ten pounds I lost already. At least, I think he has guessed who stole it, and, of course, it may be the same person who committed the murder. But about the dinner, you can see for yourself it hasn't done them any harm. I know Mrs. Lethbridge is looking a little pale, but she was too upset to make her face up. We didn't dress or anything. We really hadn't the heart."

"That is quite all right, Lady Lupin," said the inspector soothingly as the others left the room, "there is no need for you to worry about it at all. But I should be very grateful if you would just answer a few questions."

"Yes, of course, ask me anything you like and if I know the answer I'll tell you. In fact, I'd better be quite frank with you from the word go. The truth is I am not a very good housekeeper, it is no use pretending I am because I am sure you will find out. I mean, when I go to the fishmonger's, he always calls to his boy, 'Here comes Lady Lupin Hastings, bring out that codfish that we found lying on the sands last August!' I know that some people can tell all about fish by gazing into their eyes, but I always think that fish have such unresponsive eyes, especially when they are dead, don't you?"

"Yes, quite, but about this little dinner party of yours . . ."

"Oh, it wasn't really a party, only just Mr. Young and Miss Stuart besides ourselves; but I could have easily understood if everyone had been poisoned, but why only one? I mean, it's so odd."

"Then there were you and the vicar, Mr. and Mrs. Lethbridge, Miss Stuart and. . ."

"Water! Yes, of course, that's it, none of the rest of us touched it. It's an acquired taste, isn't it? But I knew there must be a solution if we could only hit on it. Method, that is the great thing, isn't it? I have read a lot of detective stories, and I know how important it is to marshal one's facts in the right order."

"You think there may have been something wrong with the water?"

"Yes, one is always reading of people getting things from drinking water, isn't one? It seems a dangerous habit."

"But was Mr. Young the only one at the table to drink any water?"

"I imagine so. I don't see why anyone else should have done, but he was one of those total thingummybobs, you know, who revel in water and lemonade. I ought to have had some lemonade made for him. It was very remiss of me, but I had forgotten that he was one. I wish I had thought of it. It was his last dinner, too."

"You could not be sure that no one else touched the water?"

"No, I didn't notice; but it doesn't seem likely. Besides, if they had done they would be dead, too," she added triumphantly, proud of her logic.

"You are assuming that Mr. Young was poisoned at your dinner table ?"

"Oh, dear, no; what a horrible idea! Why should he have been? None of us wanted to poison him. We liked him very much; at least, I am sure we should have done if we had known him better, and he wasn't feeling frightfully well at dinner either, poor thing. I wish I'd. . ."

"Wasn't he well when he arrived?"

"Well, he had a boil on his neck, and he seemed quietish at dinner. I thought it was because of the boil. It would make anyone feel awkward, and there were other reasons, too, but they were private, so I can't tell you."

"I would be glad if you were to tell me anything that might have a bearing on the case, Lady Lupin."

"I wonder if I ought. Well, of course, you are a police inspector, aren't you? Rather like a doctor in a way, or a clergyman. It is only that I think—not that he actually told me so himself—but, well, I think he was in love with Miss Stuart."

"And she did not reciprocate his affection?"

"No, especially after she had seen him with the boil. Well, I mean, you would have to be frightfully in love, wouldn't you? And I don't think she was ever that. Though, of course, some people are very reserved, aren't they?"

"Yes, very. Now Miss Stuart and Mr. Young were the only guests besides your house party, weren't they?"

"Yes, if you call them a house party, they are only my greatest friend and her husband and my husband's nephew."

"Which left first?"

"How do you mean, they are still here."

"I mean Mr. Young and Miss Stuart."

"Oh, I see what you mean. I thought you meant my friend and her husband. Mr. Young and Miss Stuart left together. Oh, what have I said? I know what you are thinking, but I am sure she didn't. She is not that sort of girl at all. She is a perfect dear, everyone likes her. You will like her yourself when you get to know her."

"I am sure I shall. What time did they leave?"

"Oh, let me think. Early, yes, very early. Mr. Young wasn't feeling well, but he wouldn't go without Miss Stuart. Naturally he was looking forward to the walk, and she is frightfully kindhearted; she saw how he was suffering so she said she would go. We were playing rummy. I think we must have had one round. Do you know I had four kings dealt me in one hand and the first card I picked up was the joker? Still, I should not have enjoyed it a bit if I had known. Isn't there a piece of poetry something like that: 'Alas, unmindful of their doom, the little victims play'? That was like us last night, playing and laughing as if we hadn't a care in the world except for poor Mr. Young's boil, and now he is dead."

"I can appreciate your feelings, Lady Lupin, and now I will not detain you any longer. What you have told me has been most helpful."

"Oh please don't go off and arrest June Stuart. I am sure she didn't do it, and in any case she is the only person I feel at home with in the whole of Glanville. If she's marched off with gyves upon her wrists I don't know what I shall do."

"Don't worry yourself about that, Lady Lupin. I don't think that I am at all likely to put gyves on Miss Stuart's wrists. Now might I interview your servants?"

"Oh, must you? Cook is sure to give notice if you accuse her of poisoning Mr. Young. She is so temperamental. She sulked for days just because I told her that her omelettes tasted of brown boots."

"I assure you that I will be very tactful."

"Will you really?" Lupin rang the bell. "One has to be awfully careful with servants nowadays. They are so touchy and they could probably get much better jobs if they left. Oh, Sara, this is Inspector Poolton. He wants to ask you all some questions to find out if any of you poisoned poor Mr. Young."

CHAPTER 11

"WELL, after all, it won't help poor Mr. Young at all if we don't enjoy our Christmas, will it?" remarked Lupin as she proceeded to open her Christmas presents.

They were all sitting round the breakfast table eating sausages and cold ham in the intervals of undoing delightful-looking parcels wrapped up in colored paper. They had all been to church and were feeling hungry and quite cheerful.

"No, I votes we give the tragedy a miss today," remarked Tommy. "I say, are these really meant for me, Lupin? They will give the spectators a thrill the next time I turn out for the Old Borstalians."

"Oh, I am sorry, they are meant for Duds—Duds, have you got Tommy's present?"

"No, I don't think so. Andrew, you really are a darling, how did you know I was longing for a pair of earrings like these?"

"Well, you told me pretty plainly," replied Lupin, "so I told Andrew as I imagined that was what you intended me to do. But where is Tommy's present?"

"Yes, where is it?" asked Tommy, "that is what we all want to know."

"Look what Andrew's given me," and Lupin kissed the top of her husband's head. He smiled wanly and tried to join in the general hilarity, but it was obviously an effort.

"June Stuart looked rather sad, I thought," remarked Duds. "I wonder if she were really in love with him."

"Here you are, Tommy, I knew it was somewhere. Black socks for evening wear. I don't think she was really, but one would feel rather sad if someone who loved one died, wouldn't one? Even if you didn't love them, I mean, it forms a sort of bond. I'd be sorry if Stephen died, though I gather he has stopped loving me now."

"So you did notice the hole in the heel the other night. Well, I am rather glad you did as things have turned out. Thank you very much, a most acceptable gift. I thought we were ignoring that macabre subject for the day."

"What are you murmuring about crabs for?" asked Duds. "Look what Jack has given me. Isn't it sweet of him, when he only met me for the first time yesterday?"

"That's why, I expect," replied her husband sourly. "I can't say you improve on acquaintance. If I do happen to use a word of more than one syllable you are unable to follow me."

"Yes, I forgot," said Lupin, "so we were. Mrs. Grey seemed in good spirits. I don't think she can have guessed that I am not going to have a baby, do you?"

"Why does she want you to have a baby?"

"Well, she has a thing called the Mothers' Union, and I suppose she wants to get as many members as possible, and as the parish seems to be full of spinsters, she has fixed her hopes on me."

"Looking round the congregation, I shouldn't think she can have much hope," agreed Duds. "Miss Gibson isn't likely to oblige, and I should hardly think Diana Lloyd would, but, of course, there's your Miss Simpkins."

"Yes, but I am afraid there will be a disappointment there. Oh, don't say that that is Inspector Poolton coming up the drive. I hoped we were free from suspicion by now. I suppose he wants to examine the remains of the food."

"There aren't many remains," pointed out Tommy.

"Never mind, there is heaps of food in the house. That is one good thing about being a vicar's wife, one gets lovely presents—whiskey and *foie gras* and caviar, not to mention flowers. Wasn't it lucky? I was just going out to buy some yesterday, when Mrs. Grey arrived with armfuls. Even Miss Gibson sent me a book of devotions. I must go and greet the poor inspector. After all, it is Christmas, and it must be horrid to arrive at a strange house and feel that no one wants to see you." She walked into the hall just as Sara was opening the front door. "Oh, good morning, Inspector. I am so glad to see you. Do come in; will you have a sausage or some ham? Or do you want to take away things in bottles and have them examined? I am afraid we are in rather a mess here, but we have just been opening our Christmas presents. A happy Christmas, by the way."

"Thank you, Lady Lupin, the same to you. I am sorry to be such a nuisance on Christmas Day, but I should just like a few words with the vicar. I shan't keep you long, sir."

"We are delighted to see you," said Lupin, "only do you mind not referring to the murder? We've decided not to mention it today, as it is Christmas."

"Will you come this way, Inspector?" said the vicar, leading the way to his study.

"Oh, dear, Andrew doesn't look at all well. He hardly ate any breakfast. I do hope he wasn't disappointed with my present. I thought it was rather dull looking, but he said he wanted those books."

"I expect he is worried about Mr. Young. After all, he was his curate."

"I do hope the inspector won't think that he did it. I expect he really wants a dose of something, only I didn't like to suggest it last night because of the early service; but it does make one look as if one were concealing something, doesn't it? Of course, he doesn't mean it, but you know what men are, and it will be dreadful if Inspector Poolton thinks it's guilt. I had better see if Cook has got any prunes in the house. The great thing with the police is to be absolutely frank. If they think you are hiding something from them they conclude at once you are guilty; they make no allowances for people being out of sorts."

In spite of a cheerful beginning, and the avowed intention of most of the house party to banish all unpleasant thoughts from their minds, it was not a really successful Christmas Day. Andrew continued out of sorts, and to make matters worse, Miss Young arrived that afternoon. Lupin was full of sympathy for her and had tried to arrange for her to sleep in Andrew's dressing room, but on seeing the strained look on Andrew's face decided not to do anything that might depress him further and fell in with Mrs. Grey's suggestion that she should go to her. However, she was determined to do all she could to show every attention, and she went to the station to meet her.

Pacing up and down the drafty station between her husband and Mrs. Grey was a depressing occupation for a Christmas afternoon, but Lupin fortified herself with the thought that she was doing the Christian thing and helping those in affliction. It would no doubt cheer the poor girl up to see someone young and decently dressed; most of the people in Glanville wore such depressing clothes. Lupin had put on a black hat as suitable for the occasion, but it was the sort of hat which would at once convey that the wearer, though sad at the moment, was not of a naturally gloomy disposition. In fact, after weeping together to start with, she might gradually be able to cheer up Miss Young and get her to take an interest in life once more. Thoughts of the beautiful friendship which were unrolling themselves before Lupin's eyes were rudely broken into by the arrival of the train and the meeting with Miss Young. From the first moment Lupin realized that any idea of a beautiful friendship, or in fact of any friendship at all, was quite out of the question.

Miss Young was a good many years older than her brother, and her parents had unkindly given him all the good looks that they had to bequeath. However, though plain, Miss Young had no need to look quite so repulsive as she did. She was one of those who rejected all aids to the appearance and seemed to glory in wearing the most unbecoming clothes that she could find. Her features were not relieved by any expression of amiability. Nor was she softened by sorrow. She glared at the three who awaited her with ill-concealed dislike, but Lupin felt that though some of the dislike was leveled at Andrew and Mrs. Grey, she led the field by a long way. She had prepared several gracious little remarks while she was waiting, but they fell flat under the glare of that baleful eye. She was thankful to seat herself in the front of the car with Andrew, while Miss Young sat at the back with Mrs. Grey. Even Mrs. Grey herself seemed a little subdued, though she wrapped her guest up solicitously with rugs and placed a cushion behind her unyielding back. For some time they drove in silence then Mrs. Grey rallied a little and began:

"Are you sure you are quite warm, my dear?"

Lupin, wanting to do her duty as a vicar's wife, anxiously joined in. "Yes, I do hope you are quite warm; there is nothing so bad as being cold, I mean, everything seems worse when one is cold. I remember at my grandmother's funeral . . ."

Miss Young broke in. Beyond a grudging "How do you do?" and a yet more grudging "Thank you" for the rugs, she had not spoken; she had seemed like an unpleasant automaton. Now, unexpectedly, her harsh voice broke out, silencing Mrs. Grey's hearty tones and Lupin's light chatter. "I shall feel neither heat nor cold, hunger nor thirst, until I have found my brother's murderer and laid him low."

It was a dark afternoon. The sea and the sky were gray and cheerless. Sleet was beginning to fall, and a piercing wind was blowing through the leafless trees that bordered the roads. As Lupin told Duds afterwards, it was the sort of afternoon in which ghosts might easily walk abroad, and Miss Young, tall and gaunt with her scarecrow of a hat, and wisps of graying hair and her strange voice proclaiming strange words, was a creepy figure. Lupin instinctively put out a hand and clutched Andrew's arm, plunging the car and its occupants into acute danger.

"There, there," murmured Mrs. Grey, at a loss for once.

Andrew managed to keep the steering wheel steady in spite of having his left arm clutched violently. "We do not yet know that your brother was murdered, Miss Young," he said quietly.

"I know," replied Miss Young. "You will try to bring it in as suicide to avoid a scandal. But I know Charles would never have committed suicide, my little brother, whom I nursed on my knee, whom I cared for and taught as a child. We were all in all to each other. He would never do a thing like that, Why should he? If he had been in trouble, he would have told me. Besides, I have proof. I had a letter from him this morning asking me if he could come to me for a night or two in the New Year. Would he have written to me like that on the very day he died if he intended taking his own life?"

"It doesn't sound like it," agreed Andrew. "Let us hope we reach the truth, whatever it is; but it does not lie in our hands."

"I should have thought that as his vicar you would not have rested until you brought his murderer to justice. I should have thought the whole parish would have banded themselves together to seek for the criminal in your midst."

Luckily at this moment they arrived at Mrs. Grey's house. Another minute and Lupin felt that she might have banded herself together to neither rest nor eat nor drink until the murderer was found, and very tiring it would have been.

Mrs. Grey pulled herself together. "Ah, here we are," she said, "you will feel better after a nice hot cup of tea."

Andrew helped Miss Young out of the car, but she recoiled from him and followed Mrs. Grey into the house with barely a word to either of the Hastings. Lupin watched her sinister form as it moved through the murky gloom and disappeared into Mrs. Grey's cheerful house, certainly an incongruous setting for such a figure.

"Oh, Andrew, darling, I do hope you won't be murdered," she cried suddenly.

"You are getting morbid, dear. Let's talk of something else."

"Yes, let's; but it just came over me how awful it would be to be in trouble, and to have Mrs. Grey being kind to one."

It was a relief to turn into the warm vicarage and to leave the gloom and the strange Miss Young outside. "Oh, my dears, it was too frightful," said Lupin, "a horrible creepy afternoon, and you can't think what Miss Young was like. I went prepared to be frightfully sorry for her and to like her awfully, but she wouldn't speak to us except practically to accuse us of murdering her brother. I thought the people in Glanville were rather frightening, but she makes Miss Gibson seem kind and Miss Oliver normal. It was all like something out of Pope. Do I mean Pope, Andrew?"

"No, I think you mean Edgar Allan Poe, darling."

"Yes, of course, or Edgar Wallace. You know what I mean, absolutely too eerie for words, all wind and rain, and the sea looking too unfriendly, and then this woman just like a witch. I know *Macbeth,* that was what I was really thinking of. I can just see her stirring her cauldron:

'Fillet of a something snake,
In the cauldron boil and bake.
Tongue of newt and wool of frog,
Toe of bat and eye of dog,
Adder's sting and blind worm's fork,
Lizard's leg and owlet's stalk,
For a charm of something trouble,
Like a hell-soup boil and bubble.'

"You remember, Duds, we learned it at school. It was frightfully grisly, but isn't it wonderful the way I remember it after all these years? It must have made a great impression on me. Do you remember Miss Jones and Hiss Hope?"

"Yes, but I don't think you've remembered it quite right all the same."

"Haven't I ? Oh, well, near enough I expect. 'By the pricking of my thumbs, something evil this way comes.' No, it's all right, it's only Diana and June. A Happy Christmas, I simply loved the ashtrays, and John is thrilled with his ball. Are you bringing in Bill? John will be delighted. He looks on him as one of the family now, but I am not sure about Rufus. Oh, and, June, what luck you didn't marry poor Mr. Young, you would have had his sister as your sister-in-law, she is too frightful for words, she even inspired me to recite *Hamlet*, or wasn't it *Hamlet*? Well, anyway, it was Shakespeare, because we learned it at school; but I am glad Diana wasn't here, because she would have known it was all wrong. Oh, dear, I do hope I am not being unsympathetic and heartless. I am most frightfully sorry about it all, really."

"Well, I had better remove Rufus before any mischief is done," broke in Tommy. "Shut up, you fool, though I must say all this talk about witches and murders and whatnots is enough to upset anyone; come on, old fellow, and what with Duds and Lupin starting on the dear old schooldays, stop it, I tell you. I'm so sorry, Miss Lloyd, he is the best-tempered dog in the world, really."

At last Jack had his wish and was introduced to June Stuart. She was feeling rather sad. After all, Charles Young had been her friend, and he had been in love with her, and perhaps she had been rather unsympathetic about the boil on his neck. Then he had died so suddenly—suppose it had been suicide owing to her unkindness! She would never be able to forgive herself: However, Captain Scott was very nice, and it was pleasant to be sitting by the warm fire, drinking tea and eating Christmas cake. Gradually she became rather more cheerful. She and Jack quite forgot the rest of the party as they sat together talking about Bill, the spaniel, to start with, and then about other dogs, and then going on from one subject to another. June felt she had known him all her life. The rest of the party were not so talkative. Andrew tried, but it was obvious that he was trying. Tommy was feeling rather bewildered by the way things were happening. He was a simple soul and not used to being mixed up with sudden death and sinister sisters and quotations from Shakespeare. Diana was quiet, and Lupin was depressed. She rallied a little after tea and made an effort to keep the conversation going.

"It would make a wonderful plot for you, Diana, do write a book about it. I mean, a young man dies suddenly for no reason at all, and a whole lot of innocent people get dragged in, and his sister makes a vow that she will track down his murderer. The vicar and his wife, and the captain of the Girl Guides . . ."

"I thought we had agreed not to talk about it today," interrupted Duds.

"So did I," groaned Tommy, "but Lupin will keep harking back to it."

"I am so sorry. I never meant to, but it keeps coming over me, and if you had seen Miss Young, you would find it hard to get her out of your head. But do let's talk of something else. I wish you and June were coming to dinner, Diana. I am awfully fond of Phylis Gardner, but I am always rather nervous when she is here that I may do the wrong thing, like using the wrong knife or not standing up when they play *God Save the King*. Still, I expect you will get a better dinner at Ma Grey's. Cook says the turkey is all right, but I have my doubts. I have never bought a turkey before. I always thought they just came, but I say, I have just remembered Miss Young will be at Mrs. Grey's; she will turn all the food sour unless she has hers sent up to her room. I'd think she would really, all things considered. Must you go? Bother!"

Phylis arrived punctually for dinner, looking charming as usual. She never had a hair out of place, nor did her nose ever shine. Her black dress was in perfect taste. Duds and Lupin had also chosen black, and when Lupin looked round the dinner table and saw three black dresses and three black coats, she wished she had put on something else; the effect was so funereal. The crackers struck a somewhat discordant note. Lupin had been some time deciding whether to have them or not but it seemed a pity not to use them, as they had been rather expensive. Besides, it was not as if Mr. Young had been a relation or even a very close friend.

If only Andrew had not seemed so worried about it, Lupin could have put the whole tragedy out of her mind for the time being, in spite of its having made a deep impression. But the sight of his anxious face continually brought it back to her, and Phylis Gardner did nothing to dispel the gloom; she obviously thought that she was at a funeral. On arrival she had pressed Lupin's hand and said: "My dear," in a meaning way, and she had talked sadly to Andrew all through dinner, avoiding with consummate tact the subject which was prominent in the minds of all and keeping to such general but slightly mournful topics as religious persecution abroad and infant mortality at home, the toll of the roads, and the likelihood of war.

Jack was the happiest of the party. He had had a delightful afternoon. June Stuart was as charming and intelligent to talk to as she was lovely to look at, and they had arranged to play golf together in the near future. His thoughts were full of her, and he found his mind wandering during his conversation with Duds. He struggled against it, for his manners were good, but every now and then it was too strong for him. He wondered about her friendship with Diana. Had either of them a family or were they both orphans? And then there was that likeness to Andrew that he had noticed in church. Could she be a relation? But if so Andrew would have mentioned it. It must be just a coincidence. "I am so sorry, I didn't quite hear what you were saying."

"No, the others are making so much noise. It is rather difficult to hear each other speak, isn't it?" replied Duds, sarcastically. "I only remarked that I thought the soup was very good."

"Oh, rather, delicious. Lupin has a good cook, hasn't she? Do you play golf? I believe the links here are very good; Miss Stuart has promised to take me round."

Lupin and Tommy found themselves making polite conversation to each other as if they had never met before. The turkey made its appearance and despite Lupin's prognostications it turned out to be a very good one. But no one had the heart to do more than toy with their portion, and when the pudding came in decorated with holly and in a dish of flame, they all averted their eyes. Although no one ate much, Lupin noticed thankfully that the wine was going well. She hoped it might brighten the party, but not a bit of it. It merely seemed to make them sadder. The coffee and the cigarettes went round, and

Lupin looked desperately at the crackers; they were large, showy ones and seemed to strike an almost indecent note. Still, it was Christmas Day, and she had never yet missed pulling a cracker on Christmas Day. She picked up one gingerly and proffered it to Tommy. In silence everyone else followed her example. Phylis's eyebrows were slightly raised. She obviously thought Lupin lacking in taste, but she was always the perfect guest; she held an offending object in each hand and gave a watery smile to her neighbors.

They stood round the table, all six of them, crackers clasped in their hands. "Go," said Lupin nervously, feeling as if she were dancing on Mr. Young's grave. They pulled halfheartedly, and it was some time before any of the crackers came apart. At last, propelled by a strange English custom, which would probably be kept up even if the trump of doom were heard thundering through the deep, they opened their crackers and placed the paper caps which they contained upon their heads. Lupin looked up. She caught sight of five sad faces (for in spite of his inward happiness, Jack had composed his face suitably for the occasion) underneath the ridiculous paper caps, and something seemed to snap inside her. She caught Duds' eye and burst into shriek upon shriek of hysterical laughter. Duds began to gulp into her napkin, but as she saw Lupin's imploring gaze, she rose heroically to her feet and led the way to the door, coughing slightly. Tommy and Jack were seized simultaneously with an attack of coughing.

Phylis put an arm round Lupin's waist. "My dear," she said, "it has all been too much for you."

CHAPTER 12

ANOTHER dinner party was taking place in Glanville that evening. Over that, too, a cloud lay. In fact, if anything, the cloud was nearer, for Miss Young was under the same roof. As Lupin had prognosticated, she took her meal in her room, but the fact that she was there at all, brooding over her brother's death and suspecting everyone in Glanville of having encompassed it, cast a gloom and even quenched Mrs. Grey's usually unfailing good humor.

Dr. and Mrs. Brown, with their son Lancelot, a rather spotty youth with 'views' who was home from Cambridge, were in the drawing room when Diana and June arrived.

"Hulloah, Lance," said June, "a Happy Christmas!"

"How can anyone be happy at a time like this?" demanded Lancelot.

June's face clouded. "No," she agreed, "it is dreadfully sad, isn't it? But I didn't know you and Charles were ever great friends."

"I wasn't thinking about Charles Young," he admitted. "Though of course, I am sorry he is dead. But what is one death among so many?" He accepted a second glass of Mrs. Grey's excellent sherry and took a long sip. "Do you know how many people are dying of undernourishment at the present minute?" he asked.

"No," replied June, "and I'd really rather not know, if it's all the same to you. I am feeling depressed enough as it is, and I don't see what I could do about it if I did know."

Meanwhile, Mrs. Brown was grumbling to Mr. Grey. "Where Lancelot gets his views from I don't know. He wouldn't come to church today because he says he doesn't believe in organized Christianity. So rude to the vicar! And I don't know what the maids thought. Christine was there this morning, of course. The names they have nowadays, too! I wanted to call her by her surname, but it was Brown, which made it all so awkward. But of course, Cook had to stay in as we have our dinner in the middle of the day, and she must have thought it very strange seeing Lance, and the state he leaves his bedroom in, too!"

Miss Gibson and her nephew were announced just then. "I do hope Lance won't say anything about Christianity," said Mrs. Brown.

As often occurred at Glanville, there were more women than men at the dinner table. Mrs. Grey was very hospitable and there was plenty to eat and drink, but the conversation was not so plentiful. Everyone tried to avoid talking about Mr. Young, but as everyone was thinking of him, it was difficult to talk of anything else. Everyone, that is, except Lancelot Brown. He was not particularly interested in the death of a curate, but he was very much interested in his own views. He liked the sound of his own voice, and for once he was allowed the pleasure of listening to it, with nothing but a few halfhearted interruptions.

"Tell me about this Lady Lupin," he asked Diana, next to whom he was sitting.

"Which Lady Lupin?"

"There is only one, isn't there?"

"So far as I know, but you said 'this' as if you had just produced one out of a box full."

Lancelot was as much in awe of Diana as he was of anyone, so he did not annihilate her with one of his famous sarcastic remarks. He thought these out when he was shaving in the morning with dire results to his chin, which had to be adorned with patches of sticking plaster. "Why does she call herself Lady Lupin?" he asked, mildly for him.

"I have never heard her do so," replied Diana.

"You know quite well what I mean, Miss Lloyd. Why should some people be called Lord and Lady, and other people Mr. and Mrs.?"

"Don't ask me. Why are some people dark and some people fair?"

He turned to Miss Gibson on his other side. "Do you believe in class distinctions?" he asked.

"They are not a matter on which I waste any thought," she replied. "They are a purely worldly affair and of no consequence one way or the other," and she took a sip of water.

"Do you realize that you are all dancing on the edge of a volcano?" Lancelot demanded of the table in general.

"Ha, ha," responded Mrs. Grey in a tone of forced merriment.

"I don't think I am," said Diana. "My dancing days are really over, I fear."

"You are an idiot, Lance," was June's contribution.

"Do be quiet, Lance," begged his mother. "I do wish you would not be so silly."

Miss Gibson looked rather pointedly at his wine glass, which had just been refilled, and took another sip of water.

Father Gibson stopped his interested questions about June's Brownies and gazed at the young man with a look of sad surprise. He then turned back to June. "It is a splendid work," he said.

"The revolution is nearer than you think," went on Lancelot confidentially to Diana.

"Oh well, it will make a change, won't it?" she replied wearily as she tried to hide bits of turkey underneath her knife and fork.

"I can't think why you don't take your writing more seriously," he went on. "You could do something much better and more worthwhile than children's storybooks."

"What makes you think so? As a matter of fact, I am writing a detective story."

"Detective story! What is the object of a detective story? Just to take people's minds off the problems of the day. Pure escapism, that's all it is! We don't want people to escape. We want them to think. A friend of mine at Cambridge is writing a really powerful book, in blank verse, called *Despair in Birmingham.*"

June longed for the dinner to come to an end; she was not hungry and the room felt very hot. It had been a long, tiring day; she had not heard of Charles' death until this morning and it had come as a great shock to her. After all, it was only two days ago that he had asked her to marry him, and although she had not been in love with him, she had liked him; he had been her friend. Then Diana had not been like herself today; she had been quiet and dispirited. They were so close that she could always tell how Diana was feeling. Even across the table she could tell that she was not taking her usual delight in teasing Lancelot. Why should she be so upset by Charles' death? She had not liked him, and she was the least hypocritical person in the world. Still, there had been one hour during this endless day when, in spite of Charles' death and Diana's sadness, she really had enjoyed herself, and that was at the vicarage. She supposed it had been being with Lupin. She was always such fun.

Still, she often was with Lupin, but never before had she had this feeling of glamor at looking back at their times together. Was it because there had been a young man there who was neither a curate nor Lance Brown? She hoped she wasn't going to be like a silly schoolgirl, imagining romance where there was no romance. But she did rather hope she would see Jack Scott again. She turned back to Father Gibson, he was really rather nice; she must pay more attention to him. "Yes, I like children," she said.

Mrs. Brown was meanwhile continuing her tale of woe to Mr. Grey. She told him why Christine was likely to give notice, owing to Lancelot's unorthodox views and his untidy habits in the bathroom. "The floor was simply swimming in water this morning, and, of course, Mr. Young's death has unsettled them."

Mrs. Grey's Peke then made a diversion by going out to be sick in the kitchen, owing to her having been fed surreptitiously by everyone with bits of turkey and chestnut stuffing, and there was rather a long pause between the courses, during which Mrs. Grey and Dr. Brown carried on a halfhearted conversation about the difficulty of growing roses on a chalky soil.

Even Lancelot was beginning to be affected by the general apathy. He felt that Diana was not giving him her whole attention, and he liked people to give him their whole attention when he talked to them. Miss Gibson, on his other side, sat like a graven image except when she took a sip of water. He watched June across the table. She appeared to be listening to that clergyman fellow with the greatest interest. He wished he were sitting beside her. It is true that they usually quarreled, and he had always looked on her as shallow and wanting in the intelligence with which Russian women, for instance, were so plentifully endowed. All the same, she was very pretty, though he had never noticed it before.

Had he been in love with her all the time without realizing it? He wondered. His mother had told him that Charles Young had been in love with her; well, he was out of the way now, poor chap. In a story such as the one Diana was misguidedly writing, he would be suspected of having murdered his rival. He wondered if anyone suspected him.

"I do think it is good of you and Mrs. Grey to have poor Miss Young to stay," said Mrs. Brown. "The doctor and I should have loved to have had her, but I never dare to have anyone to stay when Lancelot's home."

Mr. Grey looked rather surprised. "Doesn't he like visitors?"

"I was thinking of Christine," replied Mrs. Brown.

Mr. Grey turned to Miss Gibson. "We have poor Miss Young staying with us," he explained. "She is having her dinner in her room. Naturally she is not in the mood for merrymaking."

"Quite," agreed Miss Gibson, looking round the table.

CHAPTER 13

BOXING DAY dawned cold, wet and cheerless. Andrew and Jack both disappeared soon after breakfast and Lupin, Duds and Tommy, drawing chairs round the sitting-room fire under the pretense of writing letters, prepared to spend a lazy morning.

"What I like about Boxing Day," said Lupin, "is that no one can expect one to do anything. The shops are shut, so even if there is no food, one doesn't have to go and get any. One's friends are occupied in writing thank-you letters, and the poor are usually feeling ill after their one square meal of the year, so one is bound to have a little peace for once."

"Miss Simpkins wishes to see you, my lady," broke in Sara.

"Surely not on Boxing Day! What shall I do?" she asked her friends. "I mean, why does she come to me? Mrs. Grey would know exactly what to say to her."

Miss Simpkins was in the dining room, looking plain and disheveled.

"Oh, Lady Lupin, I am in such trouble."

"Well, sit down and tell me all about it," said Lupin resignedly, inwardly cursing herself for her weakness. After all, there was Mrs. Grey longing for people to have babies and itching to help those in trouble; then there was Diana Lloyd, who used to be Gladys' Ranger captain; why on earth couldn't she go to her?

"Miss Lloyd takes a great interest in you," she began tentatively.

Gladys leaped from her chair. "What has she said?" she demanded.

"Only that you used to be in her Rangers and how good you'd always been."

"You haven't told her what I told you?"

Lupin raised her eyebrows. Of course, it was only four days ago, but it seemed years since that evening when Gladys had told her that she had been seduced and that ten pounds had disappeared, and she had collided with Mr. Young on the stairs. "No, rather not. It was ages ago, she just mentioned you in conversation."

"I'm sure she thinks I've done it."

"Done what?"

"Murdered Mr. Young."

Lupin stared at her. "What do you mean?" she gasped.

"Well, it was after the carol practice. I was feeling so low and then hearing all those lovely carols I felt I must confess. I went home and had supper and read for a bit, but I felt I could not sleep until I'd confessed, so I went round to where Mr. Young lives. Not that he really holds with confession, not like Mr. Gibson—Father Gibson, I should say—still, he was always very kind, so I thought I'd go to him. As there wasn't any light in his window I was coming away again when he arrived, but Miss Lloyd was with him."

"Miss Lloyd? You mean Miss Stuart."

"No, it was Miss Lloyd all right. She looked at me as if I'd done something awful. She must have known. I just mumbled 'Good evening' and ran off. I felt dreadful, Lady Lupin. I never slept a wink all night, and my heart was thumping like a sledgehammer, and perspiration—it was as if I'd been bathing in the sea!"

"It must have been beastly not being able to sleep."

"Well, next morning I went round to Mr. Young, and he was ever so nice. I explained that I had wanted to see him so badly and that was why I'd gone round to his rooms last night. He said that he was ever so sorry that he was out, but he had been dining with you, Lady Lupin, and that he'd stayed rather late and he had to take Miss Lloyd home."

Lupin was not a profound thinker. Her brainpower had not been remarked on at school, and her headmistress had never urged her parents to send her to college; but at this moment some thoughts began to take nebulous form in her head. She had a vague feeling that there was something strange in what Miss Simpkins was saying. Not that it was any stranger than the story of her seduction; she had probably invented it all, but it was odd all the same. Mr. Young had not stayed late at dinner. On the contrary, he had left rather early, and it was June Stuart whom he had taken home. Diana had not been dining at the vicarage. Perhaps, after he had taken June home, he had gone out again to fetch Diana. But it was unlikely, as he wasn't feeling well.

Besides, Lupin rather gathered that they couldn't bear the sight of one another. In any case, whoever he took home, why should he drag them round to his lodgings, which were in a side street quite out of the way? 'It is all very peculiar,' thought Lupin, 'but I expect it will be cleared up like Tommy and the Sweet Sadie.'

"And then he made me take a cup of tea," continued Miss Simpkins, "and he said would I pour out one for him, too. Just as I was putting in the sugar in came Miss Lloyd, and you can't think how she looked at me, Lady Lupin. I slopped tea all over the saucer. It's a wonder I didn't drop the cup. I gulped my own tea down as fast as I could; I did not like to leave it as he had been so kind and ordered it especially. He offered Miss Lloyd a cup but she refused it as if she thought it was poisoned. My head was ever so bad, I've always suffered from sick headaches ever since I was a child; throb, throb, throb, something awful.

"I meant to take a couple of aspirins with the tea. I'd got the bottle out ready before Miss Lloyd came in; in fact, I'd told Mr. Young all about it, and it was lying there on the table. It was nearly empty because I've had to have a great many lately, what with being so upset, and I was meaning to get a new bottle. I was in such a hurry to get away because I knew Miss Lloyd did not like me being there. I swallowed down that tea, though it was simply scalding and my throat still ever so sore, and I left that aspirin bottle on the table. So

Miss Lloyd will think that I put aspirin in his tea instead of sugar."

"I don't quite see why she should think that," said Lupin. "I mean, it would take a lot of aspirin to kill anyone, and besides, you've no motive."

"She's not to know that. She might have thought that I'd told him something that I didn't want anyone else to know and then decided to get rid of him."

"Well, that would have been a rather potty thing to do. I mean, why tell him to begin with? Besides you were in her Scouts, I mean Guides; she was furious when Miss Gibson said something about you."

"Miss Gibson? Now I shouldn't be a bit surprised to hear that she had done it, Lady Lupin, as she has never liked him, because he won't bow down to the Pope of Rome, and there she is with her nephew all ready to walk into his shoes."

"Well, it's no use our trying to guess who it was," said Lupin. She was longing to get rid of Gladys and to talk things over with Duds and Tommy. "The only thing to do is to be absolutely frank," she went on. "No, no, not with me, you've told me everything, I know, but with the police."

"Oh no, I'll kill myself if the police come!"

"Rot! Inspector Poolton has been asking us all kinds of questions. Naturally at first he thought I'd poisoned poor Mr. Young when he dined with us on Wednesday night, but I was absolutely frank with him and didn't keep anything back. I let him look at the remains of the food, and I don't really think that he suspects me at all now. You must do the same."

"Well, I couldn't tell him . . . you know, what I told you."

"Oh, I see. Well, you don't think that you could possibly have been mistaken about that, do you? I mean, it's so easy to think one has done things sometimes when one hasn't really done them at all. I remember once at school, I thought I'd done my history prep and it turned out that I hadn't at all. I got into an awful row about it."

Miss Simpkins looked offended. "I could hardly make a mistake about a thing like that, Lady Lupin."

"Couldn't you? I dare say your memory is better than mine. Well, then, tell the inspector everything, you'll find him most sympathetic. What is it, Sara?"

"Miss Oliver to see you, my lady. I have put her in the drawing room."

"Thank you, Sara. Will you bring Miss Simpkins a cup of tea? Now, my dear, you must not worry about any of this any more. After all, life is too short to spend it in worrying; the bird of time, the bird of time—um—you know, something about singing in the wilderness, I think it is, but it means that we're here today and gone tomorrow." 'Oh dear, that wasn't very tactful,' she thought to herself as she walked to the drawing room. 'But I don't really think that she did it, and even if she did, she'd get off for being mad.'

"How do you do, Miss Oliver? I hope you had a happy Christmas."

"I haven't had a happy moment since I saw you last!"

'Oh, dear,' thought Lupin, 'I wonder if she is suffering from the same as Andrew.' "I'm sorry," she said aloud, "haven't you been well?"

Miss Oliver laughed contemptuously. "Lady Lupin," she said, "have you ever known temptation?"

'Oh, dear, I suppose *she* has been seduced now,' thought Lupin. "I don't know," she replied, "I suppose so. Oh yes, often. I usually yield, too—repeating things I shouldn't and spending too much money, and ..."

"Money! You've always had all the money you wanted, haven't you? You've never gone without anything you wanted."

"Oh, I don't know about that."

"Except perhaps a few more diamonds and precious stones, a few more motorcars and fur coats, a few more menservants and maidservants."

"You make me feel just like the Queen of Sheba or else Marie Antoinette before the French Revolution."

"Did you realize that when you left ten pounds lying loose in your sitting room that you were putting temptation in the way of others?"

"Oh, that ten pounds. Did you—er—see it?"

"Had you missed it?" asked Miss Oliver severely.

"Yes, rather! I was going to pay the books with it and then I found it had gone, so I meant to draw another check. Then, what with it being Christmas and everything, I forgot all about it and I haven't paid the books after all."

"All you had to do was to draw another check?"

Lupin began to feel very uncomfortable and guilty. "Well, I didn't draw it," she said.

"No. It doesn't matter to you whether you draw a check or not. What is ten pounds to you? To me it meant happiness, comfort and freedom from worry. I was able to pay a bill for which otherwise I should have been sued; you wouldn't be sued for not paying your books. Oh no, it doesn't matter if rich people pay their bills or not. I was able to buy myself a dress so that I could go to a party; otherwise I couldn't have gone. I was able to buy Christmas presents for my friends, and some little comforts for my father and mother which made all the difference to them, and we had a real Christmas dinner which we hadn't expected to be able to afford."

Lupin stared at her, amazed at all that her ten pounds had done. What a good thing that Miss Oliver had taken it. She would have just paid the books with it, and that would have been all. Had Miss Oliver bought a fur coat and a diamond necklace too? Or was she saving what was left over for a trip to the South of France?

"Yes, I stole it. I am a thief."

"Oh—er—did you? Are you? Um—um—I wondered what had happened to it."

"And I have spent it all."

"Oh—er—er—have you? Yes, I suppose you have; I mean, there can't be much left."

"But what do you care? What are a few pounds one way or another to you?"

"I don't know."

"Or what does it matter to you if other people sell their souls and embark on a life of crime?"

"I'm sorry," murmured Lupin. She felt that she was the guilty one and that perhaps if she were sufficiently humble Miss Oliver might forgive her in time.

"Well, you can put me in prison if you like."

"No, no, not at all. It was my fault. Did Mr. Young see you take it?"

"Mr. Young? No, why should he? What has he got to do with it? I never saw him."

Lupin gazed at her. Was her memory going or had she imagined that collision with Mr. Young on the stairs? She certainly thought that she had seen him there and felt him, too! And surely he had told her that he had left Miss Oliver in the sitting room. But, now she came to think of it, Sara had denied showing him up there.

'Oh, dear,' thought Lupin, 'nothing makes any sense.'

"Well, what are you going to do?" demanded Miss Oliver.

"Do?" said Lupin. "Well, if it leaves off raining I may take John for a walk."

"I mean about the money."

"What money?"

"The money that I stole from you."

"Oh, that money."

"It means nothing to you, but it is the price of my soul."

"Is it?" replied Lupin feebly.

"You have only to ring up the police."

"We needn't do that. I expect Inspector Poolton is somewhere in the house. He practically lives with us now."

"Why don't you call to him?"

"I hardly feel I know him well enough."

"Lady Lupin, this is all a joke to you, but to me it is tragedy!"

"Dear, dear. I expect it's the weather, and one always feels a bit flat on Boxing Day, doesn't one? After the excitement of Christmas and then poor Mr. Young, too. Have you ever tried Kruschens?"

"Can you imagine what it is like to lose one's self-respect?"

"No, I don't think so. I don't think I ever had any."

"It was all I had and now it has gone.".

"Bad luck! I tell you what, we'll have some cocktails and then you'll feel much better."

"No, thank you. I have confessed to you that I stole your money, and I am ready to go to prison if you wish it."

"But I don't. Not at all. What would the Guides do without you? I mean, who'd read the—er—what do you call them, and send out the postcards? Don't give it another thought, please."

"I shall never think of anything else," replied Miss Oliver. "Good-bye, Lady Lupin. I thank you for your magnanimity," and she walked out of the room. As she crossed the hall, Lupin felt that she had certainly come out worst in the interview.

"Mrs. Brown is here, my lady. I have put her into the dining room."

"Was it empty? We shall have to move into a bigger house if there are many more murders. Oh, by the way, Sara, do you know of anyone who would like to go to Mrs. Brown as cook or parlormaid or anything of that sort?"

"No, my lady."

"I didn't think you would. I shouldn't care to myself if it comes to that. Good morning, Mrs. Brown," she added as she entered the dining room. "I am so sorry, but I am afraid I haven't found you any servants yet."

"Well, Christine had promised to stay on till the end of the month, but I doubt if she will as things are. The doctor has been out since first thing this morning and I don't know where to turn."

"I hope your cook . . ."

"No, she seemed rather sulky this morning, but she didn't actually give notice, but she will when she hears."

"Hears what?"

"That Lance is suspected of the murder of Mr. Young."

"Is he suspected?"

"So he says; you can imagine how upset I was when he told me, coming on the top of everything else, too! Because, of course, I've had to let both the girls have this evening off to go to the whist drive, and the doctor does hate cold supper; but one daren't say no. Lance suddenly came in and said to me, 'Mummy, I'm for it.' 'For what?' I asked. 'They think I murdered Mr. Young,' he said. He says he's been in love with June Stuart for a long time but he was afraid she preferred Mr. Young, and now that he's murdered (though the doctor says we've no right to say he was murdered), everyone will naturally suspect him."

"I didn't know he was in love with June," said Lupin.

"Nor did I. I never thought of such a thing. He's always seemed so wrapped up in his views. He calls himself a Communist, you know; such a pity because it annoys the doctor and after all, as I always say, if you gave everybody a pound on Monday, some would have ten pounds on Saturday and some none. I should only be too glad for him to get engaged to a nice quiet girl. I'm always afraid he may get mixed up with some of these highbrow young women up at Cambridge who believe in companionate marriages, whatever they may be."

"I have never heard a word about anyone suspecting Mr. Brown," Lupin assured her. "Did he see Mr. Young at all on Tuesday or Wednesday?"

"Yes, as a matter of fact, the poor young man came to tea on Tuesday and I left them alone together. I hoped he might put in a word and get Lance to come to church on Christmas Day. It looks so bad, his not coming when his father is a churchwarden. But I wish I hadn't now, as of course it looks so suspicious because he easily might have put some poison in Mr. Young's tea. Not that I think he did for a moment; he would never do such a wicked thing. He has always disapproved of killing anything; he belongs to a society for abolishing blood sports."

"I don't think anyone knew he loved June. I mean, he let concealment like a worm in the bud feed on something, so I don't see why they should suspect him."

"Well, I hope they won't. I should have gone around to Mabel Grey, but Miss Young is still there, and it has upset poor Mabel. She wasn't like herself at all last night. Comforting others takes it out of you, as I know to my cost. But I'll be grateful if you'll ask the vicar what we had better do. I must get back. Oh, dear, if only those girls weren't going out tonight . . . ."

Lupin passed her handkerchief over her brow and tottered back to the sitting room. She rang the bell for her maid. "Bring me some eau de cologne," she said, "and a couple of aspirins."

"Or would cocktails be better," suggested Duds.

"Yes, let it be cocktails then, it is all one to me. I have been passing through a terrible morning; Gladys Simpkins has been dropping aspirins into Mr. Young's tea, and the Browns' son seems to be madly in love with June and murdered his rival. I am glad Stephen did not murder Andrew, though it would have been a bit more romantic than his going quietly away and falling in love with Pamela. Oh, and you know that ten pounds—"

"Wait a minute," said Tommy. "Let me get a piece of paper and a pencil and take things down in order. Scott is the real sleuth, but we may as well show him that we can be methodical too."

"Yes, that's the great thing, isn't it, method? I'll tell you everything just as it happened. As a matter of fact, I know now who took the ten pounds, so we haven't got to find that out. But some of what I have to tell you may help in finding out about poor Mr. Young. Anyway, I may as well tell you. Yes, you'll find some paper and perhaps a pencil in my blotter."

Tommy walked across to the writing table. "Have you really found out about the money?" he asked. "Did they own up, or did you guess?" He picked up the blotter, and as he opened it ten one-pound notes fluttered to the floor.

CHAPTER 14

ON TUESDAY evening the Guiders' meeting discussed by Lupin and Miss Oliver took place. It was a great nuisance as it was Tommy and Duds' last night, but there didn't seem to be any way of getting out of it. The chief subject on the agenda was the discussion of the annual Guide party, which was to take place in the near future, but anyone dropping in would have supposed that it was the arrangements for a funeral that had brought them all together.

Phylis pressed Lupin's hand as she took her seat on her right. On her left, Miss Oliver was sitting sideways on her chair, her head twisted round the other way and an expression of guilt written all over her. Lupin nearly called out to her that it was all right about the ten pounds, then wondered whether it would be tactful. It must have been someone else's ten pounds that she had taken and spent so profitably. Well, it was all very strange. Or had she murdered Mr. Young and then forgotten which commandment she had broken?

June looked frankly miserable, but that was only natural. The man had been in love with her, and she was a nice, tenderhearted girl. Or, of course, she might be worrying about Lancelot Brown. Lupin wondered why his parents had christened him Lancelot. She had been faintly disappointed in him when his mother had introduced him to her outside the servants' registry office in the High Street that morning. She had not exactly expected 'his helmet and his helmet feather' to burn in one 'burning flame together,' but she had expected something a bit more dashing and swashbuckling, something more like young Lochinvar coming out of the west than this very pimply youth, who stared at her through large spectacles and informed her that he did not expect she would wish to know him, all things considered.

"Oh, rather not," she had said, "I mean, yes, of course. Your mother and I are such friends, and I'm sure you didn't do it."

Luckily, Phylis Gardner had passed at that moment and she had been able to get away, but she did not feel that she had made a good impression, and when the revolution started he would probably see that she got a seat in the first tumbrel, unless of course he were hanged first himself. It seemed funny that June's suitors should all be covered with boils and pimples, except, of course, Jack Scott. It was early days to tell, but she was rather hoping he might turn out to be a suitor. He and June had played golf together this morning,, and she had hoped it might have cheered the girl up, but it didn't seem to have done. Still, it was only natural that sad thoughts should obtrude themselves occasionally, and a Guiders' meeting was just the sort of place to encourage them. All the same, Lupin could not help feeling it was rather hypocritical of Diana to look so haggard. She had not liked the man, she was afraid of his marrying June, and now he was out of harm's way. What had she to be

sorry about? Unless, of course, she had poisoned him herself. In their different ways she and Miss Oliver looked equally guilty. Miss Oliver wriggled
uneasily as if something was biting her, while Diana sat motionless, her great
wild eyes fixed on space. Lupin would have preferred Miss Oliver to be the
criminal, if one of them had to be, as she liked Diana and was very fond of
June; besides Andrew . . .

Phylis was prodding her. "Yes, of course," muttered Lupin. Then out
loud, "I will now ask you all to stand for a minute in silence, out of respect to
Mr. Young, who has been such an active— who is—was—was so interested
in the—er—movement." She glanced at her two suspects. Miss Oliver was
shuffling her feet; Diana stood perfectly still.

"I will now call on the secretary to read the minutes."

"Do you really want me to?" hissed Miss Oliver, looking at Lupin in a
meaning manner.

Lupin just stopped herself from replying, "No, not at all," and hissed
back, "Yes, of course."

Miss Oliver uncoiled herself from her chair and, draping herself over the
back of it, read the minutes in a low and insinuating voice.

"Well, I don't think anything arises out of that," said Lupin, anxious to
get back to Duds and Tommy.

Miss Thompson, the Guider whom Lupin had always suspected of being
a man dressed up, rose to her feet and boomed out, "What about those Christmas stockings?"

Lupin began to feel uneasy. There had been such a rush just before Christmas. She had enrolled three sets of Guides, she had been up to London and
had a permanent wave, she had attended the confirmation and helped Miss
Gibson to fasten on the candidates' white veils, she had given away some
prizes for something, she had given two dinner parties and one sherry party,
and she had opened two bazaars, but not a thing could she remember about
any Christmas stockings.

To her great relief Miss Gardner rose to her feet. "Lady Lupin and I sent
off those that were left at the Guide headquarters to a settlement in London
that was advertised in *The Guider.* They were only dispatched last Tuesday,
and we have not yet had a reply."

Lupin heaved a sigh of relief. She remembered now that she and Phylis
had spent a dreary afternoon together over some shapeless woolen garments
and some unnatural-looking toys, although she had never realized what they
were or why. As it was the day that Miss Oliver had come to see her, and
Duds had rung up about growing her hair, and Miss Simpkins had confided
about her baby, it had all gone out of her head.

"Yes, of course," she said, "I mean, no. We shall probably hear in a day
or two. Christmas posts, you know. You must all have worked very hard to
make such lovely things." She could not remember where they had been sent

but supposed Phylis knew, and in any case they could always invent a letter if the worst came to the worst. She beamed at the room in general. "About the children's party . . ." she began.

"Did every company in the district contribute something to the trail?" demanded Miss Thompson.

"I should think so," said Lupin. "The place was full enough. One could hardly move—very nice, of course."

"No, we didn't," replied Diana. "We sent ours to a poor family Mr. Young told us about, whose father is in prison."

"Of course," said Phylis, "one is sorry for children with fathers in prison, but on the other hand, when there are so many respectable families in want, I do feel rather that they should be helped first."

"They have the satisfaction of knowing that they are respectable," said Diana. "That ought to be enough for them. You can't have everything."

"No, indeed," agreed Lupin. "And what about the party?"

"I think that everyone ought to play for the team," said Miss Thompson, in her deep voice.

"What team?" asked Lupin, bewildered, scanning her agenda paper for some mention of a hockey match. "What are they going to play? It will have to be indoors, won't it? I mean, the party doesn't start until half past-four, and there is not much room in the church house, still. . ."

"I certainly think that it would be better if we acted as a district on these occasions," said Phylis, "and not as separate individuals." She was really feeling very angry with Diana for not joining in the stocking trail, as she called it, with the others. The district meant a great deal to her. It took the place of husband and children, and she liked to feel it was hers to do what she liked with. Also, like most good organizers, she hated it when people refused to be organized. Diana was a continual thorn in her side.

"Well, well," said Lupin nervously, making her agenda into a paper boat, "the stockings are over now, let's talk about the Guide party."

"Perhaps Miss Lloyd would rather give a separate party for her own Guides," remarked Phylis in icy tones, "or for those of her Guides who have parents in prison."

"Shut up, will you?" said June, savagely.

Lupin gaped at her. The ground seemed to be giving way beneath her. June always struck her as one of the few normal people in Glanville, and here she was getting all worked up and making a scene about nothing, just like the rest of them. Lupin felt like saying, "*Et tu, Brute,*" or words to that effect. Phylis went scarlet, but did not say a word.

"That's not the way to talk to the district captain!" announced Miss Thompson firmly.

"I say, June, I mean, Miss Stuart, do let's keep our hair on. I mean to say, I'm sure Phyl . . . Miss Gardner, did not mean anything personal. After all, I dare say any of us might find ourselves in prison if it comes to that."

"Is that meant for me?" hissed Miss Oliver. "Because, if so, I should like to tender my resignation."

"No. Good gracious, no! As if I should say such a thing. I wasn't thinking of you at all. As a matter of fact, I have got something to tell you, there's some good news. I've found you know what."

"I should also like to tender my resignation," said Miss Gardner.

"Oh, dear, oh, dear, perhaps we had all better resign. I mean, we don't seem to be getting on very well, do we?"

"Miss Stuart should apologize to Miss Gardner," declared Miss Thompson.

Everyone began talking at once. "People who won't join in with others … some people think themselves too good for the district . . . I wonder what the Baden Powells are doing for Christmas . . ." (this was Lupin's contribution).

"Evidently Miss Stuart has never heard of the fifth Guide law, 'A Guide is courteous,' " remarked a Guider from the back of the room.

June jumped up. Her eyes were blazing, and her bare head shone red in the glare of the unshaded light above. "Yes, I have," she said, "and I've also heard of the second, 'A Guide is loyal,' and no one is going to nag at my mother in front of me!"

Lupin felt as though she had slipped on a banana skin. It was difficult to think of any tactful remark with which to fill in the awkward pause. She sat racking her brain for a moment or two that seemed like hours. She had not felt so uncomfortable as this since the time someone had spilled a cup of hot soup over her at a dance. As she came to the surface again, Diana was apologizing for the intrusion of her domestic matters into the affairs of the meeting and was leading the weeping June from the room. Phylis Gardner hurried after them, full of love and goodwill. No one would now guess that a few minutes ago she and Diana were in the middle of a bitter argument.

Miss Oliver, uncurling herself from one posture and working herself round into another, said that she was sure no one would think of taking any notice of what anybody said when they weren't feeling quite themselves. Miss Thompson barked out something about everyone playing cricket, which Lupin thought a rather unseasonable suggestion, and the sweetfaced Guider murmured that a Guide was a friend to all and a sister to every other Guide (or a mother, murmured Lupin, but luckily no one heard her). In fact, the meeting ended in much more harmony than any other meeting of Guiders that Lupin had ever attended.

All the same, as she walked home Lupin's mind was troubled. She heard voices in the drawing room, but instead of hurrying in to join her friends, which would have been her natural procedure under ordinary circumstances, for hers was a sociable nature, she went up to her own sitting room and asked

Staines to bring her a whiskey and soda, which was also an unusual procedure for her.

Something was worrying her, but what exactly was it? Why was it so dreadful that Diana should be June's mother? She took a drink and lit a cigarette. It had come to her in a flash, and it was best to face it. She had often wondered why June's profile reminded her of something. Now she knew what it was; it was Andrew's profile. There it was then. Diana was June's mother, and it looked as though Andrew was her father. Lupin had always thought he seemed very fond of her, and she remembered now little looks of understanding and sympathy which had passed between them that she had scarcely noticed at the time. Well, that appeared to be the situation, but very likely it would all be cleared up, like Tommy and the 'Sweet Sadie.'

Lupin finished her whiskey and soda. After all, Miss Oliver thought she had stolen ten pounds, but she hadn't. Gladys Simpkins thought she had been seduced, but Lupin would be prepared to lay ten to one against it, so perhaps Diana and June were mistaken too, and as for the profile it was probably a coincidence. She powdered her nose and strolled down the drawing room, where the others were playing bridge.

"Well? How did the meeting go?" asked Tommy, who was dummy.

"Acrimonious at first, but we ended up playing 'Kiss-in-the-Ring.' "

Jack looked up for a moment. "Everyone all right?" he asked, anxiously.

"So-so," replied Lupin. She supposed that it was June to whom he was alluding, and as the last glimpse she hid had of her was in floods of tears, she felt a noncommittal answer was the best she could do for him.

Luckily everyone was rather tired and ready to go to bed early, and Lupin soon found herself alone with Andrew. It was rather awkward to have to ask one's husband if he were someone else's father, but it was no good beating about the bush.

"Andrew," she said, "June got a bit rattled tonight and blurted out that Diana was her mother."

Andrew was about to pass on to his dressing room, but he turned at this. "In front of everyone?" he asked.

"Yes, the whole Guiders' meeting."

"That was unfortunate."

"But is it true?"

"Yes."

"Then who is her father?"

Andrew looked at her, quizzically. "Did you think I was, darling ?"

"Well, it did just cross my mind."

"I wonder if it has crossed many people's minds."

"Well, it's her profile, you know."

"I told you about my brother Stuart, who was killed in the war."

"Oh, of course. I might have thought of that. After all, if it had been you,

you'd have married the girl, and naturally you are fond of June if she's your niece."

"Now, if you will just keep quiet for a minute, I will tell you the whole story. Stuart was engaged to Diana, but her people said she was too young to get married; she was only eighteen, he was just twenty-one. They were an attractive pair," he added reminiscently. "It was wartime. Everything seemed different then; life was so uncertain, and people became a little unbalanced, I think. They went off together for his last leave and stayed at a little farmhouse in Devonshire. Of course, it was very wrong, but try not to judge them harshly. After a while Diana found that she was going to have a baby; she wrote to Stuart about it, and he told the whole story to his captain, who was very understanding and applied for special leave for him. He was killed a few hours before he was due to start, and it was only a couple of weeks before the Armistice was signed. He left a letter for me telling me everything. I tried to do what I could; I even tried to persuade Diana to marry me."

"You darling!" cried Lupin.

"Her people were very nice on the whole, but she couldn't very well live with a child without causing a scandal. Her father was a clergyman in a country parish. So she went up to London. She worked in my parish there for years, and then, when I had to give it up, it seemed only natural for her to come and live here; as a matter of fact, I felt rather lost without her. You see, she is just like a sister to me, and I am very fond of June."

"Darling, I quite understand. It used to worry me a bit, in a way. I mean, I wasn't exactly jealous, because after all you had married me, only it seemed curious, you being such very great friends, and I did think that she was in love with you."

"No, there has never been anything like that, but I am her one link with Stuart. She has never cared for anyone else, she is wrapped up in June—too wrapped up, I am afraid!"

"She didn't want her to marry Mr. Young, did she?"

"No," Andrew hesitated. "She is right there, he was a cad. Perhaps I oughtn't to say that, now that he is dead; in fact, I don't think that he was really responsible, poor fellow. But he heard us talking once. It was a summer evening, and we were sitting in the garden, and he found out the whole thing. He has been blackmailing her for months; if only she had told me. . ."

"You don't think. . ."

"No, I don't. I'm certain she didn't, but she is bound to be under suspicion."

"That's why you've been so worried the last few days?"

"Yes. I met Diana on the night of his death. In fact, she was hanging about outside, and she told me the whole thing. She has been very silly, but she thought it would spoil June's chance in the world if people knew that she was illegitimate. Young forbade her to mention it to me, but if only she had, I could have dealt with him. I took her to Inspector Poolton, and we told him about it. It would have looked very bad if it had been found out, as it certainly would have been, and in any case one wants to get at the truth."

"I should never have thought of poor Mr. Young as a blackmailer."

"Nor should I. That's the extraordinary thing about it. When I went round on Christmas Eve he tried to speak to me, but he couldn't. At last he murmured, 'It wasn't for myself.' I couldn't think what he meant, but of course when Diana told me about his blackmailing her, I understood and, putting the two things together, I guessed what had happened. He had been taking blackmail, not for himself, but for some object near to his heart. His great interest was foreign missions, so I've been looking through our accounts of the church missionary society, and I find that our total for the last twelve months is something like three times as much as it has ever been before, and there are a large number of anonymous donations for quite big sums. Some of these correspond, both in amount and date, to sums that Diana has paid. It is a terrible thought that one of the most horrible crimes that we know should be mixed up with preaching the Gospel."

"I suppose that he thought that he was doing right. Weren't there some people called Jews or Jesuits or something who thought it was all right to do a thing wrong if it was going to turn out right in the end?"

"You mean, doing wrong that good might come? There was such an idea, but it was a horrible one. It's a dreadful blow, because I liked Young. I still think that there was good in him. His mind was warped, I suppose; his sister tells me that he had always been delicate. He had a weak heart which prevented him doing many things he wanted to. I think he wanted to go out as a missionary, and that stopped him, poor fellow. We mustn't judge him harshly, but when I think what Diana has been through, it's very difficult. Still, there it is, darling, and I'm sorry I didn't tell you about Diana's and my relationship before, but it wasn't my secret. I wanted to tell you when we were first married, but she didn't want me to; she thought you'd look down on June."

"What a beastly snob she must think me."

"But she didn't know you then, did she?"

"But if Mr. Young was in love with June, how could he blackmail her mother?"

"I suppose he didn't fall in love with her until he'd begun, and then he thought that he could force her to marry him to save Diana, but I don't think June had any idea what was going on."

"No, she hadn't. She told me that she didn't think Diana liked him, but she didn't know why. I think she may know about it now; she looked awfully unhappy at the meeting—before all the upset, I mean."

"Poor child. Let's hope that they will be able to bring it in 'suicide.' Diana is bound to be suspected otherwise."

"We must prove that she is innocent, Andrew. After all, she is sort of one of the family. Don't you think that Jack could do something about it all? After all, he is in the Secret Service, and they have to detect spies and things, don't they?"

"I don't know if Jack has ever detected a spy, but he's a good boy, and I think he's got brains."

"Does he know?"

"Yes. I asked Diana to let me tell him the whole story. I thought it would be a help to talk things over with him. Now, darling, you are tired out, and must go to bed. All this worry and excitement is bad for you."

"Andrew!" cried Lupin, suddenly, long after he had imagined her to be asleep.

"Yes, darling?"

"If June is your niece, she is Jack's cousin."

"Only half cousin. Jack's mother is Stuart's and my stepsister, and in any case, I don't think it matters much so long as there are no family peculiarities to be multiplied."

"Oh, that's all right, then. Good-night."

CHAPTER 15

JUNE arrived early at the vicarage the next morning. Andrew had gone to his study, but the others were still sitting round the breakfast table. Her face was very white, and there were dark rings under her eyes.

"Hulloah, June," exclaimed Lupin, "will you have an egg or a sausage or something?"

"Hulloah," echoed Tommy and Duds, rather feebly, feeling that something uncomfortable was up.

Jack was busy, fetching a chair and coffee.

"Diana is arrested," announced June. "At least, they have taken her to the police station, and it's all my fault."

"Nonsense. No one from the Guiders' meeting would say a word. I must say they were very decent about it. In any case, I don't think you can be arrested for that."

"For what?" asked Tommy.

"Shut up!" said Jack, lighting June's cigarette. "You want Andrew, I expect?"

"Yes. He must come, he might be able to do something,"

"And I tell you what," said Lupin, "if I were you, I'd tell absolutely everything to that nice Inspector Poolton. I'm sure he'll understand, he is a family man, himself. As a matter of fact, I was a bit upset myself last night, because at first I thought it must have been Andrew. Still, I might have known he would have married her if it had been, he has such high principles. In fact, he wanted to as it was. Not that I shouldn't have loved to have had you for my daughter, though I don't quite see how you could have been, as I'd have only been about a year old. However, you aren't, and it wasn't, and, of course, with the war and everything I quite understand. I mean, it might have happened to anyone, and even Phylis Gardner was quite nice in a grieved way, and that awful, wriggly Miss Oliver, and the one like a man, and . . . oh, here is Andrew. Darling, do go quick, they are arresting Diana!"

"If only I'd married him," said June, "none of this would have happened, but I didn't know that he was blackmailing Diana."

"I don't see how it would have helped much," said Lupin. "Except, of course, they would be suspecting you of having murdered him, and I dare say you would have done. It must be awful to be married to someone you don't like, especially when they have boils. But perhaps it's rather bad taste to remember that now."

"I'm sure he has been blackmailing a lot of people," went on June, taking no notice of Lupin's attempts at consolation, "and one of them has murdered him, but it isn't Diana."

"We all know that, dear," said Andrew.

"Yes, but you don't know that she went to get some sulphur for Bill the other day, and she got two pounds for some reason or other, you know how vague she is. I ragged her about it frightfully at the time, and now the inspector wants to know all about it. I suppose that must be what he was poisoned with, but I never knew that it was a poison."

"Well, didn't you explain all that to the inspector?" asked Lupin.

"Yes, and he asked to see the packet, and we can't find it anywhere."

"But it must be somewhere," Lupin pointed out. "You can't have given Bill two pounds of sulphur in a few days. I mean, he would be dead by now, wouldn't he? And he isn't," she added, rather unnecessarily, as Bill entered the room. June had left him on the doorstep, but he had pushed open the front door and found his way into the gentlemen's cloakroom, from which he had purloined a roll of paper which he was now tactfully unrolling round the dining room. Rufus and John joined in the new game with delight, all old enmities forgotten, and the room was soon handsomely festooned. In fact, when Phylis Gardner was announced, she caught her feet in it, tripped over John, knocked over two plates and a pot of marmalade, and finally collapsed into Tommy's arms. Tommy's look of embarrassment was too much for the others, and June, who was already on the verge of hysteria, laughed louder than any of them.

"I hope I have not come in at an awkward time," said Phylis, in her well-bred voice, ignoring dogs, marmalade and paper. "Ah, June, dear, how are you this morning?"

June laughed louder than ever. "Very well," she replied. "Diana has just been arrested for murdering Mr. Young. Ha, ha, ha!"

"Nonsense!" said Andrew, sharply. "Pull yourself together, June. She has just been asked to go to the police station to make a statement. There is nothing to make a fuss about. Come along, dear, we'll go and meet her. I expect she has said all there is to say by now."

"But you don't know all," went on June, in an unnatural, high-pitched voice. "That awful Miss Simpkins has been spreading some tale about her being in his room on the last morning."

"Well, no one need believe a word she says," said Lupin. "Just tell the inspector that she told me she was going to have a baby, and then he'll know whether she is to be trusted or not. Besides, I can't see why she should poison him, even if . . . Oh, sorry, I forgot the others don't know."

"Well, I really must be getting along now," said Phylis, hurriedly, as she tried to disentangle her feet from the paper that entwined them. Tommy, very red in the face, had to perform this office for her, all three dogs leaped up at her at once, but she managed to go on behaving like a lady. "I just wanted to have a word with you sometime, Lupin, but I won't keep you now. Give my love to dear Diana, June, and say I hope to see her this afternoon. Good-bye."

"I wish Diana had been here," said June, as Andrew took her away.

"Well, you'll be able to tell her as soon as you see her," pointed out Lupin, "it will cheer her up, if she needs cheering up, that is," she added, lamely. "Oh, and do you mind if I tell the others, you know what, only we may be able to think of a plan if we all put all our cards on the table, so to speak."

"Put out any cards you like," replied June, wearily.

"Let's go up to my sitting room," suggested Lupin, "this room seems a bit untidy."

"It does a bit," agreed Duds.,

"Well, it's like this," explained Lupin. "You know all about it, don't you, Jack, but Andrew says it doesn't matter, being cousins so long as you are not peculiar. Neither of you are really, are you? Though June was a bit hysterical, but then, anyone would be if their mother had been arrested for murder."

"I haven't the vaguest notion what you are talking about," remarked Tommy. "But, what with finding strange young women in my arms before I have finished my breakfast, and things being found on the floor which one doesn't usually expect to see in mixed company, not to mention murders and whatnots, I am not really feeling myself; and in any case we ought to be starting if we are to be in London in time for lunch. You had better be putting on your hat, Duds."

"But we needn't really be in London for lunch; it's only Mary Wraights', and she never remembers whom she has asked, and who not. Last time there wasn't enough to eat. Ring her up, if you want to be a 'parfait' gentle knight, but she will never notice whether we are there or not."

"I don't believe you really need go at all. Tommy likes to think he is so invaluable in the Foreign Office, but I don't expect they notice whether he is there or not. Do stay until the inquest is over, anyway, and anyhow, you could easily get up in the morning and down in the evening. You can't leave everything like this."

"There is something in what Loops says, Tommy," pointed out Duds. "I mean, here we are in the middle of a really thrilling detective story. We must finish it. You know you don't really have to be at the office until Monday. You can easily pop up if you want to and come back in time for dinner. We can easily put off all our engagements by saying there has been a death in the family. There has, almost—"

"And I don't expect you really have any engagements," added Lupin.

"Well, get on with your story," grunted Tommy. "Or would it be better if Jack told us?"

"No," said Jack. "Lupin had better tell it in her own way."

"From what I know of her own way, none of us will be much wiser at the end of it!" objected Tommy. "But carry on."

"Andrew had a brother called Stuart," explained Lupin, "and he was in love with Diana. Stuart, I mean, not Andrew. Andrew says they were the most attractive couple, but of course it is a very long time ago, in the war, so off they went and spent his last leave together, if you know what I mean."

"We do," said Tommy, in a resigned voice.

"Of course, they were very young and inexperienced and that sort of thing, so they went and had a baby."

"Good heavens!"

"I shouldn't have thought that Diana was as old as that."

"Well, she wrote to Stuart before the baby was born, and he applied for leave and then went off and got killed before he got home, and there she was. Andrew, like the darling he is, asked her to marry him, and she very nobly said she wouldn't, and—er—then the baby was born and, of course, it turned out to be illegitimate or whatever it is, and what's more, it's June!"

"But what's all that got to do with the murder of Charles Young?" asked Tommy.

"He has been blackmailing her for over a year," said Jack. "Andrew told me about it. That's why he's been so frightfully worried these last two or three days. Miss Lloyd never told him anything about it until after Young was dead or, of course, he would have taken steps before."

"Well, I don't blame her if she did do him in," said Tommy. "Blackmail is a nasty, low-down trick, and he deserves all that he got."

He gave it all to some missionary society," said Lupin. "Wasn't that a funny thing to do?"

"Very funny," agreed Duds. "He must have been potty."

"Yes, but the law won't take that view," said Jack. "About it serving him right, I mean. We must do something."

"Couldn't we smuggle her out of the country?" suggested Lupin.

"No. That's the worst thing we could do; it would be the same thing as shouting out that she was guilty. We know that she isn't, so there is really nothing to be frightened of, but it would be a great help if we were to find out who really did do it, presuming he *was* murdered. We don't even know that. It may have been suicide, or even an accident. We shall know better after the inquest."

"Why are you so certain that it wasn't Miss Lloyd?" asked Tommy.

"Instinct, I suppose," said Duds.

"No, not altogether. I have been studying Miss Lloyd pretty closely, and one thing that strikes me is that she isn't a fool; she may be a little absent-minded in some ways, but if she undertakes a job, she does it well. If she had decided to poison someone, she would do it better than this; she wouldn't have been seen with the 'poisonee' outside his lodgings at eleven o'clock on the night before the murder. And she would hardly have burst into his room in the middle of the morning, when she knew that people would be there talking about their souls and whatnot. She must have often met the man in a social way. There seems to be quite a lot of eating and drinking together in this place; surely she could have slipped something into his whiskey or Eno's or whatever it is he drinks without haunting his doorstep."

"That's very true," agreed Tommy. "But I don't know that you would get a jury to recognize it."

"No, that's why I don't want her to be arrested," went on Jack. "But it's pretty grim, all the same." He took a paper from his table, and began writing:

1. Young had been blackmailing her for over a year.
2. He was also trying to blackmail her into persuading June to marry him.
3. She was seen outside his rooms on the evening before his death.
4. She was seen in his room on the morning of his death.
5. She bought two pounds of sulphur from the chemist a few days ago and can't produce it.

"It's all very damning, and somehow I think she would have managed better if she really had done it."

"Yes, there is something in that," agreed Tommy.

"Well," went on Jack, "I gather that all of us here are unanimous in wanting to clear her, so let us form ourselves into a band of detectives and see if we can't find the real criminal. If Diana did not do it, somebody else did; the question is, who? Probably someone else whom he was blackmailing. We must find out who else could have been blackmailed. What we want is as much information about everyone in Glanville as we can lay our hands on;

even if it doesn't seem at all important or relevant, it might turn out to be of use."

"I shall be very glad to make myself useful in any way I can," remarked Tommy, "but I don't quite see myself worming secrets out of the church workers."

"Oh, I don't know," said Lupin. "I always remember that time when I dropped a cigarette-end and burned a hole in that lovely blue frock of mine the first time I put it on, you were perfectly sweet."

"Well, if he's going to start being 'perfectly sweet' to Phylis Gardner and Mrs. Grey and Miss Gibson, I think the sooner we go home, the better!" said Duds.

"Oh, here comes Lochinvar Brown—I mean Lancelot," said Lupin, who was looking out of the window. "Perhaps you could worm something out of him, Tommy, Duds couldn't mind that."

Lancelot came in so close on Sara's heels that he nearly knocked her over, but like Phylis Gardner she kept her dignity, although he allowed her no time in which to announce him. "Captain Scott, I believe," he said to Tommy.

"No, no, not at all," said Tommy, hastily. "That's him, or should I say, he."

"I've come to give myself up," he declared.

"Did you really do it?" asked Lupin, in a tone of mingled surprise and relief.

"I'm nothing to do with the police," said Jack. "You had better go along to the station if you have a statement to make."

"Yes," said Lupin, "the station. I'll run you along in the car, but leave a statement clearing Diana first, then we'll all help you to get away. After all, it's very decent of you to tell us about it. If you're quick, you'll be able to catch the train that Duds and Tommy were going to catch, and I believe there's a boat train about two something. We needn't give the statement to the police till you are safely across, though we'll have to tell June, to put her mind at rest. But all you'll have to do is just to grow a beard. You needn't really have done it, because June was never in love with Charles, but it is no use thinking about that now. Did you put the poison in his tea?"

"Yes," said Lancelot. "It was a sudden temptation. I hadn't meant to do it, but as we were sitting at tea it suddenly struck me that if he were out of the way I might persuade June to marry me, so I suggested his looking at the sunset, and while his back was turned I slipped the poison into his tea and went on with the conversation as if nothing had happened. I even quoted some lines of poetry about the sunset, ' 'twas at that hour of evening when the setting sun . . .' "

"It was rather a coincidence that you had the poison on you, wasn't it?" remarked Tommy.

"Yes," agreed Lupin. "Like having the time and the place and the loved one all together."

"I had bought my father a tin of weedkiller while I was out, and it happened to be in my pocket. I suppose realizing that it was there put the idea into my head."

"It was clever of you to know enough pieces to keep Mr. Young amused all the time you were opening the tin," said Lupin. "I remember opening a tin of apricots once; it took me years, and then I cut myself all over them and they had to be thrown away."

"You say you put weedkiller in his tea," said Jack. "Are you sure it was poisonous?"

"Yes, it was arsenic," replied Lancelot, proudly.

"But Young was poisoned with sulphur," said Jack.

CHAPTER 16

THE INQUEST, which took place the next morning in the Town Hall, was well attended.

"What I like about Glanville," whispered Duds, "is whether you go to a party or to a carol service or to an inquest, you are sure to meet the same people. It makes it so cozy. I feel as if I had lived here all my life."

There were several Guiders present. They had evidently come to see that Diana 'wasn't put on.' It had leaked out that she had been questioned by the police. Phylis Gardner had on her 'church' face, while Miss Thompson looked as if she were umpiring at a football match and wasn't going to stand any nonsense. Mrs. Grey, of course, was among those present. She looked kind and capable, and if anyone were accused of murder she would be there to succor their friends and relations. She was chiefly occupied at the present time in trying to succor Miss Young, who was sitting beside her and who was looking more angry than grieved.

The jury filed in. They were, for the most part, local tradesmen, who looked rather sheepish and uncomfortable at finding themselves in their present situation. The coroner was a small, dry man with a great dislike for unnecessary conversation. He had a habit of cutting the witnesses short just as they were getting into their stride, which was rather disconcerting to them.

Miss Young was asked to give evidence of identification. She was on her feet almost before her name had been called and burst into a torrent of speech: "Yes, the deceased is my brother, Charles Fortescue Young. I ought to know if anyone does, considering I brought him up from a child. He has never had any secrets from me, we were more like mother and child than brother and sister, only the day on which he died, was foully murdered, I should say—"

"We don't know that, yet," interposed the coroner. "We are here to decide on how he met his death."

"I know how he met his death," went on Miss Young, unperturbed. "He was murdered! I had a letter from him on that very day, arranging to pay me a visit and asking me to invite certain old friends to meet him. Would he have done this if he had been intending to take his life?"

"May the jury see the letter?"

"Certainly. There is nothing in it that I should mind anyone seeing; my brother never wrote me any letter that he could be ashamed of. From his earliest years he was the most devout young man; his dearest wish was to be a missionary, but owing to a slight weakness of the heart he was unable . . ."

"Your brother had a weak heart?"

"Yes, from the age of fifteen. He was unable to play games like other boys, so he spent more time with me than he would have done otherwise, so I am. . ."

"That will do for the present, Miss Young. Thank you very much."

Miss Young, very angry at being stopped in the middle of her discourse, sat down, muttering: "Suppression of evidence, that's what it is. A put-up job."

"There, there," murmured Mrs. Grey soothingly. "You gave your evidence very well. It must have been an ordeal."

Dr. Brown was called next. He gave his evidence very fully. He was rather pleased with himself for being in such a prominent position, and he refused to let the coroner hurry him. Mr. Young had died of acute sulphaemoglobinaemia; owing to his weak heart he had succumbed rather quicker than was usual in such a case.

"Had Dr. Brown known beforehand that his heart was weak?"

Yes. He had. He had examined him once or twice. Young had been under him lately for a boil on his neck, and he had been taking a purifying mixture in which the predominating factor was sulphur. Dr. Brown was satisfied, however, that this medicine was not strong enough to have caused his death, even if he had taken an overdose of it.

"Not if he had taken a whole bottle of it straight off?"

Dr. Brown hesitated. "I doubt it, but in this case it is impossible. He ordered a new bottle from the chemist the day beforehe died, and only two doses had been taken. I am certain that he must have been taking sulphur in some form or other and in large quantities during the last few days. The actual cause of death was heart failure, caused by the breathlessness which is the chief symptom of sulphaemoglobinaemia."

The police surgeon corroborated the evidence of Dr. Brown as to the cause of death. Then Dr. Brown continued: "I was having tea at a friend's house, Mr. Grey's, in company with Mr.Young, when he was taken ill. I had noticed at once that he was not well. He had an unnaturally high color and seemed to behaving some difficulty with his breathing. It crossed my mind then that the sulphur was not suiting him, and I decided to change it. He only ate one small piece of cake, but he drank several cups of tea. I was just going to suggest his going home to bed when he collapsed. Mrs. Grey, with great presence of mind, produced some smelling salts and he rallied a little; she then gave him some sal volatile. Mr. Grey and I got him into my car and we took him home and put him to bed. We had to sit him up as he could hardly breathe at all by this time, but he asked for the vicar, and Mr. Grey went at once to fetch him. He died almost at once after the vicar's arrival."

"Why?" asked Miss Young. "Why should he have died as soon as the vicar arrived?"

Dr. Brown's face was a study as the meaning of the suggestion dawned on him. The jury looked embarrassed and pretended not to hear.

"Please, Miss Young," commanded the coroner.

"There, there," begged Mrs. Grey.

"He was dying," went on Dr. Brown. "I rather doubted his lasting till the vicar came, but I am glad he did, poor fellow, as it may have put his mind at rest. The police surgeon and I performed a post mortem and found a large quantity of sulphur that could not be explained by the medicine that he had been taking."

"If his heart had been sound, would there have been a chance of saving him?"

"There might have been. At any rate he would not have died at once, and there might have been a chance of counteracting the poison if we had had longer in which to do it. But his heart could not stand the strain imposed by the breathlessness."

Mr. Grey gave evidence that the deceased had had tea with him within a couple of hours of his death. He had not seemed in his usual health and spirits; he was generally a very cheerful young man. He had had one small piece of cake, in which he understood there to have been some sulphur, but Dr. Brown had had it analyzed and assured him that it could have no bearing on the case. He had helped the doctor to take the poor young man home to his lodgings and had afterwards gone to fetch the vicar. Yes, he had known the young man very well, as he was one of the churchwardens of the church. He often came in for a game of billiards in the evening. He knew his heart was weak, as Mr. Young had lamented not being able to play football with his boys' club, but otherwise he had seemed healthy enough and usually in very good spirits.

The vicar gave evidence that he had been called from the vestry by Mr. Grey just before six o'clock on the evening of the twenty-fourth. He found Mr. Young propped up with pillows and hardly able to breathe. He only gasped out five words. No, he had no objection to repeating them. They were: "It was not for myself." The vicar had not understood them at the time, but he had found out later that Mr. Young had been levying blackmail on at least one of his parishioners and that he had been giving the money to the church missionary society.

"That's a lie," interposed Miss Young.

"He evidently repented," went on the vicar, "and wished to confess the whole matter to me but was unable to speak. Those five words were all he could manage, but I understand now what he meant. He died while I was there. Dr. Brown was not satisfied as to the cause of death and called in the police surgeon."

"I think the deceased dined with you on the night before his death, Mr. Hastings?" suggested the coroner.

"Yes, he did. He did not seem very well. He was quiet and ate very little."

"Was he pale?"

"No, his color was rather high."

"Thank you very much, Mr. Hastings."

Then came the shock of the morning, when Diana was called. She answered the questions which were put to her, simply and quietly. She admitted that Mr. Young had been blackmailing her for over a year and that he had agreed to stop doing so if she would encourage her illegitimate daughter, June Stuart, to marry him. The surprise on the faces of the good people of Glanville at this disclosure was stupendous. Diana remarked afterwards that it would almost be worthwhile being hanged for. The Guiders had guarded her secret jealously, and they all stared straight in front of them. Mrs. Grey looked at Diana affectionately. The parish nurse gazed at her with her eyes almost popping out of her head, while Miss Gibson's countenance was a mixture of outraged decency that she should find herself in the same building as such a person and satisfaction that one whom she had never trusted should be proved a sinner.

"When did you last see the deceased, Miss Lloyd?"

"On Thursday morning."

"Did you quarrel with him?"

"No. He said he regretted what had been taking place between us and asked me to forgive him."

"You mean that he regretted blackmailing you and was not going to continue doing so?"

"Yes."

"You have, of course, no witness to that conversation?"

"None."

Andrew held June down by brute force and put one hand over her mouth.

Miss Young leaped to her feet. "That is my brother's murderer," she cried.

George Farmer, a local chemist, was next called. He seemed ill at ease and kept glancing apologetically at Diana as he spoke. He had sold the last witness two pounds of sulphur on December twelfth. No, she did not have to sign the book for sulphur.

"Do you remember any remarks that passed between you and the last witness on that occasion?" asked the coroner.

Mr. Farmer shuffled and cleared his throat. "The witness asked me about various poisons," he said reluctantly.

"Yes. Do you remember any details of the conversation?"

"She asked me whether strychnine or arsenic was the most efficacious, and she asked if anyone could be poisoned with sulphur."

"What was your reply?"

"I said that arsenic would be the easiest poison to kill anyone with. It is easier to get hold of, in the form of weedkiller, etc."

"What did you say about sulphur?"

"I said that it might prove fatal if taken in large quantities."

"Never will I buy another thing from that man," hissed Lupin. "To think that I gave him a huge order only last week for toothpaste and soap and I don't know what."

Diana was recalled. "Do you agree with what the last witness has said?" she was asked.

"Yes," replied Diana cheerfully. Ever since June had given away her secret at the Guiders' meeting a load seemed to have rolled off her shoulders. For years she had guarded that secret and had been in terror of its being discovered. Now that she realized that it was a secret no longer, and that in spite of being known to be illegitimate, June was just as popular and as much respected as she had been before, she found that she had been living in fear of a bogey of her own imagination. Nothing seemed to matter any more. She felt years younger, and her eyes had lost their wild, hunted look. "Yes, I asked Mr. Farmer for some information about poisons, as I am writing a detective story. I wanted to know all the different ways in which the victim might be murdered."

There was a stir in the court. Miss Young leaped to her feet once more. "There is the murderer!" she cried. "There is the woman who murdered my brother. Arrest her at once. What further evidence do you want?"

One of the Guiders called out, "It's not true!"

"Hear, hear!" agreed Miss Thompson.

"Murderess!" shrieked Miss Young.

There was a confused babbling. Mrs. Grey held Miss Young down and tried to soothe her, while Mr. Grey hovered over them, looking worried and inefficient. Two Guiders were ejected by the police for trying to make a demonstration. Andrew put a restraining hand on Lupin's knee just as she was about to stand up and speak. Jack had an arm round June and was whispering to her that she would help Diana best by keeping quiet. Miss Simpkins had hysterics and was led out by the parish nurse.

At length order was restored, and the inquest was resumed. Diana was asked why she had bought two pounds of sulphur. She replied that she had not the least idea, but that she was thinking of something else at the time.

Things looked very black against her: she had had a very strong motive for killing Mr. Young; she was known to have Inquired about poisons; she was also known to have two pounds of sulphur in her possession. What was almost worst of all was that she could not produce the remains of the large packet and could give no explanation of what she had done with it. She was in Mr. Young's room on the morning of his death and had had plenty of opportunity of putting the sulphur into his drinking water. Her friends and supporters felt very depressed.

Mrs. Jones, Mr. Young's landlady, was called. Mr. Young had always been a very nice young gentleman, and it had been a terrible shock, his dying like that. She had always looked after him as if he were her own son, and if anyone thought she would have murdered him, it was their own blackness of soul that put such ideas into their heads. Many a time the poor reverend gentleman had said, "You spoil me, Mrs. Jones." He had had some cold mutton for his luncheon, and if anyone thought you could put poison into cold mutton …

"No one is accusing you, Mrs. Jones. Had you noticed anything different about the deceased during the last few days?"

"The deceased? Oh, Mr. Young. He hadn't any disease that I know of, just a boil on his neck for which I put on a bread poultice, and if he'd stuck to that instead of taking doctor's stuff, he might have been here now!"

"Did he seem at all depressed?"

"Of course he was depressed. Who wouldn't be, with a boil on his neck? Very painful until they break, and not becoming either, especially if the gentleman is thinking of courting a young lady."

"My brother never thought of courting young ladies," declared Miss Young. "He was wedded to his religion."

"When did you last see Mr. Young before he was brought back by the doctor, Mrs. Jones?"

"At dinner, luncheon, I should say. I took him up some coffee; he had made a shocking meal, poor dear. I asked him if he would be in for supper, and he asked me to go out and get him one of those jars of meat jelly, as he found a difficulty in swallowing. And then he asked if I'd iron out his surplice against the carol service, and I did, too. A treat it looked, and he never wore it again," and Mrs. Jones subsided in tears.

"We have to consider the possibility of Mr. Young having taken his own life."

"That he never did," interposed Miss Young.

"He was in a poor state of health, I think that is proved by his having a boil, is it not, Dr. Brown?"

Dr. Brown nodded assent.

"His landlady thinks he had had some love trouble. Mr. Hastings, could you give us any information on this point?"

Andrew gave June an apologetic glance. "Yes, I understand that he proposed to my niece, Miss Stuart, on the evening before his death, and that she refused him."

A sigh of relief went round the court. Obviously it was a case of suicide; all was well.

Miss Young alone was not satisfied. "I don't believe a word of it!" she cried. "Would he have written me this letter if he had contemplated taking his life?" and she thrust a letter into the coroner's hands.

"May I read this aloud?" he asked.

"Certainly. It was written on the morning of his death, after that young woman," with a venomous glance at June, "is supposed to have refused him. I received it on Christmas Day, after I had heard of his death. It came as a message from the grave."

The letter was as follows:

Dear Susan,

This is to wish you a very happy Christmas. I sent your little gift yesterday, and I hope it will arrive safely. It is a book of St. Paul's missionary journeys, and I hope you will like it. I have got a boil on the neck, which is making me feel rather under the weather, and the vicar has kindly suggested my taking a night or two off when Christmas is over. Could you put me up if I came to you on Wednesday or Thursday? I should be so glad if you would. I haven't seen you for so long, and you might ask Basil Browne to look in; I'd like a talk with him, and also the Barbers. I am dining tomorrow with Mr. and Mrs. Grey; you have heard me speak of them. He is the vicar's warden: they are very hospitable people.

With all best wishes,

Your affectionate brother,
Charles.

The coroner read out the letter and then handed it to the foreman of the jury, who passed it round, after which it was returned to Miss Young.

The coroner summed up the case: "There are three alternatives," he pointed out. "Death by misadventure, suicide, and murder. Dr. Brown tells us that the deceased could not have died from an overdose of his medicine, and it is hard to see in what other way he could have taken such an unnatural amount of sulphur. As regards suicide, we know that he was depressed by his offer of marriage being refused, but his letter to his sister does not suggest a broken-hearted man. If he had been intending to take his life, would he have asked her to put him up the following week and gone into details about whom he wished to meet while under her roof? His landlady, too, tells us that he had specially asked for a special dish for his supper, and that he wished to have his surplice ironed in readiness for the carol service. Mr. Hastings tells us that he was not very well on the night of the twenty-third. He mentions his having a color. This looks, according to the doctor, like symptoms of sulphaemoglobi-naemia, so he may have been taking the sulphur in small doses over a period of . . . at any rate, two or three days. A man wishing to take his own life would hardly do it in so uncomfortable a manner." He droned on, referring to the former evidence. It looked very black for Diana; her friends gave up all for lost.

At last the jury left the room. The atmosphere was very tense. No one spoke; even Miss Young was silent. Every eye was on the door through which the jury must reappear, except Diana's. She alone appeared uninterested in the proceedings. There was a faraway expression on her face, such as she often wore when thinking out a new plot.

Fortunately, the coroner's jury were careful men. They did not want to accuse anyone wrongfully. Incidentally, most of them knew Diana. She was popular with the working population of Glanville. Not that this would influ-ence them in any way in the course of their duty, for they were conscientious men, but they could not help feeling how impossible it would be for her to commit a murder. She was not the sort of person to do it at all. Of course, they were shocked to find out that she had had a daughter all these years without being married; but, after all, these writing people did often have funny ideas, and in any case it was a very long time ago.

The verdict was given: wilful murder against some person or persons unknown.

Miss Young protested, and Mrs. Grey had some difficulty in getting her out of the court. Andrew hurried Diana to his waiting car. A certain section of the community hissed as she passed, but this was counteracted by a volley of cheers from the Guiders. A photographer caught Andrew and Diana just as he was helping her into the car.

"That's torn it," said Diana. "They will all think that you are the father of my child and that we murdered Charles Young between us. After all, she is very like you to look at."

"Well, it can't be helped now."

Jack took June home, and Tommy drove Lupin and Duds.

"Oh, dear," said Lupin, "what are we going to do? Diana is as good as hanged already. Whatever made her go and ask that beastly little man Farmer all those questions about poison, when she might have guessed that Mr. Young was going to get himself done in?"

"But she didn't know it," pointed out Tommy. "That is just the point. If she had meant to do it herself, she wouldn't have been such a fool."

"No, of course not, but you'll never get the police to see that. Most people are such fools and they judge others by themselves. I thought she was going to be arrested then and there; I was absolutely dripping from every pore. I shall have to change everything I've got on. Anyone would think I had been playing dozens of sets of tennis. However, it's very slimming, I believe. That ghastly sister of Mr. Young. She gave me an awful look just as I was in the middle of making up my face. It gave me such a fright that I put lipstick all over my nose. Does it show?"

"Yes," replied Duds.

"Well, I don't care. Though if I do have to go to the scaffold I should like to be looking my best. Oh, dear, do you think that they'll arrest Andrew? June is the living image of him; they'll never believe it was his brother. What are we to do? I'm sure we had better leave the country. Let's go to New Zealand. I believe the climate is very nice there, and we could all settle down and make a new life. Andrew could preach to the natives, and Diana could turn them into Girl Guides, and the rest of us could enjoy ourselves. Oh, my dear, what is that man doing outside Diana's house?"

"I was hoping you wouldn't notice," replied Duds.

"I expect he is a commercial traveler or something," said Tommy, frowning at his wife, "selling vacuum cleaners, very likely."

"No, I have seen them too often at weddings; there is no mistaking them, whatever hats they wear. I shouldn't mind if it were Inspector Poolton; he is so understanding. Still, I dare say that this one is very nice when you get to know him, but it doesn't look as if it would be much good trying to smuggle Di off if they've got their eyes on her. We must try to find the real criminal without delay, or it may be too late."

Andrew and Jack stayed to luncheon with Diana and June and afterwards Jack went round to the police station to have an interview with Inspector Poolton. He had been working in the Secret Service and had received a good deal of training in observation and in the fitting together of facts. He felt certain that he could solve this particular problem if he were given time and opportunity. For one thing, so much depended upon it. He had fallen in love for the first time in his life, and he longed to prove himself a knight errant and save the mother of the girl he loved from the scaffold. He did not word his feelings in such high-flown language even to himself; it would have made him blush to the roots of his hair to think of such a thing, but nevertheless they were very much after that fashion.

"It sticks out a yard," he said to Andrew, "that Diana was not the only one of Young's victims. What we have to do is to find out who else in this town, probably in this parish, was blackmailed, too."

CHAPTER 17

"YOU KNOW, Inspector, just because I've had a year or two in the Secret Service, I don't for a minute imagine that I know anything about detective work, so don't think I fancy myself as Sherlock Holmes or Peter Wimsey—or anything of that sort. It's only that, staying as I am at the vicarage, I see a good many people and they talk in front of me, while they're a bit inclined to close up at the sight of a police inspector, if you know what I mean."

"Yes, sir, I quite see your point, and we shall be very glad of your help. In fact, the chief constable said we were to give you every facility, but it's an awkward situation for you being, so to speak, a friend of the family. You cannot help being somewhat biased, if you will forgive me for saying so."

"You are quite right, I am biased. I do not want Miss Lloyd to be proved guilty, but then I quite definitely believe her to be innocent. If I thought that she was guilty I should be wiser to keep out of the business altogether, but as it is, I want to have a chance of clearing her. Honestly, Inspector, does she strike you as a fool?"

"No, she doesn't. I don't mind telling you that I don't like the case. No woman would behave as she has done unless she was either completely inno-cent or else a lunatic. And yet the evidence is overwhelming. Of course, she may have asked the questions at the chemist's in perfect good faith in relation to her book, and the thought of using the poison in real life may never have occurred to her until later on, when, driven to beyond bearing point, she de-cided to murder the man and didn't stop to think."

"Just pushed into his rooms and bunged the stuff into his drinking water, you mean?"

"More or less."

"Hardly true to type. Her whole life is centered round Miss Stuart. She has paid away nearly all her capital to prevent people knowing that she is her daughter. Would she go and commit murder without taking precautions that Ju . . . Miss Stuart wasn't going to be branded as the daughter of a murderer?"

"No, it doesn't seem likely, but it's going to be a difficult business to find anyone else with as good a motive."

"There are several other people with rather fishy stories."

"There always are," replied the inspector, "but we can't get much from them, though, of course, they are all under observation. You'd like to see the notes on the case?"

"Thank you very much," and Jack took the sheath of papers from the inspector.

'Charles Young, son of the Rev. George Young of St. Mary's, Layden, Dorset, who died February, 1936, and Mrs. Young, who died July, 1914. Came to Glanville October, 1936; previously curate to the Rev. John Smith, St. Peter's, Lashmere, Somerset.

'Was taken ill at Mrs. Grey's house on December 24th at about 4:30 p.m. Symptoms, breathlessness and peculiar change of color. Dr. Brown was present. Diagnosis, heart failure. His heart always weak. At doctor's request Mrs. Grey administered sal volatile.'

"I suppose it was sal volatile and not something else given by mistake?"

put in Jack, looking up.

"No, the glass was left just as it was and thoroughly examined. Mrs. Grey was very anxious about it; I remember her saying, 'Oh, I couldn't have made a mistake, could I, and given him something else?' She gave us the glass and the bottle from which the sal volatile was poured."

Jack returned to the notes. 'Young taken back to his lodgings and became seriously ill. Asked for the vicar, who was sent for at once. When he arrived, Young was dying; managed to say the words 'It wasn't for myself', then died about 6:15 p.m.

'Doctor's diagnosis is "Heart failure owing to advanced form of sulphaemoglobinaemia." Dr. Brown reported that he had prescribed him Sulphonamide P. for boils. If this is mixed with any other form of sulphur it brings on sulphaemoglobinaemia, or too much sulphur in the system. This is especially serious if the heart is weak.'

Jack looked up again. "Do you think he was given one big dose or several small ones?"

"It's difficult to tell, that's what makes it so complicated. One can't narrow down the time."

"In fact, anyone who had a meal with him during the last few days is suspect?"

"Just so. Almost anyone in the parish could be guilty, but one wants a motive."

"Don't you think that Young may have been blackmailing one or more other people besides Miss Lloyd?"

"It seems most likely. The sums that he has been paying into the church missionary society are much larger than the money he extracted from Miss Lloyd warrants. Of course, he may have collected it in some perfectly legitimate way, but the vicar finds it difficult to account for it. The trouble is to narrow down the field. He knew so many people and had been in so many different houses during the past few days. Of course, if blackmail was the motive, one would expect to find the guilty person to be among the well-to-do."

"Miss Lloyd is not very well-to-do."

"No, I suppose not. Of course, he might have collected small sums from poor people. However, I should say we'd be more likely to find him or her among the less poor. For instance, Young might have been blackmailing your uncle. It would not have done him any good to have the fact of his brother and Miss Lloyd's relations published to the world, and incidentally, if you'll forgive my mentioning it, we haven't any actual proof at present that it was his brother and not he who was the father of Miss Stuart. There is also Lady Lupin. He might have found out something there that she did not want her husband to know."

"But she would have blurted the whole thing out," objected Jack.

The inspector smiled. "Unless she is a most accomplished actress," he remarked. "Then there are Mr. and Mrs. Grey. They had plenty of opportunity. Young had been in there several times within the last few days. He played billiards with Mr. Grey on the evening of the twenty-second, called in to see Mrs. Grey about some parish matter on the morning of the twenty-third and had tea there on the twenty-fourth. There are also Dr. and Mrs. Brown. Young called there about his boil on the morning of the twenty-second. On the afternoon of the twenty-third he went in about some society of which Dr. Brown is the secretary and had tea there, and on the twenty-fourth he met them both at tea at the Greys'. However, I am not supposing that either of those respectable couples have anything they wish to hide."

"You can never tell," said Jack thoughtfully. "One thing strikes me as strange. Why, if Brown knew that Young had a weak heart, did he give him this sulphur medicine?"

"I think that is all right," replied the inspector. "I have consulted the police doctor and there seems to be no reason why that form of sulphur should affect the heart. He must have been given a very large dose of sulphur in some form or other that, in connection with the medicine, had the fatal effect."

Jack turned over the notes, occasionally jotting down something in his pocketbook. It was mostly reiteration of the evidence that had been given at the inquest. The case against Diana looked very black.

The inspector went on with his list of possible suspects. "Then there is his landlady, of course. She had the best opportunity of anyone for getting rid of him if she wished to do so. And there is Miss Gibson. You'll find that he went to see her on the morning of his death."

"By Jove, so he did!" said Jack, referring to the list of times and places. "That is interesting."

"Why? Surely that lady hasn't got a past?"

"I don't say she has, but the cognizi tell me that feeling was very high between her and Young. Religious difficulties, you know; there is nothing like them for producing bad feeling from the time of the Inquisition onward. I gather that she wanted her own nephew here as curate and did her best to cramp Young's style on every occasion."

"I doubt that she would have cramped it to that extent, though she is a bit of a tartar by all accounts. Thinks for the tip, though."

"Oh, here you've got down Miss Simpkins. . . 'Saw Miss Lloyd in Young's room morning of the 24th' … but what was she doing there herself, that's what I'd like to know? I've heard some funny tales about her."

"She is rather a fishy customer," agreed Poolton. "Weeps a good deal, too, which always complicates things. She was certainly as thick as thieves with Young at one time, so of course; there is always the chance of the *crime passionel,* as the French call it. But as regards blackmail, I hardly think he would have blackmailed a shopgirl. And then there is that other woman, Miss Oliver. Why does she deny having seen him on the evening of the twenty-second? Lady Lupin seems convinced that they were both together in her sitting room. She is not very definite as a rule, so that when she is, I feel it must be true, unless, of course, as I said before, she is the guilty party and acting all the time. It is very difficult to tell who is speaking the truth and who isn't. You, mixing with them all as you do, have a chance of sifting some of the facts out of the muddle, and we shall be very grateful if you will. We don't want to make a mistake. Miss Lloyd looks guilty enough on the face of it. He had been blackmailing her for over a year, and she had got rid of more than half her capital. Also she was afraid of his marrying Miss Stuart. She had plenty of sulphur and can't account for it. She had been making inquiries as to the best way of poisoning someone, and she was in his room on the morning of the murder. If anyone ever looked guilty, she does. Yet, as you say, it is too obvious. Would any woman be such a fool? Unless, of course, she argued to herself that that is just what we would say."

"Well, she is under observation, so she can't get away without your knowing it, and in the meantime I am going to follow up the life stories of some of these other people you've got down in your dossier. I'd like to get the truth out of Miss Simpkins and Miss Oliver."

"Of course, there's that young son of Dr. Brown," went on the inspector. "They say he was in love with Miss Stuart, too, and he was alone with the deceased on the afternoon of the twenty-third."

"Well, he came to me and said that he'd poisoned Mr. Young by putting arsenic in his tea."

The inspector burst out laughing. "There are always a lot like that, confessing to crimes they haven't committed for the sake of a spot of notoriety; though," he added reflectively, "if he really had done it, it would be rather an artful dodge to make up a tale like that, so that we should wipe him off the slate as dotty."

"Yes, there is that, but I don't quite see what he had to gain by murdering Charles Young. I mean," and he went rather red, "he had no reason to think that Miss Stuart would look at him, curate or no curate."

The inspector gave him a shrewd glance. "I guess you're right there, sir," he said. "Though, of course, he may not have realized that. I should think he's a young man with a pretty fair opinion of himself. Still, I think he just wanted to draw attention to himself, like when he made a speech in the marketplace last year. The doctor was pretty sick about that, as you can guess. But the lad will grow out of it, no doubt. No, I don't think we need bother ourselves about Master Brown."

"I don't think I am worrying about him either," said Jack, smiling shyly. "Thank you most awfully for being so helpful, Inspector, and for not minding my putting a finger in the pie. I'll get my spies to work and let you know the results of our investigations."

"That's all right, Captain. Good luck to you."

Jack walked home slowly and thoughtfully. He was rather relieved to find that the others were all out. He rather wanted a little quiet time in which to think. He lit his pipe and read his notes slowly, then he went into Andrew's study where he found *Crockford's Clerical Directory* for 1936. He looked up Young, George, late vicar of St. Mary's, Layden, Dorset, and was interested to see that he had been chaplain to Dartmoor penal settlement from 1910 until 1929.

'That is interesting,' said Jack to himself. 'Young would have been born there and lived there until he was about eighteen. I wonder if that has any bearing on this case.'

CHAPTER 18

"WELL, we don't seem to be getting much further," said Duds.

They had all gone round to Diana's house to discuss the situation. "Surely, between us all, we might be able to discover one murderer?"

"Are we absolutely certain that it was not suicide?" asked Tommy hopefully.

"I'm afraid we are," replied Jack. "There was a list of visits for the future that he had just made out, all lying ready on his writing table; and there was the letter that he had written to his sister suggesting a visit to her in the near future and mentioning people he wished to see. Also there was the jar of meat jelly that he had ordered for his supper. Oh! And the surplice that he had asked his landlady to iron for him."

"Mightn't he have done all that on purpose to make it look like murder just to spite Diana because she had prevented him from marrying June?"

"She didn't prevent me. I didn't want to marry him, though I wish I had now; then none of this would have happened."

"Why not?" asked Jack.

June paused. "I don't know," she admitted. "But I might have been able to stop it."

"Until we know who was the murderer and what was the motive we can't say one way or the other about that. But I don't think he would have done what Tommy suggests," went on Jack. "I should say that his was a single-track mind. Unpleasant as he was, he seems to have acted from a perverted sense of duty. He wanted to collect money for the missionary society. I don't think he would have taken his own life for the pleasure of getting Diana hanged. It would amount to murder, and he would have hardly wanted to die with that on his conscience. After all, he tried to confess about the other thing when he found he was dying."

"I feel that a fellow who went in for blackmail would not stop at much," remarked Tommy. "But I dare say the idea is farfetched. What about his hav-ing taken an overdose of sulphur by mistake?"

"That solution would save a lot of trouble, but I'm afraid it won't work. There was not enough taken out of the bottle to have killed him, and the police can't find that he ordered any more from the chemist."

"But couldn't he have got some without anyone knowing anything about it?" asked Lupin.

"It would have been very difficult as he would have had to produce the prescription; but he might have got some sulphur, of course, if he wished to commit suicide. But we have just decided that he didn't."

"I think it was Miss Oliver," announced Duds.

"Why on earth?" asked Tommy.

"There is something very fishy about her. I mean, why did she invent that tale about the money?"

"I should think that she is probably mad, but that is no proof that she murdered Mr. Young."

"No, but listen. She was alone in Lupin's sitting room on Monday evening. She saw the ten pounds and took it. As she did so Young came in. He said, 'Give it to me or I'll tell on you,' or words to that effect, so she did. Then he said, 'Now you'll write me a confession that you have stolen ten pounds.' He fetched the blotter and made her write it, but I suppose he lost his head or something and left the notes there by mistake. Anyway, she was not to know that, but she did know that he had gone off with her confession in his pocket and that there was nothing to prevent him blackmailing her in the future. Getting desperate, she went round to his rooms the next day and put sulphur in the drinking water in his bedroom."

"That's no good. It was analyzed."

"Well, perhaps she got there before lunch and put it in his beer or what-ever he drank for lunch."

"Water," put in Lupin. "That wouldn't have been analyzed because they would have emptied the jug before they knew that he was going to be mur-dered."

"It is just possible," said Jack thoughtfully, "but I don't see how she could have got in and out without being seen. I mean, you can't just go wan-dering about in other people's houses without having to give a reason."

"But why?" asked Tommy. "If she murdered Young for fear that some-one should hear of her stealing ten pounds, why did she then come round and tell Lupin all about it?"

"I suppose she got frightened, realizing that Lupin would miss the ten pounds and would suspect her as having been alone in the room and, knowing her kind nature, thought she would tell her herself and throw herself on her mercy, so to speak."

"That is the weak point," said Jack. "Why not go to Lupin straight away instead of complicating things by murdering Young? Besides, how was she going to get the confession away from him? If she had shot him or stabbed him it would have been a different matter, but as it was she wouldn't have been there when he died and would have practically no chance of getting the thing back, and it would have been found among his papers. No, I don't think that will do."

"Well, she went to his rooms to hunt for the confession and couldn't find it, so in desperation she put some sulphur in his water."

"But one doesn't carry sulphur about in one's handbag," objected Lupin. "At least, I don't, though I wouldn't put it beyond Miss Oliver now I come to think of it. Nothing she did would surprise me, as a matter of fact."

"But why sulphur?" inquired Tommy. "That's what seems so funny to me. I never even knew it was a poison. I should have used weedkiller or something like that. Besides, if he hadn't been taking this sulphur medicine for his boils it wouldn't have done the trick, would it, Jack?"

"No, I don't think so. I think who ever gave him the sulphur must have known about the boils."

"We all knew about them," remarked Lupin. "One could hardly help knowing. I mean, a boil is a pretty obvious sort of thing, isn't it?"

"Must have known that he was taking sulphur already, I should have said," went on Jack, "and that he would be affected by some more. Of course, the Girl Guides do learn all about poisons in their first aid classes, don't they, Lupin?"

"Very likely," agreed Lupin. "As a matter of fact, I have never found out what it is they do learn about, but I am sure it is very useful."

Diana, who was sitting quietly smoking and listening to the conversation of the others in a detached manner, now broke in with a cynical laugh. "Very useful," she said, "as things have turned out."

"Well," said Jack, "we had better explore every avenue. Miss Oliver is certainly keeping something back. I don't think that she is the actual criminal, but she might be able to throw some light on this case. Who would like to take her on? What about you, Duds? You might pretend to be a visiting Guider who wishes to discuss Guiding with her."

"Can't you think of something a little more likely?" begged Duds.

Lupin was not at all clever, but occasionally she came across a good idea by mistake; she did so now. "I think June had better go," she announced.

"Me?" asked June, surprised. "Why?"

"Well, I think Miss Oliver rather likes you, at least, she doesn't positively dislike you, which is more than she could say about anyone else. And she certainly seemed rather inclined to be sympathetic the other evening at the Guiders' meeting."

"That's not a bad idea," said Jack, "I should lay all your cards on the table, explain that you are worried to death about Diana, and ask her if she will help you by elucidating the two points that are obscure: One, why did she say that she had stolen ten pounds when they were in the blotter all the time? and two, why did she say that she hadn't seen Mr. Young when she obviously had? If she is innocent, as I think she is of the murder, at least, she will very likely give you an explanation, especially if you appeal to her better feelings."

"But do you think she has any?" asked Duds pessimistically.

"Probably, most people have. The trouble about this case is that there are so many suspects, almost anyone in the town might be the murderer. My idea is to eliminate as many people as possible so as to narrow down the field."

"Yes, but if you eliminate all the others it will make it all the worse for Diana," pointed out Lupin.

"Unless you succeed in eliminating me, too," remarked Diana, "and that will require some doing."

"It shall be done," replied Jack gravely.

"Thank you, Jack," said June. "Then I'll go after Miss Oliver. It's not the sort of job I like, pretending to be friendly with someone when I am really trying to worm things out of them, but I'll ring her up and see when she'll be in. It's hardly the time for being squeamish."

"It certainly is not," agreed Jack, as he opened the door for her. "Now the next on the list," he said to the others, "is Gladys Simpkins; her story also needs explaining. It is very thin. She wanted to confess to Young that she had been seduced by someone and was going to have a baby. First, that seems an unlikely tale. Second, according to her it wasn't her fault, so what was there to confess? Third, Young wasn't given to hearing confessions, and in any case, surely Andrew would have been more suitable for a tale of that sort, being married and everything. We know that she was seen outside his lodgings on the evening before and also that she was sitting in his room drinking tea with him on the morning of the twenty-fourth. She had ample opportunity for murdering him, but we don't at present know of any motive. I think someone must see if they can get a true statement from her."

"Don't you think, Diana," suggested Duds, "that if you went to her and told her the true story of what you were doing at his lodgings, she might reciprocate with the true story of why she was there?"

"I wonder," said Diana thoughtfully. "We might have been great friends, only I told her that she was too old for the Rangers; no, it's no good pretending that that went well. Still, she was very fond of me once. Perhaps the old fascination will work once more and she will tell me all. The only trouble is where and when? I can't move without being watched—even when I'm in my bath I'm always expecting to find a policeman disguised as the towel rail. If Gladys and I are seen conferring together they will probably think that we are both in it and that we are planning fresh murders."

"I don't see why. The rest of us come and go quite freely. Miss Simpkins is no more suspicious a character than Andrew or Lupin."

"Oh, dear," cried Lupin. "Do they think it was us? I am sure that nice Inspector Poolton doesn't. I explained the whole thing to him and he quite understood. After all, if it had been the fish, Mr. Young wouldn't have been the only one. In fact, he ate less than anyone, and after all it would have been more the fishmonger's fault than ours. Not that I want to get anybody into trouble, and he is really a very nice man apart from his fish . . ."

"I think we'll leave the fishmonger out for the moment," said Jack. "It is really Gladys Simpkins that we are concentrating on at present. You can easily ask her to come and see you here, Diana, and then talk to her as girl to girl."

"I don't quite see how I can do that," objected Diana. "My best friends could hardly call me a girl, and Gladys is less of one still by a matter of ten years, I should say. Oh, dear, here comes Phylis! As you say, one visitor more or less will hardly be noticed. All the Guiders come to see me every day, and some twice; they work off their good turns that way. I should think that I am easily the most popular member of the movement at the moment. It is a pity I paid all that money to Mr. Young for keeping my guilty secret, because now that it is out, I am a much greater success than I was before. I don't expect I shall have a minute to call my own when I am in prison, and I had been looking forward to having a little quiet time there in which to finish my book. Hulloah, my dear!" she said, turning to Phylis. "How nice of you to come. I'm still at large, though expecting to be arrested at any moment."

"Diana, dear." Phylis kissed her tenderly, then looked round sadly at the others. They all composed their faces, and Tommy nervously put out his pipe for fear that he should not seem sympathetic enough.

There was an awkward pause. "I believe that prisons are more comfortable than they used to be," said Lupin, feeling that someone had better say something.

"Lupin, my dear," protested Phylis sorrowfully.

There was another silence. Phylis broke it herself this time. "And where is dear June?" she asked.

"My child is out trying to prove her mother's innocence," replied Diana. "Isn't that beautiful? If I live long enough I shall write a book about it."

"Well," said Lupin, "I think there is always a month after the trial, and then if you appeal you can draw it out a bit longer; or perhaps if you said that you were writing a book they might give you an extension."

"I don't think you quite know what you are talking about, Lupin, dear."

"No, nor do I," agreed Lupin. "I am feeling a little distraught."

"So are we all, dear, but we must keep our heads, mustn't we?"

"I will, if they will let me," remarked Diana brightly. "I am glad we haven't the guillotine in England, it must be so untidy."

"Now, my dear, you are quite unhung, I mean unstrung." She stopped, quite overcome by her solecism, which was not improved by Lupin and Duds bursting into shrieks of laughter.

"What about some sherry?" suggested Diana. "I don't know why it is, but everyone seems a little bit depressed this evening. Perhaps it's the weather. Sherry will do us all good."

The sherry was brought in and conversation became a little easier. In the middle Miss Thompson was announced, and she strode breezily into the room. "Evening, Miss Lloyd. Evening, everyone. Thought I'd just look in, what? All stick together, you know."

June returned to the room. She looked slightly ruffled at the sight of the visitors but greeted them politely and didn't fidget too perceptibly when Phylis kept hold of her hand and called her "childie."

"Well, I've fixed up that interview," she remarked cheerfully, "ten o'clock tomorrow morning."

"We are all doing detective work," Lupin explained to Phylis.

"Jolly good fun," put in Miss Thompson. Then, catching Phylis's cold eye fixed on her, she muttered something about "looking on the bright side of things."

At last the party broke up. Diana heaved a sigh of relief. "I was afraid that they were going to stay to dinner," she remarked, "and I knew there were only two cutlets and a little toasted cheese."

"I wish they were all in hell!" said June savagely.

Diana raised her eyebrows. "All?" she inquired.

CHAPTER 19

JUNE started out early the next morning and found her way to the narrow street with semidetached villas on either side where the Olivers lived. She had felt rather a beast when Miss Oliver had so cordially assented to her suggestion of coming to see her but, as she had already remarked, "it was not the time for being squeamish"—and Diana's life might depend upon this interview.

Miss Oliver was on the lookout for her and opened the door herself. She did not want June to encounter the little maid-of-all-work. She had been wanting to be friends with June for a long time. She represented that world to which Violet Oliver had always wanted to belong—that world where people were sure of themselves and had no need to try and impress each other. She knew that Diana and June were not well off; like the Olivers they only kept one servant, but theirs was an old family retainer who would always open the door with an air, even if she had been interrupted in the middle of peeling potatoes or cleaning the grate.

Violet's feelings toward people in that enviable world were mixed. She half-admired them and half-hated them. June she could not hate, she was attracted toward the girl in spite of herself, but Diana always struck her as a perfect example of arrogance and self-complacency, and she had therefore accorded her a respectful dislike. After the startling disclosure the other night, however, her feelings had changed. Then had come the still more astounding news that Diana was suspected of murder, and now she longed for a chance to show her friendship. The irreproachable Miss Lloyd with her lazy drawl and superior air was just an ordinary person in trouble and disgrace, and there was something rather piquant about it.

Violet took June up to her bed-sitting room. It was small but scrupulously clean and tidy; the divan bed had a rug thrown over it. There were two reproductions of old masters on the walls and the shelf of books by the bed included *Mansfield Park, The Forsyte Saga, The Lighthouse by* Virginia Woolf, and the *Oxford Book of English Verse.* A bowl of hyacinths, not yet out, stood on the writing table. It struck June as rather pathetic that Miss Oliver should live in this awful house smelling of cabbage, in a drab and clingy street, and yet try to make a life for herself with something of beauty in it. 'I do hope that she didn't kill Mr. Young,' she thought impulsively.

"It's awfully good of you to let me come and see you. I thought perhaps you would help me, we are in terrible trouble. Diana, my mother, you know, is suspected of this awful murder. I expect you have heard all about it."

"Yes. I am terribly sorry." Violet put June in a comfortable chair and gave her a cigarette. She was really very sorry for her, and for the moment her self-consciousness and self-absorption left her and she forgot to wriggle.

"Well, we were talking about it to Lady Lupin. She has been very nice about it, and she thought that you might be able to help us."

"Why me?" asked Violet, half flattered and half suspicious, and beginning to wriggle again.

"Well, it's like this," explained June. "Naturally she wouldn't have mentioned it in ordinary circumstances, but things being as they are, we are all trying to remember everything that might have some bearing, however indirectly, on Mr. Young."

"Naturally."

"So she told us that you had been in her sitting room with Mr. Young the evening just before the murder, and that you had told her you had—er—taken ten pounds off the writing table."

"And so you think that I killed Mr. Young?" Miss Oliver sounded rather gratified.

"No, I don't see why you should have done. Besides, you didn't really take the ten pounds, did you?"

Miss Oliver subsided like a pricked balloon. So they had found that out, had they? What a fool they must have thought her. She twined herself round the back of her chair in agony. She would much rather be thought a thief or even a murderer than a fool. Perhaps she would be the principal figure in this business after all. She thought of Diana with her photograph in the papers, and their captions of the 'tragic mother' and 'blackmailed Guider.' Everybody was talking about her, everybody was interested in her. Should she invent some interesting secret for herself, something for which she might have been blackmailed? An illegitimate child? No, that would be copying. A husband in jail? A secret liaison with some important person? That would do. She had stolen the ten pounds to pay Young for his silence. For some reason or other he had left it behind him, but she had not discovered that until she had murdered him ..."I will tell you everything," she said, tilting her chair and looking at June sideways.

June put out her hand. "Thank you," she said, and Miss Oliver saw that the girl's trustful brown eyes were full of tears as she turned to her in gratitude.

Violet untwisted herself, sat up straight, and said in a somewhat different voice: "Not that there is much to tell. I was with Lady Lupin doing some Guide business when she was called to the telephone. She was away a long time, and I got annoyed at having to wait. I felt that she did not take Guiding or any of the Guiders seriously. I walked about the room fuming, and then saw ten pounds lying loose on the writing table and I thought of how ten pounds meant nothing to her and of all that it would mean to me."

June looked at the bowl of hyacinths and at the Medici prints and sympathized with her. She obviously wanted so badly to have nice things about her.

"I picked it up and thought of all the things I could do with it, then suddenly I had an idea. I'd hide it somewhere and see if she ever missed it. I hid it in her blotter. Then she came back and I left almost at once."

"But what about Mr. Young?"

"Lady Lupin asked me that and so did the police inspector and several other people, but honestly, I never saw him."

June noticed that she was talking quite naturally now, and was sitting perfectly still, and she felt convinced that she was speaking the truth.

"But he told Lady Lupin that he had seen you in her sitting room."

"He may have been told by the maid that I was there, or he may have even looked into the sitting room while I had my back to the door."

"If he had seen you with ten pounds in your hand he would have started blackmailing you at once."

"I doubt it. He would know that I hadn't any money."

"Well, poor Di hadn't much and she has less than ever now. She says she is never going to give another penny to foreign missions as long as she lives."

Miss Oliver looked at her curiously. "You know, I admire Miss Lloyd very much," she said.

"I don't see how anyone could help that," replied June simply. "But I say, what made you tell Lady Lupin that you had stolen ten pounds when you hadn't?"

Violet shrugged her shoulders and wriggled a bit, then she sat bolt upright. "I expect you will think that I am an absolute fool," she said. "In fact, I don't see what else you could think. It's so hard to explain. But for one thing I was longing to find out if she had missed it or not and to have a chance of rubbing in how careless she was with money and how poor people had to live as well as rich. I'm a bit of a Communist, you know. And then—er—well, I suppose I wanted to appear interesting. I lead such a dreary life and the people I'd like to know never take any notice of me—I almost told you that I'd committed the murder because I thought you would all have to take notice of me then. It would be fun to be important for a little while and to have my photo in the papers."

June shuddered, Violet blushed. "I'm sorry," she said, "I didn't mean to be a beast."

"No, I know, you didn't. But you would not like it really, you know. And it's worse when it's someone you are fond of."

"Yes, I see that. Well, anyway, I went to see Lady Lupin, as you know. I found she had missed it after all, so I told her I'd taken it and told her a sad story about my poor father and mother not getting enough to eat. Of course, it wasn't true, but she swallowed it all. Did she find the ten pounds?"

"Yes. That was what we couldn't understand at all."

"Oh, it's easy enough. I just wanted some limelight. But I wish I could help you in some way, only I really didn't see Mr. Young that evening. He must have been prowling about the house for some reason or other."

"Well, come and join our band of detectives," suggested June. She was grateful to Miss Oliver, for she felt she had really been sincere for once, and it must have been very unpleasant to have to own up to the sort of thing she had owned up to. She was the type who would mind ridicule more than anything else. She had brains of a kind, too, and definite histrionic gifts that might come in useful.

Violet's sallow face flushed. "Do you mean that?" she said. "I should simply love to."

They walked back together and found several of the Guiders rallying round Diana. Lupin and Duds were also there looking through the picture papers with a certain amount of interest.

" 'Earl's daughter gives evidence at inquest . . .' Personally, I should have arrested you at once," remarked Duds. "I have never seen anyone look so guilty."

" 'Vicar takes tragic mother home . . .' That one looks as if they had both been attending the mothers' meeting and were discussing whether nonconformists might be members or not. Hulloah, June!"

"Here is Miss Oliver, come to join the detectives," June explained.

"Then it wasn't you who did it?" said Lupin, "Thank goodness for that. You owe me half a crown, Duds."

"This is hardly the time for joking, dear," pointed put Phylis.

"Getting money out of Duds never is a joke, as you would know if you had known her as long as I have."

"Well, I must be off," said Miss Thompson. "Glad I've seen you though; we must all stick together."

The sweetfaced Guider took her leave sadly. "I shall be thinking of you," she said to Diana.

"It's difficult to think of anything else, isn't it?" remarked Lupin. "My maid gave me an odd stocking this morning, and I put it on without noticing, we were both talking so hard. Then Sara forgot to put any sugar on the table for breakfast and the cook never told me what we were going to have for dinner. She thinks that it must have been the landlady, she has never trusted her. She did her down at the butcher's over a leg of mutton, I think, or was it the best end of the neck?"

"You don't mean that you discuss this affair with the servants, do you, Lupin?" said Phylis, aghast. As it was exactly what Lupin had meant, no reply was possible. "Well, I must go now, Diana. If there is anything I can do for you at any time you will let me know, won't you?"

"Well, if you could just find out who really killed Mr. Young, it would be a great help:"

"Oh!" and Phylis smiled wanly, "I only wish that I could. What about your Guides, would you like me to take your meeting for you?"

"Thanks awfully, but I think I'll take them myself so long as I am at large. I have got an idea for a patrol competition—detective work, you know. The first patrol to find out who killed Mr. Young will get a good-conduct mark."

"My dear, you wouldn't mention such a subject to innocent little children, would you?"

"I don't expect the innocent little children speak of anything else at the moment. I expect I will get a full house this evening. They'll all want to see a murderess at close quarters, and the other children at school, not to mention their parents, will hang on their words."

Phylis hurried away, telling herself that poor Diana talked very wildly, but that she was naturally upset, and that in spite of appearances to the contrary she was innocent of the murder of Mr. Young. After all, she was a member of the Girl Guide movement, and in spite of her strange ways, no one could doubt that she was a pukka sahib.

"I wish someone had thought of taking a photograph of Phylis," said Diana. "Loyal Guider visits suspect's house, or just a Guide is a friend to all and a sister to every other Guide no matter to what criminal class the other Guide belongs."

"Oh, do stop about the photographs," burst out June. "This is important. Miss Oliver didn't really see Mr. Young. He might have gone into Lupin's sitting room when her back was turned, but she doesn't know anything about it."

"I am afraid I made an awful fool of myself about those ten pounds, Lady Lupin, I don't know what possessed me . . ."

"Oh, that's all right. Don't bother about that. I've made a fool of myself often enough and so has Duds. Do you remember that time when you went to the Hunt Ball in fancy dress . . ."

"I didn't. At least, anyone might have mixed up the dates, and anyway, I never let my dog loose on the golf links on the day of the men's open meeting."

"What has happened now?" asked Jack, following the maid into the room. "Any fresh developments, or merely a wrangle between a couple of old school chums?"

"Oh, hullo, Jack," said Lupin. "It really is most frightfully exciting. Miss Oliver didn't murder Mr. Young. In fact, she never even saw him, and she was just explaining that little blunder about the ten pounds if you know what I mean, and I was saying it might have happened to anyone."

"Quite," agreed Jack. "You didn't really take them, did you?" he said to Violet.

"No, I picked them up and I thought how easy it would be to take them, and then I hid them. I wanted to know whether Lady Lupin would ever miss them."

"She was feeling a bit socialistic, you know," explained June kindly. "One does sometimes."

"Yes, rather, of course," agreed Lupin, "though I hear it isn't really most frightfully comfortable in Russia just now. You never seem to know what times the trains are going or if they are going at all. Must make it very difficult if you want to go anywhere, I mean. But then, I don't think I should really like it frightfully in those Fascist or Nazi countries either. You seem to be expected to have dozens of babies all the time, and—"

"You picked up the ten pounds," went on Jack, "and thought what you would do with them if they were yours, and how careless it was of Lady Lupin to leave them lying about. Then you thought you would teach her a lesson by hiding them, so you put them in the blotter?"

"Yes," replied Miss Oliver in a low voice, and wriggling a little.

"Then what did you do?"

Violet twined herself round her chair. "I walked up and down the room, and looked at the books and smelled the roses."

"And thought how extravagant it was of Lady Lupin to have roses in December?"

"Well—er—yes, I did as a matter of fact. I really don't know what else I did do, I just walked about and felt rather annoyed."

"Are you quite sure that Mr. Young didn't come in?"

"I am quite sure that I didn't see him. I can't swear that he didn't come in while my back was turned."

"But why should he have gone up there at all?" asked Duds. "Sara showed him into the drawing room, didn't she?"

"I suppose he got tired of waiting there for me. You know, if only you hadn't told me that you had grown your hair, none of this would have happened. Then you went and cut it off again after all, so you've caused all the trouble for nothing."

"Wouldn't it be rather a funny thing for Mr. Young to do?" suggested Duds, ignoring Lupin's last remark, "I mean, you weren't very intimate with him, were you?"

"No, not at all, and he was always very polite. It was rather a funny thing to do, now I come to think of it, but he certainly was on the staircase and he did look rather embarrassed. Oh, do you think that perhaps he was looking for somewhere else?"

"Not upstairs, you idiot! And he must know the gentlemen's cloaks by now—by then, I mean."

"What did he say to you when you met him on the stairs?" asked Jack.

"Well, I'm not quite sure. I was feeling rather flustered myself because I didn't know how long I'd been on the telephone and I was naturally excited about Duds' hair and he gave me an awful kick on the shins. But I do remember feeling surprised at finding him on the stairs, and I noticed that he looked as if he had been stealing a chicken. And I know he said that Miss Oliver was in my sitting room, and I realized how rude I had been, so I didn't stop to chat. It was only really afterwards that I thought much about him looking funny."

"I know!" said Duds excitedly. "You told me that Miss Oliver was in your sitting room. You described—er—I mean you told me about the interesting talk you were having, and he overheard."

"But he was in the drawing room."

"No he wasn't. You met him on the stairs just afterwards. He must have been waiting in the hall or else in gentlemen's cloaks."

"I believe Duds has got it," said Jack. "He saw Lupin at the telephone as he came in, he was conducted to the drawing room by Sara, and as soon as her back was turned, he slipped out and hid somewhere. Probably, as you suggest, in the cloakroom, hoping to hear Lupin say something which might give him some reason for blackmailing her."

"The horrid thing!" exclaimed Lupin indignantly. "Oh, I'm sorry, I suppose I shouldn't say that now he is dead. But it wasn't a very nice thing to do, was it? Besides, what on earth did he think that he could find out about me?"

"Well," said Jack impartially, "we all know that you are a good girl, pure as the driven snow, as the saying goes, and an ideal vicar's wife, but it's no good pretending that you look it."

"Just the opposite from me," said Diana pensively.

"Well, anyway," went on Jack, "you must have come away from the telephone sooner than he had expected because he hadn't time to get back to the drawing room; he just made a dash for the stairs. Or, of course, he may have been there all the time. I wonder whether you could hear the telephone from the stairs? We must try. Naturally he was embarrassed and invented some lame excuse of having been in your sitting room, which would have struck you as strange if you hadn't been so absorbed in Duds' hair. I think that explains Young's movements for that evening and also explains why Miss Oliver never saw him."

"And about me saying I had taken those ten pounds," said Violet, tipping back her chair to a dangerous angle and twisting her head round her left shoulder, "I suppose that wants an explanation?"

"I don't think so," broke in June. "I mean we all understand that you were feeling a bit bolshie and you wanted to bring it home to Lupin that she had been putting temptation about the place."

"Yes," said Jack, "I don't feel we need go into that, and I hope it will be a lesson to my respected aunt not to leave money lying about another time. I think we may clear this suspect for the time being:"

"I hope that all the Guiders will be cleared," said Diana, "including myself, for Phylis's sake. She would feel it a slur on the movement if anyone were to be arrested for murder."

Duds turned to Violet. "I am afraid you were my choice," she said apologetically. "I do hope you don't mind."

"Not at all, Mrs. Lethbridge," replied Violet, tying herself into such a frightful knot that Lupin wondered if she would ever extricate herself again.

CHAPTER 20

DIANA had written a note to Gladys Simpkins and she came round that evening after her shop was closed. Diana received her alone.

"Well, Gladys," she said "it is very nice of you to let bygones be bygones and to come and see me. After all, we are in the same boat, aren't we?"

"What do you mean, Miss Lloyd?"

"Well, we were both in Mr. Young's room the morning of the day he died, so either of us might have poisoned him, mightn't we?"

"Do you believe that I poisoned Mr. Young?" asked Gladys.

Diana looked at her thoughtfully. "No, I shouldn't think so. Do you believe that I did?"

"No, I don't."

"Well, then, let's tell each other exactly what we did do, and why we were there, and see if we can make any sense out of it all. I expect you know by now that Miss Stuart is my daughter and that Mr. Young had been blackmailing me for months. Well, the evening before his death he brought Miss Stuart home from the vicarage, where they had both been dining. I was standing on the doorstep. I was very worried and felt that I must get into the air. I had got to pay some more money to Mr. Young and I didn't know where to get it from. I had sold out nearly all my capital as it was. When I saw him I decided to try reasoning with him once again, so I told Miss Stuart to go in, pretending that I wanted to talk to Mr. Young about the Guide church parade. Then I was rather afraid that she might overhear us, so I said that I would stroll a little way along with him.

"Mr. Young said that if I would persuade Miss Stuart to marry him, he would stop blackmailing me. If she had known about it, she would probably have insisted on sacrificing herself or doing something tiresome. I walked with him toward his rooms. It was a lovely night. Mr. Young was half-inclined to relent; falling in love with Miss Stuart seemed to have softened him, and yet in some strange and perverted way he thought it was his duty to wring money out of me for his beloved missions. However, we parted more amicably than we ever had done before, and he asked me to meet him the next morning. I rather foolishly arranged to go to his rooms, because I did not want him in my house. Well, I went round and saw him, and we had a chat. He had lain awake all night thinking about things, and he said that he realized now how wicked he had been, although he had done wrong that good might come. He said that it was since he fell in love with Miss Stuart that all his values had changed. We talked for a bit, and he asked me to forgive him. I said he must give me time. He had made me suffer so much I couldn't do it all at once, but I wish I had, for I never saw him again."

Diana stopped talking and sat staring at the fire for some minutes without speaking; then she turned to Miss Simpkins. "I have been absolutely unreserved with you, Gladys," she said. "Will you be the same with me?"

"Very well, Miss Lloyd, I will," and Gladys fixed her rather prominent eyes on Diana's face. "Ever since I was a tiny child I've been mad on missions. I used to love missionary stories and missionary pictures, and I made up my mind that one day I would go out as a missionary myself. Then when I grew up I had to start earning my living and I did not know how one set about being a missionary, so I went into a shop, thinking that perhaps I'd find out later on. But the years went by, I got, well not so young, and it got further and further away, but it was always a sort of dream at the back of my mind to be a missionary, and then Mr. Young came along, and he preached a lot about missions, and one evening after he had preached a lovely sermon, I stayed behind to ask him questions about it, and after that he was ever so nice to me, and he used to talk to me quite a lot, and bring me letters that he got from a missionary in China, and then—oh, I can't tell you, Miss Lloyd."

"You fell in love with him, I suppose?"

"I know it was foolish of me, him being a real gentleman and so much younger, but he did seem to like being with me. I see now it was because of me liking missions and that, but it's so easy to think things when you're keen on someone."

"Yes, I quite understand that."

"Well, then he stopped talking to me so much and I realized that he had fallen in love with Miss Stuart, and I wanted to kill myself. I even lost my interest in missions. It was all him by then. Nothing else mattered."

"Yes?"

"I suppose I went a bit mad. I felt that I must get his interest back whatever happened, and suddenly the idea came to me to pretend that I had got into trouble. I was in the road when he went into the vicarage, and I hung about waiting for him to come out, and that is when the idea came to me. I thought I'd wait till he came out and then tell him that I had been seduced by a man and that I was going to have a baby, but when he did come out he was with the vicar, so I couldn't, and then I saw Lady Lupin at the door, and I thought I would go to her first, and then she would tell the vicar and Mr. Young, and they would all talk about it and decide what was to be done. Anyway, everyone would make a fuss of me, and I'd seem sort of interesting. It is so dull always being good and plain," and she looked enviously at Diana.

"Yes, my dear, I quite understand how you felt, but they were bound to find out in the end that you had invented the story and that would have been rather embarrassing for you."

"I didn't bother about what was going to happen afterwards. I did it all on the spur of the moment. I thought Mr. Young would be interested in me again, and that was all I minded about. Clergymen are always more interested in girls who've gone wrong. And I imagined you all talking and saying, 'Fancy—Gladys!' and things like that."

The pathos of it all hurt Diana. "So you told Lady Lupin," she said.

"That's right, and she was ever so kind, but she didn't suggest telling Mr. Young, and I was afraid that perhaps she wouldn't after all. She didn't really seem very interested, though she was so nice. I suppose being in society and that she doesn't think much of those sort of things."

Diana lit a cigarette to conceal her smile. "Well?" she said, encouragingly.

"Then I thought I really would go and tell Mr. Young myself. I would say it was on my conscience, and perhaps it had really been partly my fault. I would pretend that I had led the man on a bit, not that I ever have led a man on, but I thought if I seemed a bit wicked he would take more notice. I mean, it would be his duty to convert me. Oh, dear, how could I? I have always been to church so regularly, and to think that I wanted to be a missionary, and then to think of all these wicked things!

"Well, I hardly slept that night, and the next day I couldn't do my work, and I couldn't make up my mind one way or another. And at last, after Mother had gone to bed, I slipped out and went along to his lodgings, and then I saw you come along with him, so I hid behind a house till you had gone. Then I went up to him and asked if I could speak to him privately, because I was in great trouble. He was ever so nice and asked me to go round the next morning, and so I did, and when I got there I was so upset I couldn't say anything, and I realized how wicked I was to think out all those lies. And I just broke down and said I'd been ever so wicked, but I couldn't say what it was, and he ordered me some tea. He said I'd feel better if I had some tea, and I took out my aspirin because my head was so bad. I'd hardly slept at all two nights. And then you came in, and afterwards I thought you'd seen me with something in a bottle and would suspect me of having poisoned his tea."

"You old silly. As if I would suspect an ex-Ranger of such un-Guide-like behavior." Diana's eyes were twinkling, but Gladys took her in all seriousness.

"Well, that's what I said to myself, Miss Lloyd. I said I knew Miss Lloyd wouldn't do a thing like that, being a Guider. After all, one can always trust a Guide, can't one?"

"Oh, absolutely," replied Diana solemnly. "Well, Gladys, I am glad that we have cleared this up, and that we believe each other. Drop in to one of our Ranger meetings one Monday, if you feel like it."

"Oh, Miss Lloyd, I should love it. Thank you ever so."

Diana saw her out, then slipping on a coat went out of the front door. A man was leaning up against a lamppost, smoking a cigarette. She turned to him brightly. "Good evening," she said. "I am just going along to the vicarage for a little while."

The man threw down his cigarette and rubbed his head. He did not quite know what he ought to say or do. "That's all right, miss," he muttered eventually, looking rather sheepish.

June was sitting with Lupin in her sitting room and they were both eager to hear the result of the interview between Diana and Gladys Simpkins.

"No, it wasn't Gladys," said Diana thoughtfully when she had finished her account.

"And I'm sure it isn't Miss Oliver," put in June.

"It is a very funny thing," said Diana reflectively, "that both Miss Oliver and Gladys Simpkins should be so anxious to attract attention by pretending to have done something wrong, when they are in reality blameless, while I have spent all my life and most of my money in trying to appear blameless, when in reality I was not."

"Oh well," said Lupin, "one always wants to be different from what one really is, I suppose. I was always hankering after black hair when I was a child, but my cousin who had it wished hers was fair. It just shows!"

"Oh, do shut up about your cousins and your hair," broke in June irritably.

"I'm sorry," said Lupin imperturbably. "But I tell you what I think: I believe it was his sister who did him in. She's a nasty piece of work if ever there was one."

"But how could she have done it if she weren't here?" objected Diana.

"Oh, that's nothing to go on. The better the alibi the more likely the murderer; they always tell you that in detective stories."

"Good," said Diana. "That's something to be thankful for, because I've no alibi at all."

"No, nor you have. I suppose you didn't do it, by the way? No, no, June, I don't mean it offensively, but after all she had got a very good reason. I shouldn't blame her at all if she had."

"It is a funny thing," replied Diana, "but I never thought of it; if I had done I might have murdered him, of course. I can't say whether I should or not."

"Diana," exclaimed Lupin suddenly. "Do you remember saying once that Miss Gibson would be capable of committing murder for the sake of her religion?"

"Did I? I think perhaps she would under certain circumstances. But I don't see what that has to do with this case. The death of Mr. Young could not affect her religion one way or the other."

"Why? I thought Mr. Young was High Church or something and that she was on the other side, and that she wanted to put her nephew in his place."

"But she could not put her nephew in his place, that is Andrew's business. No, I was not thinking of anything like that; she might murder someone's body to save their soul. I think that must have been what I had in mind. But she'd never conceal what she had done. She would glory in it. I don't think it's Miss Gibson."

"Anyway, I think I'll go and see her. Yes, now, at once, before I change my mind. Will you wait here till I come back? Andrew will be in soon. I had better have one more drink before I go. I shan't get one there. This is a far, far better thing than I have ever done."

"She is a brick, really," said June, "but she can be perfectly maddening."

"Can't we all?" replied Diana.

Lupin arrived at Miss Gibson's forbidding-looking house. 'Why use chocolate paint even if you are religious?' she wondered.

A severe-looking maid ushered her into a grim drawing room and turned on an electric radiator. The sofa and chairs were all set at right angles; the ornaments on the mantelpiece were placed symmetrically; the books, chiefly volumes of sermons, were arranged on their shelves according to their authors, not one was out of place. 'No one has ever read a book in this room,' thought Lupin, 'nor done a piece of knitting, nor made love, nor played a game of cards, nor eaten, nor drunk nor smoked. They have just come in to view the corpse,' she decided, 'and gone straight out again.' She shivered and drew near the radiator.

Miss Gibson walked in. "Good evening, Lady Lupin, won't you sit down?"

"Good evening, Miss Gibson. I just called in to ask about—er—the Sunday School treat."

"Oh yes?"

"It is next Tuesday, isn't it?"

"No, on Wednesday."

"Oh, of course, how stupid of me. Wednesday, so it is. I hope it will go off well, I take so much interest in the Sunday School."

"Do you?"

"Yes, rather. I hope the new curate will take an interest in it."

"I hope that he will."

"I mean it is so nice if you get a curate who is interested in religion and that sort of thing, isn't it?"

"Yes, it is." Miss Gibson was looking at Lupin in a strange sort of way, and she felt that she was not being a success.

"I wonder if he will be High Church. The curate, I mean," she said.

"You know the vicar's views and what he is likely to look for in a curate."

'Oh, yes, of course. That is, I know he would like a religious kind of man, who would come to church and visit the poor, and all that sort of thing."

"Really?"

"I expect your nephew is awfully good at all that sort of thing."

"My nephew is an earnest-minded young man, but his views differ from those of the vicar, and in any case he has just been offered the living of St. James the Less at East Croydon."

"Oh, then that washes him out, doesn't it? Did you know that before Mr. Young died?"

Miss Gibson did not often register any expression except that of disapproval, but she did look a little surprised at this question. "Yes, my nephew told me on his arrival here. As a matter of fact, I mentioned it to poor Mr. Young when he called in on the day of his death."

"Oh, did he call in here?"

"Yes, just before luncheon to discuss arrangements for the Sunday School treat, in which you are so much interested."

"Did you give him a cocktail or sherry or—er—any lemonade or anything?"

"Are you suggesting that I poisoned Mr. Young, Lady Lupin?" and the surprise on Miss Gibson's face gave way to an expression of grim amusement.

"No, rather not, nothing of the sort," replied Lupin, confused. "But we are all under suspicion, if you know what I mean. After all, he dined with us the night before, and I was fearfully afraid that it might have been the fish, but it doesn't seem to have been. But some of us are sort of scouting around, trying to collect evidence and things. They are awfully keen on that sort of thing in the Guides and, of course, we are frightfully anxious to clear poor Diana Lloyd, because it is rather sickening for her, everyone thinking she has done it. And June feels it like anything."

"I see. And I am on your list of suspects, I gather?"

"Well, it is only that I knew that you didn't approve of his religious views, you know."

"Hardly a sufficient motive for murder. No, I didn't murder Mr. Young, so I'm afraid I cannot help you there, but I hope you will succeed in clearing your friend. Things look bad for her, very bad, at the present. But I don't believe she did it."

"Thanks awfully for saying that. I am glad you believe in her."

"I don't believe she is a murderess, if that is what you mean," replied Miss Gibson.

Lupin hurried home only to find that June and Diana had left. She hurried to the telephone. "Hullo! Is that you, June? No, it's all right, I'm not the press. I only rang up to say that Miss Gibson said she didn't do it."

"Well, did you expect her to say she had?"

"No, well, not exactly. I see your point. Still, I'd hardly think she would tell a lie, do you? I mean, a Sunday School superintendent and everything. Oh, and her nephew had been offered a living somewhere before Mr. Young was bumped off, so that rather queers her motive, doesn't it? Oh, and she doesn't think Diana is a murderess."

"I'm sure we are very grateful to her for her kind opinion," said June heatedly.

"Do keep calm, my dear. What I meant was, if she had done it herself wouldn't she try to put the blame on someone else? Well, I'll tell Jack what I've done and leave him to judge, but we don't seem to be getting much further, do we? Everyone seems so beastly innocent. Miss Oliver, Miss Simpkins and now Miss Gibson. I'm beginning to wonder if I did it myself in my sleep."

"I shouldn't be surprised. Anyway, thanks awfully for going and bearding Miss Gibson, it must have been foul. We really are grateful to you. I hope you are not quite worn out with it all. You had better go and have your dinner. Di is shouting to me. We are having an omelette and she says her good name can wait and the omelette won't."

"That's true. I must fly, too, I forget what we are having, rissoles I expect. Well, anyway, I shall have a nice quiet evening for once. Good night, love to Di."

CHAPTER 21

"WELL, whatever else the life of a clergyman's wife is, it isn't dull," declared Lupin, as she lay in a large armchair after dinner that evening. "Do you remember, Andrew, how you said I'd find it very dull after the life I'd been leading? When I think of the vegetable existence I led in London, going to parties, dining somewhere, and perhaps dancing and going to a few quiet plays and films! No one ever got murdered or blackmailed, or even had illegitimate children, so far as I know. Since I came to live here it has been one thrill from beginning to end. Plots, and counterplots, and whatnot. One can't speak to anyone without wondering if they are a murderer in disguise. I shouldn't be a bit surprised if that nephew of Miss Gibson turned out to be her son all the time. By the way, she says she didn't murder Mr. Young."

"They mostly say that," pointed out Jack.

"I know, but I think Miss Gibson is one of those tiresomely truthful people who would tell you you were looking plain just when you hoped that you were looking your best. Besides, her nephew had just been offered a living. How I ever could have thought foxhunting thrilling, I don't know. Still, it is very discouraging now that all the suspects are flopping. Miss Oliver, Miss Simpkins and Miss Gibson."

"I don't see that we have any direct proof that they are innocent."

"No, only womanly intuition, I think it's called. Never mind, it is probably someone we never thought of. There is Phylis Gardner. I wonder what dark secret she is hiding. Or Mrs. Grey. Now I come to think of it I am sure she didn't really like Mr. Young, and I remember she looked very funny once . . . wait a moment, I know! He asked her if she had ever been in Dorset, and she got confused. I expect she was staying there with a lover and he was blackmailing her about it."

"Are you sure that it was Dorset?"

"No. It was somewhere beginning with D… Devonshire! Of course, because Mrs. Brown went there for her honeymoon and the cream made the doctor sick. What about the doctor! He would know all about poisons, and doctors are very susceptible to blackmail, and he was there when he was taken ill. Of course, it all fits in. What fools we were not to think of it before. Do ring up the inspector, Jack, and tell him we have solved the whole thing."

"I think I *will* go round and see him," said Jack. "There is something I want to discuss with him. You needn't start choosing another doctor yet."

"What does he mean?" Lupin asked Andrew.

"I don't know, but he has evidently got an idea of some sort. Leave it to him, darling, you are wearing yourself out over this wretched business."

"Well, so are you. You know that you are worried to death about Diana."

"Yes, but I don't know why you should be."

"You are a silly idiot, aren't you? After all, we are practically relations, and I'm awfully fond of June, although she is a bit quick-tempered some-times. I mean, she flies out at one for no reason at all, I suppose it is her red hair. I wish I had got red hair. I wonder—"

"You are leaving your hair alone, if that is what you are wondering."

"Shut up, you great bully! I'll spread it about the parish that you are a wife-beater. Poor Mr. Young could have blackmailed you if only he had known. Sh-sh!"

"Miss Oliver, my lady. I've shown her into the drawing room."

"Oh, dear, I wonder what she is going to confess to me now! No one has committed arson so far. Perhaps she has set the church on fire. Is it insured? It would be nice if we could get rid of those windows."

Miss Oliver was wriggling nervously when Lupin went into the drawing room. "I am so sorry to bother you, Lady Lupin, especially in the evening, but I thought it was best to come to you first. Of course, there may be nothing in it."

"In what? The church?"

"No. In the Girl Guide headquarters."

"Why? What do you think is in it?" asked Lupin, conjuring up visions, of burglars or wild beasts.

"The sulphur."

"The sulphur? What sulphur? You don't mean *the* sulphur, do you?"

"Well, there is some sulphur there."

"Let's go and get it at once, Andrew! Andrew! Here is Miss Oliver. She thinks she's found the sulphur."

Miss Oliver writhed. Lupin was not sure, but she thought that she twisted her head right round on her neck and then twined her left leg round it.

"Where do you think it is?" asked Andrew.

"In the Girl Guide headquarters."

"It would be," said Lupin. "It's just the sort of place one would expect things like this to happen. I wonder if it was Miss Thompson all the time? I expect that Mr. Young knew that she was a man and was blackmailing her about it. I shouldn't be a bit surprised if she were married to Phylis Gardner."

The Girl Guide headquarters was a large basement room. It was brightly furnished with scarlet cushions and curtains. In spite of this it had a vaguely depressing air and a perpetual smell of wet mackintoshes. Cupboards ran along one side of it, while on the opposite wall were some photographs of Guides and Guiders evidently taken just after they had received bad news. Miss Oliver led the way to one of the cupboards in which were some cups and saucers for the use of any members of the movement who might wish to have tea down there. On the bottom shelf were bowls and brushes for washing up. In one of these bowls was a packet done up in newspaper. Miss Oliver picked it up, bowl and all, turned down a corner of the newspaper and showed a yellow powder.

"Is that sulphur?" cried Lupin. "Andrew, is that really sulphur?"

"It looks like it, certainly," said Andrew. "I'll get Jack to come and have a look. We'd better not touch it more than we can help because of the finger-prints."

"There is just one thing," said Miss Oliver, wriggling nervously. "This newspaper is the *Morning Courier,* and I remember at one Guiders' meeting Miss Gardner asking us if we had read an article in the *Morning Courier,* and Miss Lloyd said something rather scathing about not being in the habit of perusing that periodical."

Andrew chuckled. "No," he said, "she wouldn't."

"But Phylis Gardner reads it, I'm sure," put in Lupin. "It's full of the British Empire and British Israel and pukka sahibs, of course it's hers. I see it all now. She is married to Miss Thompson—or should I say Mr. Thompson?—and Mr. Young was blackmailing her about it, so she poisoned him with Diana's sulphur. Then she wrapped it up in her newspaper and brought it here. After all, being district captain or whatever she is, she uses this place more than anyone else."

"I use it a good deal," pointed out Miss Oliver.

"So you do, but you didn't murder Mr. Young, did you? We've crossed you off once, for goodness' sake don't muddle us by going and getting into it again."

"I don't think we'll do any good by discussing it further," said Andrew. "We'd better go and find Jack."

"Well, it's lovely to think of Di being cleared, but I'm sorry about Phylis; she's really very nice and it will be so sad for her mother."

"It may not have been her," said Violet Oliver.

"No, but it must have been one of the Guiders. I knew when they made me a district commissioner it would lead to no good. I must go and ring up Duds, it was a nuisance her and Tommy having to go off just at the critical moment, but they'll be back on Saturday, all being well."

"I think I'd wait till you see them, and tell them then," suggested Andrew.

"Oh, darling, are you begrudging me the shilling or whatever it is? Be-cause, if so, I'll pay it myself."

"I can't imagine any of your telephonic communications with Duds work-ing out at a shilling or anything like it; but I'm not begrudging you the price of the call. After all, I have endowed you with all my worldly goods and I should not think of criticizing the way in which you use them. I was merely thinking that until we are really certain who committed the murder, we should be wiser to keep our suspicions to ourselves."

"Oh, all right. But we'll have to tell Di and June because that is where Jack will be."

"Well, I'll say good night," said Miss Oliver.

"No, you won't," said Lupin. "This was all your discovery, you must come and explain," and she dragged an unwilling and writhing Violet into Diana's sitting room where, true to her prognostications, they found Jack.

"We've found the sulphur!" cried Lupin, forgetting that Miss Oliver was to have broken the news. "And where do you think it was?"

"In Andrew's boot cupboard?" suggested Jack.

"In Miss Gibson's reticule?" hazarded June.

"In my nightdress case?" was Diana's contribution.

"Neither!" cried Lupin triumphantly. "You tell them, Miss Oliver, you found it."

Miss Oliver looked painfully embarrassed, so that Jack murmured, "Perhaps she would rather tell Miss Lloyd in private."

"No, no, it wasn't there," said Lupin. "It was in the Girl Guide headquarters."

"In the Girl Guide headquarters?" repeated Diana, and she began to laugh.

"Whatever made you put it there?" asked Lupin.

"What do you mean?" demanded June.

"I don't, of course, I don't. How silly I'm being. It is just the excitement. I always get overexcited. My nurse used to tell me I would end in tears, and I usually did. Besides, I know who did it, as a matter of fact; the whole mystery is cleared up."

"Who did it?" asked her audience eagerly.

"Phylis Gardner."

"Phylis Gardner?" Even Diana was surprised. "But she would never do a thing like that, she wouldn't think it right."

"Well, it was wrapped up in the *Morning Courier,*" said Lupin, triumphantly.

"I certainly never wrapped it up in that," agreed Diana. "It was in a brown paper bag the last time I saw it. You remember, June? You and Mother Grey laughed at me for buying such a lot."

"I'd like to see it, if I may," said Jack. "Can I go into this Girl Guide headquarters?"

"Certainly, as far as I'm concerned," said Diana. "I don't know if Phylis would like it though. Perhaps we ought to ring her up and ask her."

"Don't be so silly," said Lupin, "naturally she would say no when she knows her old sulphur is there, wrapped up in her own *Morning Courier.*"

"Anyway," said June, "it is for you to say, Lupin; after all, you are the head of the Guides."

"Am I? Yes, I suppose I am. Well, come on then, one and all, and hand in hand, and who will bid us nay?"

"I don't expect Miss Gardner is the only person in Glanville who reads the *Morning Courier,*" reflected Jack.

"No, I suppose not, but its being found in the Girl Guide headquarters is very suggestive."

"I wonder," said Diana. "I think that if I had done it, I should have hidden the sulphur in something belonging to the Sunday School or to the Mothers' Union."

They all trooped into the Guide headquarters, and Jack was led in triumph to the newspaper package. He examined it, then turned to Diana. "Is this your sulphur?" he asked.

"My good man, do you think that I can tell my, sulphur from anyone else's sulphur? It looks much the same, that's all I can tell you about it. But mine was in a brown paper and there was a good deal more of it, but of course some may have been used since I saw it last. However, I'm sure you're wrong about Phylis Gardner. Even if she so far forgot herself as to commit a murder, she would never have walked through the streets carrying a parcel wrapped up in a newspaper. She has the highest standards."

"Well, if you don't mind, I will carry it to the police station just as it is, basin and all."

"You can't," said June, aghast. "Suppose you were to meet Phylis."

CHAPTER XXII

"OH, GOOD MORNING, Mrs. Grey," said Lupin. "How nice of you to call. As Miss Thompson would say, 'All we suspects must stick together.' "

Mrs. Grey laughed her jolly laugh. "I don't think that anyone suspects you or me, Lady Lupin, at least, I hope not. But it's a bad business about poor Diana. I wish I'd known before that she was in trouble. I might have been able to help her."

"Who do you think did it?"

"I haven't the least idea. I shouldn't like to suspect anyone. I always try to see the best in my neighbors."

"How nice. I can't think how you were able to find any 'best' in Miss Young, all the same."

"Well, poor thing, she was a little difficult. But then it was a sad blow for her to have her only brother die suddenly like that. Still, I must admit I was rather relieved when she decided to go up to town yesterday; though, of course, I was only too glad to have her so long as I could be of any help to her. I am afraid she will move heaven and earth to get poor dear Diana arrested."

"But didn't you tell her that she hadn't done it?"

"Yes, I assured her that she was a most respectable young woman and had been working in the parish for years, and a most exemplary Guider, always at church with her company on the first Sunday in the month. Of course, there was that little lapse, but after all she has lived that down now. It would be hard if people were to be held responsible for what they did twenty years ago, wouldn't it? But I'm afraid I couldn't get Miss Young to listen to me. What I really wanted to ask you was whether you would come and talk to my Mothers' Union again one Monday afternoon?"

"Oh, dear, do you really want me to? I'm afraid I'm not much good at talking. Besides I'm not a mother. I say, I hope I didn't mislead you into thinking that I was going to be one?"

"Well, I had hoped; but never mind, these disappointments will happen, and you have plenty of time before you."

"Yes, so long as they don't arrest Andrew for killing Mr. Young."

"I can't see any reason why they should."

"No, but you never can tell, can you? I say, why don't you ask Diana to address the meeting? After all, she is a mother."

"Er—er—yes, in a way," replied Mrs. Grey, dubiously. "But we don't want to draw too much attention to that. Not that I'd hold it up against the poor girl for a minute, but one has to be rather careful in the Mothers' Union. Their motto is 'Purity,' you know."

"How nice."

"So you will give them a talk, won't you? Tell them all about the fashions and what the smart set are wearing. They love that sort of thing."

"Oh, dear, I don't really know at all what they are wearing. Perhaps my maid does, though. I'll do what I can, but I shall die of fright. I mean, I'd never spoken in public before I came here, except at my twenty-first birthday party, and then I was a little drunk, but that wouldn't really do at the Mothers' Union, would it? Oh, Jack, you've met Mrs. Grey, haven't you? She wants me to talk at the Mothers' Union about what the smart set are wearing. I don't think I know any of the smart set; do you?"

"How do you do, Mrs. Grey? I saw you at the carol service on Christmas Eve, but I do not think that we were introduced, were we? I have heard what a good golfer your husband is."

"Oh, he is nothing out of the ordinary, but I believe he plays quite a decent game."

"I suppose he wouldn't care to have a round with me one day?"

"I am sure he would simply love it. How long are you here for?"

"That is the worst of it. I have only got another day or two. I don't expect he is free tomorrow by any chance, is he?"

"Unfortunately the poor old dear is suffering from rheumatism very badly at the moment. Sciatica, I suppose it really is, in his left leg. Frightfully painful. I am afraid that it will be some days before he gets round the links again. What a pity you are not staying longer. He would have enjoyed a game with you. I left him grumbling like anything this morning, poor fellow. He does miss his game, especially during this nice dry weather."

"I am sorry. I do hope he will be better by the next time I come down. I have heard so much about his play. Didn't he win the men's open meeting last year? I am afraid I shan't give him much of a game."

"Oh, I am sure you will. Well, I must hurry back to my poor invalid. Good-bye, Lady Lupin, and thank you so much. Will Monday week at three o'clock suit you?"

"What a ghastly hour! I'm so sorry. I mean, of course, that I shall be delighted. Do I radiate charm, Jack? Duds says that a vicar's wife ought always to radiate charm."

"Ring up Mr. Grey and ask him after his rheumatism."

"Oh, do you think so? I think it is rather overdoing things. I mean, if I am as charming as that he may get fresh."

"Hurry up, I want you to ring up before Mother Grey gets home. Just say rheumatism. Don't mention leg."

"I suppose you know what you are talking about. Is this the great detective at work or something? Here goes—two five one. May I speak to Mr. Grey, please? Oh, Mr. Grey; is that you? I felt I must ring you up and ask about your rheumatism. It is such a beastly thing, isn't it? I know, because my father gets it and he is like a bear with a sore head. What? Oh, haven't you? I thought you had; your wife told Captain Scott that you had. He had been hoping for a game of golf with you. Oh, I see, in your shoulder. How beastly! Have you tried Beltona? It did wonders for Daddy. You are sure you couldn't play golf? Oh, dear. How horrid. Well, I do hope that you will soon be all right again."

"Well?" said Jack.

"First he said he hadn't got it, and then he said it was in his shoulder. Do you think he murdered Mr. Young? But what's his having rheumatism got to do with it? And now I come to think of it, Mrs. Grey said it was in his leg."

"Exactly. She suspects me of being able to worm something out of her husband so she doesn't want him to play golf with me."

"Oh, I see. But why did she say his rheumatism was in his leg when it's really in his shoulder?"

"Darling, you are very beautiful, but if you had been born into the working classes you would have been sent to a special school."

"What sort of school?"

"For borderline cases. They don't differentiate in the same way among the rich, so they never get cured. But try to get this into your pretty head: Mrs. Grey invented the rheumatism in his leg. He knew nothing about it so he gave himself away by saying it was in his shoulder."

"That was why you wanted me to ring up before she got back?"

"Brilliant!"

"But does that really mean that he killed Mr. Young, and that Diana is cleared? Because, if so, that is too wonderful. Do hurry round to the police station at once and tell them to remove the civic guard from her house."

"It isn't quite as simple as all that, but I'll go round to the station. I think that we are on the right track and, strange to say, it was really you who led me there, so I will take back anything unkind I have said about your brains."

"No! Really? Do you mean it? Do tell me what it was. Oh, are you in a hurry? Yes, of course, do hurry, don't wait for anything. May I go and tell Diana and June?"

"No, I think I'd rather you waited a little longer. But we may have something to tell them this evening."

Jack found the inspector at the station. "Well?" he said inquiringly as he sat down and accepted a cigarette..

"Mr. Grey was at Dartmoor for three years for embezzlement, from 1921 till 1924, under the name of White.

"His wife, Maud White, who was a trained nurse, ran a nursing home at Plymouth from 1921 till 1930.

"She came in for a considerable sum of money from a relative in 1930, whereon she sold her nursing home and they came to live in Glanville under the name of Grey. They took up parish work and soon became respected in the place.

"During the last two years she has been drawing out very considerable sums of money, payable to herself, from the bank, and has also sold a good deal of her capital."

"We can guess where that has been going," said Jack, as the inspector put down his notes. "Young's father was chaplain at Dartmoor at that time. Young as a boy probably knew some of the prisoners by sight and had been black-mailing them ever since."

"Her, at least. He does not seem to have had any money of his own."

"She would know about poisons, too, I suppose, being a nurse. Yes, I should think she was the active partner. It has been jolly quick work on your part; how did you get hold of it all?"

"As soon as you gave us the tip we got hold of their fingerprints and sent them to Scotland Yard. His, of course, were there. After that it was mere routine work. But what put you on to it?"

"My aunt, funnily enough. Naturally, once I'd found out that Young's father was chaplain at Dartmoor, I was on the lookout for a possible convict. Then, by the merest chance, Lady Lupin remarked that Mrs. Grey had looked funny when Mr. Young asked her if she had ever been in Devonshire and, well, there it was."

"It was good work, sir. I thought you might get something in the way of ordinary conversation, so to speak, and it was a lucky hit. It gave us something to go on."

"And the *Morning Courier*?"

"There are some of Mrs. Grey's fingerprints on it, but they are not the only ones. We mustn't go too fast. Mr. Grey was in prison for three years, that is the only thing we know for certain against either of them. It is true that she has been drawing out very large sums of money, and a rough calculation shows that when these are added to the sums paid to Mr. Young by Miss Lloyd they add up to approximately the amount paid by him to the church missionary society, but that is not proof."

"There are her prints on the *Morning Courier;* also she was at Miss Lloyd's house when she arrived with her packet of sulphur."

"Have you proof of that?"

"No, but I could probably get it. It just came out in the course of conversation, and I did not want to draw attention to it till I had more to go on."

"Well, we will have to go into that. As regards the fingerprints, hers are not the only ones on the paper. Have you anything else to add to what we already know?"

"Yes. That is really why I came hurrying round so early. Mrs. Grey called on Lady Lupin this morning. She came to ask her to speak at the Mothers' Union. You know, I admire that woman,"

"Well, it is no good being sentimental in our profession. I hope that you are not going to try to clear her now."

"Aren't you glad now that I persuaded you not to arrest Miss Lloyd?"

"I don't know that you did persuade me. There was something about that I never liked. But to stick to the point, what about Mrs. Grey's visit this morning?"

"I was glad to see her as it gave me an excuse for suggesting a game of golf with her husband, which is what I had been wanting to do. I felt that if I could have a clear and uninterrupted conversation with him I might learn a thing or two. Whether she suspected anything I don't know; she may have guessed that I have been sleuthing round a bit. It is not exactly private property. Anyway, she wasn't risking her husband out alone with me, so she said that he had very bad rheumatism in his left leg. The moment that she had left the house I got Lady Lupin to ring up. He seemed surprised at first and said he was quite all right. Then, when she referred to his wife he said, yes, he had got it in his right shoulder."

"Of course, she may have been frightened of you finding out that he was an ex-convict. After all, that is what she has been at such pains to hide all these years."

"You haven't questioned her at all yet, have you?"

"Only about the tea party at her home on the day of Mr. Young's death. We shall have to do so, of course, but I did not want her to think that she was suspected until we had collected as much evidence as possible. And even if we find, as I think we shall, that she has been blackmailed, that does not make her guilty of murder any more than Miss Lloyd. They both had plenty of motive and plenty of opportunity."

"You do know that Mrs. Grey is a trained nurse and knows all about poisons and their effects. She is one of the few people here who would have known that sulphur would have affected Mr. Young."

"We know that Miss Lloyd had been making inquiries about poisons, but the thing we want to follow up is this sulphur that you found in their Girl Guide headquarters. It was undoubtedly wrapped up in a *Morning Courier* and it undoubtedly had Mrs. Grey's fingerprints on it, but there are other fingerprints that we haven't succeeded in tracing yet."

"Probably the news agent, the paper boy, and the parlormaid."

"Very likely. That can easily be ascertained."

"Well, anyway, Miss Lloyd never takes in the *Morning Courier.*"

"But, for the sake of argument, she could have abstracted a sheet from Mrs. Grey's house. These ladies seem to spend a lot of time going round to each other's houses, for one reason or another."

"But were there any of Miss Lloyd's fingerprints on it?"

"A lady who writes detective stories would naturally have worn gloves."

"A lady who writes detective stories would have refrained from inquiring in a public place the best way, of poisoning someone just a few days before doing it. Also—"

"Excuse me, sir, but we have been through all this before. We won't get any further on these lines. I'd better go and question Mrs. Grey, or rather Mrs. White, about her past life, while one of my men looks out for the fingerprints on this *Morning Courier.*"

A policeman came into the room. "There is a lady to see you, sir, the vicar's wife, Lady Lupin Hastings."

Jack and the inspector exchanged glances. "Show her in," commanded the inspector.

"Oh, dear, is it all right me coming in here? I didn't know what to do. But I went round to see Mrs. Grey and took her a bottle of Beltona for her husband's rheumatism, in case he really had got it. It used to do Father a lot of good, and so it did Andrew when he had a stiff neck. At least, it would have done but I spilled most of it on his pajamas, such a lovely pair, too, blue silk with—"

"Did you see Mrs. Grey?"

"Yes, that is just what I am telling you. When I was crossing the hall whom should I see but Pa Grey simply nipping down the stairs on both his legs and carrying a huge suitcase in both his arms. I couldn't help feeling that, after all, his rheumatism couldn't be so very bad. When he saw me he dropped the suitcase and I dropped the Beltona, and it broke all over the place, I felt such a fool. Then Ma Grey appeared in her hat and gloves, carrying an enormous handbag. She said that they were just off to Brighton for a few days, so I said 'What about the Mothers' Union?' and she said she'd be back by then. They'd only just decided to go but she thought a change of air would do her husband good, and I must say he did look awful. Quite green in the face and goggling."

"Were they going by car?"

"Yes, the car was at the door, I think they were in a hurry to start. They were quite friendly, but somehow I felt I was a bit in the way. Then it struck me that I'd better let you know, because, of course, if it were they who murdered Mr. Young, one wouldn't want them to escape before Diana was cleared."

Inspector Poolton was already at the telephone.

"Thanks, Lupin," said Jack. "That was a good bit of work of yours."

"I feel a bit of a beast. I mean, it does seem rather a shame just when they were getting off, poor things. But, after all, if they did do it they had no right to put the blame on Diana. Besides, it's so upsetting for June, she is looking a perfect wreck. It would be too awful if she were to lose her looks, wouldn't it? Though I am sure you'd love her just the same, wouldn't you, Jack?"

"Yes, I think I should. Now you had better run along home. You have been a great help to us and you deserve a nice rest."

"Yes, perhaps I will; and of course I didn't mean that I thought June was losing her looks at present. She just looks pale and interesting, but if anything happened to Diana she would be dreadfully upset, and I hate to think of her being unhappy. Not that I like to think of poor old Mrs. Grey being unhappy either. I dare say they didn't do it, and even if they did, there were faults on both sides. Well, I must be getting along. I haven't seen the cook yet this morning; she always likes to tell me what we are having for dinner. I can't think why. Say good-bye to the inspector for me. He seems rather busy and I don't quite like to interrupt him."

"Yes, he is rather busy, but the policeman will take you downstairs. Good-bye, my dear. Thank you very much."

CHAPTER 23

"WHEN they're laughing with you,
When they love you so,
When they beg you to remain,
That's the time to go,"

chanted Diana, as her friends expressed their regret that she was leaving Glanville.

"No, I am not going to live with June and Jack, but I shall have a nice little flat somewhere near so that I can pop in and interfere whenever I feel like it. I couldn't very well stop on here being a pillar of church now that everyone knows my guilty past. Especially as I shall no doubt soon be presented with dozens of guilty grandchildren."

Diana's sitting room was very full; the whole of Glanville seemed to have flocked to her farewell party. All the Guiders were there, and most of the Sunday School teachers, not to mention several district visitors, parish magazine distributors and sidesmen. Even Miss Gibson had appeared for a short time and had congratulated Diana on not having murdered Mr. Young. She obviously considered that the sixth commandment was the only one which she had left unbroken, but she was broad-minded enough to rejoice that there was even so much to be thankful for. She left a little book behind her, which Diana assured Lupin was the touching story of a prostitute who had been converted and who afterwards married the local secretary of the Church of England Temperance Society.

Dr. and Mrs. Brown were there. He was gazing pensively out of the window at Diana's little strip of garden, which was not particularly interesting in the twilight of a wet February evening. In fact, Diana had drawn the curtains and shut out the dusk, but the doctor had pulled one back and was peering out through the gloom. His wife was busy asking each of the Guiders in turn to find her a maid among her Guides or Rangers.

Duds and Tommy were there. They were staying at the vicarage for the weekend. The atmosphere of Glanville entranced them; it was so different from any place in which they had stayed before, and they felt quite a proprietary interest in Diana, for had they not been part of the detective club which had finally proved her innocence? They imbibed a good deal of Diana's excellent sherry, together with the various conversation of the other guests.

Jack and Andrew acted as hosts and handed round plates of sandwiches, glasses of sherry and boxes of cigarettes untiringly. Lupin ran eagerly from one group to another, talking at random and drinking, smoking and eating all at the same time.

But, in spite of the friendly atmosphere, in spite of the relief which was still predominant in the minds of most of the guests at the freedom of Diana from suspicion, in spite of all the laughing and talking and all the eating and drinking that was taking place, there was a cloud over the assembly. Everyone was conscious of a feeling of bereavement at the loss of one who had, for many years, been the life and soul of every party in Glanville. It seemed incredible that she should be gone, that the door would not open suddenly and her hearty tones boom out 'Good evening, everybody.'

Mr. and Mrs. Grey had already left their house on that fateful morning six weeks ago when Inspector Poolton had arrived, but their car was easily traced, and on arriving at Folkestone Harbor they were stopped by an official who asked for a few words with them. Mrs. Grey had just got out of the car and her husband was preparing to unstrap the luggage. She gave one look at the official, tried to speak, and fell down with a stroke from which she never recovered. She died in Folkestone hospital that same evening.

Poor little Mr. Grey was utterly bewildered and heartbroken, and it was some time before he could give a coherent account of all that had happened. But at length he unburdened himself and seemed relieved at having done so. In the beginning he had had no suspicion of the real facts of the case; he did not even know that his wife was being blackmailed. The money practically all belonged to her, and he knew very little about it. He had always been content to leave everything in her hands; she was a very capable woman.

At the time of the murder he had assumed, like most other people, that Miss Lloyd was guilty, but when he had said so in front of his wife she was quite angry with him. She had been unlike herself during the last week or so, and he had wondered if she had anything on her mind. It was not until it became rumored that there had been other victims of blackmail that the first awful suspicion had occurred to him. His wife had seemed a little short of money lately, and he remembered once or twice her saying that she could not afford something and he had been rather surprised, as she was very comfortably off. He knew only too well how easily his wife might have been blackmailed, for she had fought so hard for their return to respectability. She had been a wonderful wife to him, and he struggled with his suspicions, trying to dismiss them from his mind as treasonous; but, try as he might, he could not help noticing that she was wrought up about something.

Then came the morning when Lady Lupin had rung up to ask after his rheumatism, and he had been unable to understand what had made her do such a thing. His wife had returned home and explained that she had not wanted him to play golf with Captain Scott; he was a clever young man and might have got something out of him as to his past life. When Mrs. Grey realized that her husband had given away her subterfuge to Lady Lupin, she had exclaimed: "It is all up. We had better try to get away. I have been a bad wife to you after all." His suspicions were naturally aroused by these words, but he had assured her that she had been a wonderful wife to him, and whatever happened he was on her side. Then Lady Lupin had arrived with the lotion; after that they knew escape was hopeless, but it seemed to be better to be doing something than just to wait where they were, and it was on the journey to Folkestone that Mrs. Grey told her husband her story.

Mr. Young knew that Mr. Grey had been in prison because his father had been the prison chaplain during the period of his incarceration, and he had soon started blackmailing his wife; it was she who had the money, and it was she who so longed to be respectable. She had established herself and her husband at Glanville; he had become churchwarden and they were both looked up to in the parish. They had settled down to the kind of life for which she had always hankered, and when Mr. Young arrived on the scene he had made her life a misery: She had been left a nice little income by an aunt, and she and her husband were very comfortable. Gradually, owing to Mr. Young's demands, her capital dwindled, for she had to sell out stocks to meet them. She had to cut down her subscriptions to various charities, of which she had always been a staunch supporter; she had to economize in clothes and in food, and she was even contemplating getting rid of her two excellent maids and managing with a general servant; and during all this time the dread of exposure hung over her.

She told Mr. Grey that the thought of murder had never really entered into her head until one morning when she met Diana carrying home her huge packet of sulphur. She was laughing at her for buying such an immense quantity when it suddenly flashed across her: 'Charles Young is taking a strong sulphur prescription; I heard him mention it to someone yesterday. A good stiff dose of this in addition might finish him off; I wish he would take some by mistake. What a lovely world it would be if Charles Young were no longer in it.'

Diana Lloyd had asked her to go in for a drink before lunch and she had done so. June joined her in laughing about the quantity of sulphur which Diana had brought home. She had undone the packet and put a little in Bill's water, leaving the rest on the hall table. As Mrs. Grey was passing out, Diana turned for a moment to speak to June. In that moment, acting on a sudden impulse, Mrs. Grey had picked up the brown paper parcel and put it in her shopping basket, and it was at that moment that the intention to murder Mr. Young was born.

Diana and June evidently forgot all about the sulphur for the next few days. Mrs. Grey took a larger quantity out of the bag and put it into a bath-salt jar. She wrapped up the rest in a newspaper and hid it in the cupboard in the Girl Guide headquarters. She had not done so with the purpose of incriminating anybody, but the idea had been put into her head by Miss Gardner.

Mrs. Grey had asked her if she might borrow some cups and saucers from the Guides for her Mothers' Union tea, as they were having some visiting mothers in addition to her own. Miss Gardner replied that the might have as many she wanted as the Guides never seemed to use them. Mrs. Grey thought that that would make an ideal hiding place, as no one seemed to go near the cupboard from one year's end to another. Why Miss Oliver happened to be poking round there when she did was a mystery. As a matter of fact, she had been tidying the place, and had just taken a cursory glance at the crockery cupboard when her eye was caught by the newspaper packet.

Once the sulphur was in her possession, Mrs. Grey started work. Mr. Young came in that night to play billiards with her husband, and she put some sulphur in his lemonade. The next morning, when he came to discuss some parish business, she insisted on his having some coffee. There was nothing unusual in this, she was always a most hospitable woman. The next day, Christmas Eve, he came to tea. There was a sulphur cake, as she had admitted freely at the time, but she also took the precaution to put some in the tea. None of the rest of the party were affected, but Mr. Young, who had been absorbing large quantities of sulphur, both in his medicine and in Mrs. Grey's concoctions, during the last few days, succumbed.

Mrs. Grey had not expected it to take effect so soon, as she did not know about his weak heart. She had not the least wish for his being taken ill in her house, and she had had some nasty moments when she realized that the police might be arriving at any moment to ask awkward questions and to examine the remains of the tea.

Luckily for her, her parlormaid had been going out that evening to the carol service and had washed up the tea things as soon as she had cleared the table, so that when Mrs. Grey, bluffing bravely, had begged Dr. Brown to have the tea analyzed in case there was anything in it, they were told that there was none left. She then expressed her fears about the sulphur cake, and to satisfy her, Dr. Brown consented to have it analyzed. He explained matters to the police officer, and added that he did not think the tea could have any bearing on the case as he and his wife had both drunk it and had noticed nothing unusual. The glass with its few remaining drops of sal volatile was produced, and was, of course, perfectly innocent.

In the overwhelming evidence against Diana Lloyd, the police gave little thought to anyone else. Although, when they had heard that Mr. Young's father was a prison chaplain, they tried to check up on anyone in Glanville who might have been in prison. The respectable Mr. and Mrs. Grey were naturally exempt from any such suspicions. It was not until Lupin gave Jack Scott the idea by saying that Mrs. Grey had looked 'funny' when Mr. Young asked her if she had ever been in Devonshire that the police had found themselves on the right track. It had given Jack the clue for which he was looking, and he at once communicated his suspicions to the inspector who, by means of fingerprints, soon dug up the whole story. Mrs. Grey had only precipitated matters by running away.

One thing Mr. Grey kept on assuring the police: his wife would never have allowed Miss Lloyd to be hanged, he was sure of that. "She was driven to murdering that brute," he declared, "but she was really a good woman, and she was a wonderful wife to me." Then he had broken down.

Dr. Brown was thinking of his friend as he looked out of the window at the darkening garden, and Mrs. Brown was thinking of her friend as she bustled about from Guider to Guider. 'If only Mabel Grey had been there,' she thought, 'she would soon have found me a maid.' What a good friend Mabel had always been to her! She missed her and would always miss her.

"Well, Miss Lloyd, we can congratulate each other," said Lancelot Brown. "It looked as if one of us were for it at one time, didn't it?"

"It did, indeed," said Diana, kindly. Somehow she did not want even to tease Lance any longer. Her bitterness had left her; all this time when she had had a secret to keep, and when Charles Young was making life so hard for her, she had relieved her feelings by looking down on the people of Glanville and by trying to annoy them; yet they had all stood by her when the crisis came, and it made her feel very humble. If only she had been brave and had refused Charles's demands, perhaps it would have influenced him, and poor Mrs. Grey would have been spared too. She wished that she had not been such a coward.

"This experience will enrich our whole lives," said Lancelot, ponderously. "I feel that I have been reprieved because I have serious work to do. I have started an epic poem on the world situation."

"That sounds an ambitious undertaking."

"It is ambitious, I am ambitious. I shall take each country in turn and try to portray something of the misery of its inhabitants. May I send some of it to you to read?"

Diana bit back the words, 'Yes, do, it sounds very jolly,' and replied, cordially, that she would be very much interested.

"And what about your own work?" he asked. "Don't you feel that you must tackle something more worthy of you than children's stories and detective novels? After all, it isn't every day that one escapes from the gallows."

"One hopes it won't occur again," agreed Diana.

"What do you hope won't occur again?" asked Lupin, wandering up.

"Lancelot and myself escaping from the gallows," replied Diana.

Lupin pondered this; it conjured up rather an entrancing vision. "Well, if you get there, I hope you escape," she said. "Though I don't really quite see how you could. This is a lovely party; even Miss Watson was most affable, she said she had made a point of coming, as she always believed in doing the Christian thing; she drank three glasses of sherry and ate three sandwiches, so I suppose she believes in doing the Christian thing thoroughly. Father Gibson is rather a lamb, he likes dogs; I quite wish he were coming here as curate, it will be so awkward if we get one who doesn't like it if John and Bill come to look for us in church, like they did last Sunday. Oh; and Miss Gibson drank a whole glass of lemonade and ate a macaroon, I think that was very unbending of her, and there's Phylis, smoking a cigarette in spite of wearing a Guide trefoil. I almost wish you and Mr. Brown could escape from the gallows once a week, if it means such a nice party."

"I always thought she was frivolous and worldly minded," said Lancelot, as Lupin moved on.

Diana was about to retort to this when her eye was caught by June's radiant face as she stood beside Jack Scott, receiving congratulations, and she felt sorry for Lancelot. It must have been a great blow to him. "I hope we may see you sometimes in London," she said.

"Thanks awfully, I'd love to come," he replied, evidently gratified, "and we can talk about our work. I suppose I must go and congratulate June. The best man won, after all," he added. Not that he really thought that Jack was the best man, but he had been thankful to learn of his engagement to June. It had struck him that after all the excitement of having been suspected of having murdered his rival he might find that he was expected to marry June himself, and although she was very pretty, he feared she was rather shallow, and in any case he did not want to get married. In fact he was not at all sure that he approved of marriage, and he couldn't possibly afford it if he did. So he went up, very willingly, to congratulate June and Jack.

People were beginning to take their leave. "Well, good-bye, Diana, dear," said Phylis. "We shall miss you terribly at the Guides."

"The Guiders' meetings will be rather dull, won't they," agreed Diana, "without you and me having a stand-up fight every time?"

"Oh, my dear, I am sure we have never had anything approaching a real quarrel," said Phylis, "just a little friendly disagreement from time to time! After all it would be a dull world if we all thought alike. I do hope," she added, lowering her voice, "that the vicar will be able to find a sahib to take your place. I do feel that is so very important."

"Well, it will be something if he can find someone without any improper appendages. However, I hope, for your sake, it will be someone who can eat asparagus properly. Such a help at a company meeting."

Phylis moved doubtfully away. It was always so difficult to know when dear Diana was being serious and when she wasn't.

"Well, good-bye," said Miss Thompson, striding up and seizing Diana's hand in such a way that, for some minutes afterwards, she thought every bone was broken. "Sorry you are going. It will be a loss to the side."

"Good-bye, Miss Lloyd," said the sweetfaced Guider. "Isn't it wonderful how the cloud has lifted? Do you remember how I always told you, even in the darkest days, that all would work out for the best?"

"Did you?" replied Diana, rather vaguely. "Unfortunately what is best for one isn't always necessarily best for everyone else," and she thought of Mrs. Grey with regret.

Dr. Brown approached her. "Perhaps in London you could sometimes see Tom Grey," he suggested diffidently. "I shall run up and see him when I can. It would be awkward for him to come down here, but people will leave him alone in London. He may be lonely, though."

"Yes, I shall love to see something of him," Diana assured him. "I shall be lonely myself when Jack and June are married. They will like to see Mr. Grey sometimes too, I am sure."

"Thank you," said the doctor simply, and he moved on.

"How lucky you are to be able to take your maid with you," said Mrs. Brown. "I had been hoping to get her after you had gone. You might let me know if you hear of any decent girls in London."

Miss Oliver wriggled up. "Good-bye, Miss Lloyd. I am awfully sorry that you are going away."

"Well, it's a great deal owing to you that I am going to London a free woman," replied Diana, "instead of languishing in the condemned cell. Do come and see me if you are in London any time. It won't be so thrilling as visiting me at Wormwood Scrubbs, but we can always gossip about the Guides, and you'll be able to tell me all the Glanville scandals, if they have any when I'm gone."

"Thanks awfully, I shall simply love to," and she wriggled away.

Diana watched them all go. Friends of many years' standing, at whom she had laughed, with whom she had disagreed, but all of whom had stood by her when she was in trouble. It was rather a wrench leaving them all and starting off on a new life by herself. 'Oh well, this is the time to make a good exit,' she told herself, as she walked back into the sitting room, where a few remaining friends were still gathered. 'While they beg you to remain, that's the time to go!'

"Hulloah, what's happened?" she asked aloud, feeling alarmed, for Lupin had suddenly and unaccountably burst into tears. June and Duds were helping her on to the sofa, while the men were falling over each other in their desire to help. They finally arrived, each with a separate glass of sherry, collided, and spilled it all over Lupin.

"I am sorry to be so silly," gulped Lupin. "But I believe what Mrs. Grey hoped for is going to happen, and she won't be here to see it."

THE END

About The Rue Morgue Press

The Rue Morgue vintage mystery line is designed to bring back into print those books that were favorites of readers between the turn of the century and the 1960s. The editors welcome suggests for reprints. To receive our catalog or make suggestions, write The Rue Morgue Press, P.O. Box 4119, Boulder, Colorado (1-800-699-6214). The Rue Morgue Press tries to keep all of its titles in print, though some books may go temporarily out of print for up to six months. The following list details the titles available as of September 2001.

Catalog of Rue Morgue Press titles December 2001

Titles are listed by author. All books are quality trade paperbacks measuring 9 by 6 inches, usually with full-color covers and printed on paper designed not to yellow or deteriorate. These are permanent books.

Joanna Cannan. The books by this English writer are among our most popular titles. Modern reviewers favorably compared our two Cannan reprints with the best books of the Golden Age of detective fiction. "Worthy of being discussed in the same breath with an Agatha Christie or a Josephine Tey."—Sally Fellows, Mystery News. "First-rate Golden Age detection with a likeable detective, a complex and believable murderer, and a level of style and craft that bears comparison with Sayers, Allingham, and Marsh."—Jon L. Breen, *Ellery Queen's Mystery Magazine.* Set in the late 1930s in a village that was a fictionalized version of Oxfordshire, both titles feature young Scotland Yard inspector Guy Northeast. *They Rang Up the Police* (0-915230-27-5, 156 pages, $14.00) and *Death at The Dog* (0-915230-23-2, 156 pages, $14.00).

Glyn Carr. The author is really Showell Styles, one of the foremost English mountain climbers of his era as well as one of that sport's most celebrated historians. Carr turned to crime fiction when he realized that mountains provided a ideal setting for committing murders. The 15 books featuring Shakespearean actor Abercrombie "Filthy" Lewker are set on peaks scattered around the globe, although the author returned again and again to his favorite climbs in Wales, where his first mystery, published in 1951, *Death on Milestone Buttress* (0-915230-29-1, 187 pages, $14.00), is set. Lewker is a marvelous Falstaffian character whose exploits have been praised by such discerning critics as Jacques Barzun and Wendell Hertig Taylor in *A Catalogue of Crime.* Other critics have been just as kind: "You'll get a taste of the Welsh countryside, will encounter names replete with consonants, will be exposed to numerous snippets from Shakespeare and will find Carr's novel a worthy representative of the cozies of two generations ago."—*I Love a Mystery.*

Clyde B. Clason. Clason has been praised not only for his elaborate plots and skillful use of the locked room gambit but also for his scholarship. He may be one of the few mystery authors—and no doubt the first—to provide a full bibliography of his sources. *The Man from Tibet* (0-915230-17-8, 220 pages, $14.00) is one of his best and highly recommended by the dean of locked room mystery scholars, Robert Adey, as "highly original." It's also one of the first popular novels to make use of Tibetan culture. Locked inside the Tibetan room of his Chicago apartment, the rich antiquarian was overheard repeating a forbidden occult chant under the watchful eyes of Buddhist gods. When the doors were opened, it appeared that he had succumbed to a heart attack. But the elderly Roman historian and sometime amateur sleuth Theocritus Lucius Westborough is convinced that Adam Merriweather's death was anything but natural and that the weapon was an eight century Tibetan manuscript.

Manning Coles. The two English writers who collaborated as Coles are best known for those witty spy novels featuring Tommy Hambledon, but they also wrote four delightful—and funny—ghost novels. *The Far Traveller* (0-915230-35-6, 154 pages, $14.00) is a stand-alone novel in which a film company unknowingly hires the ghost of a long-dead German graf to play himself in a movie. "I laughed until I hurt. I liked it so much, I went back to page 1 and read it a second time."—Peggy Itzen, *Cozies, Capers & Crimes*. The other three books feature two cousins, one English, one American, and their spectral pet monkey who got a little drunk and tried to stop—futilely and fatally—a German advance outside a small French village during the 1870 Franco-Prussian War. Flash forward to the 1950s where this comic trio of friendly ghosts rematerialize to aid relatives in danger in *Brief Candles* (0-915230-24-0, 156 pages, $14.00), *Happy Returns* (0-915230-31-3, 156 pages, $14.00) and *Come and Go* (0-915230-34-8, 155 pages, $14.00).

Norbert Davis. There have been a lot of dogs in mystery fiction, from Baynard Kendrick's guide dog to Virginia Lanier's bloodhounds, but there's never been one quite like Carstairs. Doan, a short, chubby Los Angeles private eye, won Carstairs in a crap game, but there never is any question as to who the boss is in this relationship. Carstairs isn't just any Great Dane. He is so big that Doan figures he really ought to be considered another species. He scorns baby talk and belly rubs—unless administered by a pretty girl—and growls whenever Doan has a drink. His full name is Dougal's Laird Carstairs and as a sleuth he rarely barks up the wrong tree. He's down in Mexico with Doan, ostensibly to convince a missing fugitive that he would do well to stay put. The case is complicated by three murders, assorted villains, and a horrific earthquake that cuts the mountainous little village of Los Altos off from the rest of Mexico. Doan and Carstairs aren't the only unusual visitors to Los Altos. There's Patricia Van Osdel, a ravishing blonde whose father made millions from flypaper, and Captain Emile Perona, a Mexican policeman whose long-ago Spanish ancestor helped establish Los Altos. It's that ancestor who brings teacher Janet Martin to Mexico along with a stolen book that may contain the key to a secret hidden for hundreds of years in the village church. Written in the snappy hardboiled style of the day, *The Mouse in the Mountain* (0-915230-41-0, 151 pages, $14.00) was first published in 1943 and followed by two other Doan and Carstairs novels. "Each of these is fast-paced, occasionally lyrical in a hard-edged way, and often quite funny. Davis, in fact, was one of the few writers to successfully blend the so-called hardboiled story with farcical humor."—Bill Pronzini, *1001 Midnights*.

Elizabeth Dean. Dean wrote only three mysteries, but in Emma Marsh she created one of the first independent female sleuths in the genre. Written in the screwball style of the 1930s, *Murder is a Collector's Item* (0-915230-19-4, $14.00) is described in a review in *Deadly Pleasures* by award-winning mystery writer Sujata Massey as a story that "froths over with the same effervescent humor as the best Hepburn-Grant films." Like the second book in the trilogy, *Murder is a Serious Business* (0-915230-28-3, 254 pages, $14.95), it's set in a Boston antique store just as the Great Depression is drawing to a close. *Murder a Mile High* (0-915230-39-9, 188 pages, $14.00), moves to the Central City Opera House in the Colorado mountains, where Emma has been summoned by am old chum, the opera's reigning diva. Emma not only has to find a murderer, she may also have to catch a Nazi spy. A reviewer for a Central City area newspaper warmly greeted this reprint: "An endearing glimpse of Central City and Denver during World War II. . . . the dialogue twists and turns. . . . reads like a Nick and Nora movie. . . . charming."—*The Mountain-Ear.* "Fascinating."—*Romantic Times.*

Constance & Gwenyth Little. These two Australian-born sisters from New Jersey have developed almost a cult following among mystery readers. Critic Diane Plumley, writing in *Dastardly Deeds*, called their 21 mysteries "celluloid comedy written on paper." Each book, published between 1938 and 1953, was a stand-alone, but there was no mistaking a Little heroine. She hated housework, wasn't averse to a little gold-digging (so long as she called the shots), and couldn't help antagonizing cops and potential beaux. The Rue Morgue Press intends to reprint all of their books. Currently available: *The Black Coat* (0-915230-40-2, 155 pages, $14.00), *Black Corridors* (0-915230-33-X, 155 pages, $14.00), *The Black Gloves* (0-915230-20-8, 185 pages, $14.00), *Black-Headed Pins* (0-915230-25-9, 155 pages, $14.00), *The Black Honeymoon* (0-915230-21-6, 187 pages, $14.00), *The Black Paw* (0-915230-37-2, 156 pages,

$14.00), *The Black Stocking* (0-915230-30-5, 154 pages, $14.00), *Great Black Kanba* (0-915230-22-4, 156 pages, $14.00), and *The Grey Mist Murders* (0-915230-26-7, 153 pages, $14.00).

Marlys Millhiser. Our only non-vintage mystery, *The Mirror* (0-915230-15-1, 303 pages, $14.95) is our all-time bestselling book, now in a fifth printing. How could you not be intrigued by a novel in which "you find the main character marrying her own grandfather and giving birth to her own mother," as one reviewer put it of this super-natural, time-travel (sort-of) piece of wonderful make-believe set both in the mountains above Boulder, Colorado, at the turn of the century and in the city itself in 1978.

James Norman. The marvelously titled *Murder, Chop Chop* (0-915230-16-X, 189 pages, $13.00) is a wonderful example of the eccentric detective novel. "The book has the butter-wouldn't-melt-in-his-mouth cool of Rick in *Casablanca*."—*The Rocky Mountain News.* "Amuses the reader no end."—*Mystery News.* "This long out-of-print masterpiece is intricately plotted, full of eccentric characters and very humorous indeed. Highly recommended."—*Mysteries by Mail.* Meet Gimiendo Hernandez Quinto, a gigantic Mexican who once rode with Pancho Villa and who now trains *guerrilleros* for the Nationalist Chinese government when he isn't solving murders. At his side is a beautiful Eurasian known as Mountain of Virtue, a woman as dangerous to men as she is irresistible. Together they look into the murder of Abe Harrow, an ambulance driver who appears to have died at three different times. First published in 1942.

Sheila Pim. *Ellery Queen's Mystery Magazine* said of these wonderful Irish village mysteries that Pim "depicts with style and humor everyday life." *Booklist* said they were in "the best tradition of Agatha Christie." *Common or Garden Crime* (0-915230-36-4, 157 pages, $14.00) is set in neutral Ireland during World War II when Lucy Bex must use her knowledge of gardening to keep the wrong person from going to the gallows. Beekeeper Edward Gildea uses his knowledge of bees and plants to do the same thing in *A Hive of Suspects* (0-915230-38-0, 155 pages, $14.00). *Creeping Venom* (0-915230-42-9, 155 pages, $14.00) mixes politics and religion into a deadly mixture.

Charlotte Murray Russell. Spinster sleuth Jane Amanda Edwards tangles with a murderer and Nazi spies in *The Message of the Mute Dog* (0-915230-43-7, 156 pages, $14.00), a culinary cozy set just before Pearl Harbor. Our earlier title, *Cook Up a Crime*, is currently out of print.

Juanita Sheridan. Sheridan was one of the most colorful figures in the history of detective fiction, as you can see from Tom and Enid Schantz's introduction to *The Chinese Chop* (0-915230-32-1, 155 pages, $14.00). Her books are equally colorful, as well as showing how mysteries with female protagonists began changing after World War II. The postwar housing crunch finds Janice Cameron, newly arrived in New York City from Hawaii, without a place to live until she answers an ad for a roommate. It turns out the advertiser is an acquaintance from Hawaii, Lily Wu, whom critic Anthony Boucher (for whom Bouchercon, the World Mystery Convention, is named) described as an "exquisitely blended product of Eastern and Western cultures" and the only female sleuth that he "was devotedly in love with," citing "that odd mixture of respect for her professional skills and delight in her personal charms." First published in 1949, this ground-breaking book was the first of four to feature Lily and be told by her Watson, Janice, a first-time novelist. No sooner do Lily and Janice move into a rooming house in Washington Square than a corpse is found in the basement. In Lily Wu, Sheridan created one of the most believable—and memorable—female sleuths of her day. "Highly recommended."—*I Love a Mystery.* "This well-written. . .enjoyable variant of the boarding house whodunit and a vivid portrait of the post WWII New York City housing shortage, puts to lie the common misconception that strong, self-reliant, non-spinster-or-comic sleuths didn't appear on the scene until the 1970s. Chinese-American Lily Wu and her novelist Watson, Janice Cameron, are young and feminine but not dependent on men."—*Ellery Queen's Mystery Magazine.*